Looking for Jane

Judith Redline Coopey

To Carolyn,
I hope you enjoy
Looking For Jane!
Judith Redline
Coopey

Looking for Jane

Author's Declaration

Published by Fox Hollow Press and the author, Judith Redline Coopey
Interior design by OPA Author Services, Scottsdale, Arizona
Cover design by Albert Chui, San Jose, California
Cover illustration: a detail from a 1903 Edward Lamson Henry painting, "An October Day." Born in Charleston, South Carolina, on January 12, 1841, Henry, with a bent for nostalgia, became a noted painted of super-realistic genre scenes of early 19th century rural America.

ATTENTION CORPORATIONS, UNIVERSITIES, COLLEGES, AND PROFESSIONAL ORGANIZATIONS: Quantity discounts are available on bulk purchases of this book for educational or gift purposes, or as premiums for increasing magazine subscriptions or renewals. Special books or book excerpts can also be created to fit specific needs. Contact Fox Hollow Press.

**FOX HOLLOW
PRESS**

Dedication

For John,
who made being a mother
easy and fun.

Acknowledgments

The sources I found most useful in researching for this novel include: The Johnstown Flood by David McCullough, Calamity Jane, the Woman and the Legend by James D. McLaird, Old Deadwood Days by Estelline Bennett, Steamboat Legacy and Steamboat Kid by Dorothy H. Schrader, Buffalo Girls by Larry McMurtry.

Thanks are due to Chuck and Jan Carlbom of Interior, SD, and to Clifton Stone of Springfield, SD, and Renee Harris of Oglala Lakota College, Kyle, SD, for their help with the geography and lore of the White River area. The Wounded Knee Museum in Wall, SD and the Allen Museum in Deadwood provided a deeper and wider understanding of the South Dakota Territory and its people. Dr. Donald Coopey answered my questions about cleft palate and its treatment in the 1890s.

Additional thanks are due to the following people who helped with my research and did preliminary readings for me: Mary Agliardo, Elissa Ambrose, Charles Bauder, Erin Coopey, Kathleen Davis, Kimberly Davis, Amy Dominy, Kryston Eckelbarger, Linda Kehoe, Dave Lettick, Jeff Nicklaus, Pat Park, Janelle Raupp, Genie Robine, Vincent Set'tle, and, as always, Lou.

Chapter 1

1890

Johnstown, Pennsylvania

They say my mama sinned against God, and that's how's come I got no roof in my mouth. That's what the nuns say, anyway. I guess they'd know, being so close to God and all. I ain't sure, myself. I can't recall meeting the woman. Wouldn't know her if she walked right in here and kissed me, which she wouldn't, 'cause I ain't what you'd call pretty. It ain't no harelip or nothin' like that. You can't tell nothin' about the hole in my head from the outside. It's just that I wasn't born comely, as they say. So I guess one look at me, inside *and* outside, and she decided to drop me off at the nearest house of God and go on her way. Her name was Jane. Sister Helen Gethsemane told me that. My Mama's name was Jane.

It ain't been *so* bad, living in the convent. I had my belly fed and clothes on my back and all the religion I could tolerate. Just nobody to call me their own is all. I'm fifteen or thereabouts. Don't know for sure how old I am or how old I was when Jane whosomever it was left me at the convent door. I wasn't teething yet. I know that, and my name is Nell. The nuns named me that. That's all I know.

Some of them—the nuns, I mean—was nice. Some of the time. What I think about nuns mostly is this: somebody must've been pretty hard on them when they was little, else they wouldn't have so much meanness to hand out. But once in a while you come across a nice one. One that gives you a wad of dough when they make the cinnamon buns or a piece of red ribbon to wear in your hair come Christmas.

Sister Mary Patrick, the cook, was giving orders this morning before I was even done with my oatmeal. "Nell," she says, "Take the wagon and go get the supplies. The relief is handing out flour and sugar today."

Going downtown ain't necessarily a treat, you see. It's been right nigh a year since the flood—you heard of it, the Johnstown Flood—and it still looks like hell. I don't say that in front of the nuns. There's a lot I don't say in front of the nuns. Anyway, Johnstown is strugglin' to come back, and it has, a lot. But it still stinks when it's damp, which it is, most of the time.

Rivers on two sides, hills all around. Some folk don't like that closed in feeling you get around here. Say they wanna see what's over the next hill and whatnot. I don't care for that. These hills close us in all right, but they feel cozy to me. I just can't get over why they ever built a town here, though. Should have been a park or something—it's that beautiful. But any fool would know it was a prime place for floods. Live here three years, and you'll witness two, for sure.

Course there's floods, and then there's *floods*. The one that come through here the day after Memorial Day in '89 was more than a flood. Flood don't describe the wall of water that come down the valley of the Little Conemaugh after the South Fork Dam broke. That wasn't no rise in the water level, no sir. That was a torrent. A conflagration of water. That was hell broke loose and tearing down the valley for the devil's own infernal purpose. Churned up the whole world and left it piled up and burning at the railroad bridge, that one did. Wiped out Johnstown, near about, and killed a whole lot of people. Some of 'em you couldn't even tell who they was—had to be buried in unmarked graves. You could say we've come a long way in a year, but it still stinks, 'specially when it rains.

I get on my wraps, drag the wagon out of the shed and start downtown. It's painted red, but that was a while ago. Now it looks rough brown. The iron wheels is rusty and they make a lot of rattly noise over the bricks in the sidewalk. I wish I didn't have to take it. Makes so much noise the whole world knows you're coming. I do what I'm told, most of the time, but I ain't anxious to be out and about today. Going downtown is iffy. It might be fun 'cause I get to watch people. Other than nuns, that is. Or it might be awful if I run into the tormenters. Them's three boys, older than me, that likes to tease me—and worse, sometimes. I always watch out for them, 'cause you never know when they're going to turn up or what they're going to get it in their heads to do to you.

I know I ain't pretty. What I mean is, my teeth is all crooked, like there's too many of 'em, and they have to twist and turn to keep from being crowded out, and I can't shut my mouth very good. It's hard to pull my upper lip down over all those twisty teeth. But I guess I got nice brown eyes. Sister Helen Gethsemane said I did, once. And people sometimes make a fuss over my auburn hair, but I get more blank looks and turn-aways than anything else. Except from the tormenters. They're mean. The way I see it, how I look ain't no reason to make fun of me. Nobody can help how they look.

I turn round the corner of Franklin Street and there they are— Roddie Yon and his two friends—walking along hollering and laughing and pelting each other about a half block ahead of me. I slow down, hoping they got business someplace and won't notice me. But the wagon makes a lot of noise, bumping along, and I wish I could quiet it. I mosey along real slow, like I'm looking in the shops. The tormenters keep on going for about a block before one of them turns around and sees me. He nudges the other two, and they slow up and double back. It ain't a minute before they're laughing and making fun.

"Hey, Nell! How's the hole in your head?" Roddie hollers. "Getting any bigger?" Then they all laugh real loud.

I look around for a way to skedaddle, but the darn wagon rules that out. I could leave it and duck between the buildings, but they'd just follow me and I'd be trapped back in the alley. I should be used to it by now. They make fun of me every time they see me. Sometimes they used to hit me, but now mostly they just laugh and holler insults.

This ain't nothing new. They been bothering me ever since I started sneakin' out of the convent when I was five. I'd wander out into the yard and down by the hedge that separates the kitchen garden from the little courtyard out by the alley. The fence picket nearest the gate was loose on the bottom. You could wiggle the nail out and slide the picket crooked and squeeze through. When no one was looking I'd let myself out and wander around, lookin' in backyards or windows. That's how I learned about the world outside the convent. Heard and seen a lot of life through open windows. Sometimes, if nothing was going on, I'd sit down and tell myself stories.

One day when I was about six or so I was in the alley leaning against the back fence making up a story when Roddie and his friends come along and heard me talking and mocked me, talking through their noses and laughing. I curled up by the gate and made myself small so they'd go away.

"My ma says you got a hole in your head," Roddie said, acting all friendly of a sudden. "Could we see it? Would you show it to us?"

I thought they'd be nice if I let them look, so I opened up my mouth and they all peered in and hooted and hollered and laughed their mean laughs. I heard a lot of mean laughs in my life. I know what a mean laugh sounds like.

"Ughhh! That sure is ugly!" the fat one said. "How can she eat? Don't the food get all messed up in her brain and come out her nose?"

"You fool! That's why she's idiotic! Got oatmeal for brains!"

I shrank back against the gate, wishing I'd stayed inside. They was older than I was, and bigger. Their jeers echoed in my head long after they'd lost interest and wandered on down the alley, throwing rocks and battering the fences with a barrel stave.

That was the first time they bothered me. After that it happened just about every time I went out. Now here they are again. I try my best to give them a wide berth, but they got other ideas.

"What do you think, Frank? Is she addled or just stupid?" Roddie asks.

"Prob'ly both," Frank says, "and ugly."

I look to cross the street, but they block my way. "Leave me be," I tell them.

"*Leave me be!*" Roddie mimics, holding his nose and talking funny.

"Let's take her in the alley and poke her." That's the third one, the fat one with a cast in his eye. He's got his shirt full of crab apples they must of stole from somebody's tree.

"Yeah, let's!" says Frank. He grabs the iron handle of the wagon and rams it into my gut. It knocks the wind out of me. I suck in my breath real sharp, bent over, hoping somebody'll happen along to stop them.

"Leave me be!" I shout.

"*Leave me be!*" they chorus, dancing around me throwing punches into the air.

I grab the wagon handle and give it a shove, catching Frank in the shin. Bark his shin good.

"Now you done it," he roars. "Now you're gonna be sorry, ugly bitch!" He grabs the handle, flips it over and reaches for me.

A shout comes from the other side of the street. It's old man Yingling, the rag and bone man, shaking his fist and hollering at the tormentors. "Leave off of that girl!" he yells. "She ain't done nothing to you. Leave off of her." He steps away from his old, flea-bitten horse and rickety wagon and crosses the street in bent over strides, his hands drawn up in wrinkled fists. He's dealt with these three before.

I take advantage of the distraction to right my wagon and shove it at Roddie, but he sidesteps and looks around. "Hey! Here comes old man Yingling, the crazy old coot! Let's get him!"

Just that fast they forget about me and start into throwing crab apples at old man Yingling and his bony horse. He shakes a skinny fist and hollers in rage, but he's no match for their meanness. He takes a hit that knocks his old wool hat off and turns back to calm his horse while the tormenters tear down the street past me and cut up an alley.

"Thank you, sir," I call to him, pulling myself back together.

He waves me off, muttering about ornery, no-account ruffians and turns back to his sorry looking horse and wagon.

I rattle on to the commissary, a yellow board building near the railroad tracks. I give the convent's ticket to the commissary man and he totes the sacks of flour and sugar out and loads them on my wagon. The weight quiets the wheels a mite. I drag the heavy load back up Franklin Street, bent over and pulling with both hands, all the time keeping an eye out for the tormenters. Just like them to come by and dump my load in the street. They done it before. It's a long haul pulling that old wagon loaded with flour and sugar. I'm bushed when I get to the back gate.

The church still sits heck west and crooked from the flood, and the convent ain't much better. I know I should feel lucky to have this place, but I'm not exactly the pet here. Not one of the perfect little girls in aprons and braids that go around looking like they're praying all the time. The nuns think I'm simple-minded. Dull-witted. Idiotic. That's what they say when people ask, and they don't think I can hear them. My hearing is extra fine. It's a talent I've developed over long years of listening to whisperers.

I guess I look dull-witted, that's why they think it. Why they didn't bother to send me to their school. Since I talk funny and ain't nothing to look at, they think my brain's addled, too.

My brain's just fine.

Anyway, I can read. That squiggly one, looks like a snake? That's a S. Salt. Sugar. Like it's printed on the bags at the commissary. Figured that out all by myself. It makes a snake sound, too: Sssssss. And that humpbacked one? That's a M. Like a couple of mountains hooked together. And the V one—looks like a valley. Taught myself from the Bible they let me have. It ain't really mine. It's just in the drawer of the table in my room. So I pull it out and look at it after they put out the lights. I use my candle. Sister Grace Aloysius is always growling about how many candles I use. I read in the kitchen, too. They got books of receipts there. How much of which do you put in to make bread, or a cake or a pie. Sister Mary Patrick is fat, and the other nuns think she's lazy, but she's nice to me, most of the time. I'm supposed to be her helper. Scullery girl, they call me. Sometimes Sister Mary gets into the communion wine and falls asleep on the settle behind the stove. That's when I sneak out.

I lug the heavy sacks of flour and sugar into the kitchen. Sister nods her head toward the pantry, so I haul it in there and shove it on the shelf. I brush the flour off my dress and hang my shawl on a peg by the door.

"Go wash your face and comb your hair. Make yourself presentable. Sister Grace Aloysius wants you in her office."

Chapter 2

From the minute Sister Mary Patrick tells me the Mother wants me in her office, I know it ain't good. The Mother only talks to me to scold. I search my head for my trespasses, which are many. Cussing, lying, staying up after evening prayers, shirking my chores, giggling when Sister Joseph Magdalene tripped over her habit and sprawled out prone in front of the altar. Hell, it could be anything.

I stand in front of the heavy wooden office door, thinking on all the places I'd rather be. One of the nuns comes by, sees me, and clicks her tongue. Like tsk, tsk. You in trouble *again?* I pull a nasty face at her retreating back and screw up my courage to knock.

The Mother is sitting behind her big, new, wooden desk, a donation from the Pittsburgh diocese. Her hands are folded on top of some papers. Behind her is shelves of books. I'd sure like to get in there and read some of them. Our eyes lock, and I get all the way into the room before I notice two people sitting on a straight-back bench along the wall next to the door. Poor country folk. Ragged, I'd say. The woman peers up from under her eyebrows, looking timid and fearful. She's skinny and hunched over. Beaten down. The man has the smell of the farm on him. Cow dung. Pig dung. Whichever. He looks mean. Big, rough, meaty hands, fumbling with his old beat up hat. Defiant little pig eyes. Like maybe most of the world looks down on him, but here, with nothing but women to deal with, he can more than hold his own.

"Nellie, this is Mr. and Mrs. Brownlow. Mr. Brownlow farms outside of Geistown. They need someone to help with the chores and the housework." She talks so sweet I have to blink to make sure it's her talking. "Mrs. Brownlow isn't well. There are five little ones. I've told them you'll be glad to accept their offer of employment and purpose for your life."

I know I'm supposed to kneel and take her hands in mine and thank her for all these years of tender care. Kiss her ring. Promise to work hard to make myself worthy of this fine opportunity. I don't. I look from her to them and back again.

"I'll get my things," I say. I'm out the door before she can say Abraham Lincoln and down the stairs to my basement room. I grab my other dress, underskirt and shift, roll them into a bundle and head back for the kitchen. Sister Mary Patrick is into the wine again, so she only opens one eye as I grab my shawl from the peg and tear out the back door. I'm through the garden and out the gate before anyone knows I'm gone.

It's a chilly Saturday afternoon for early June, and I don't have but this thin shawl for a cover-up. I think of the heavy wool coats in the Poor Closet at the convent. It's going to warm up soon, but I'll still need more than this shawl. I'm not going back, though. I know what awaits me at the hands of the Brownlows. I might not be much to look at, but I'm sure Mr. Brownlow won't mind after a few shots of whiskey from the keg he keeps in the barn. And Mrs. Brownlow won't mind, neither, not getting hit and rutted and knocked up on a regular basis. I head down Locust Street with a purpose—but without a plan.

I keep to the alleys and walk with my head up as though I'm on some errand until I come to the river bank. Few trees survived the flood, but here and there one that did stands big and fully leafed out. Good place to hide while I think what to do. I climb up a big maple whose branches droop almost into the water and sit for a while. I think to get out of Johnstown before they send the constable out looking for me, but my reason tells me they probably won't. The sisters are likely glad to get rid of me, and the Brownlows will just have to find some other feebleminded work horse to prey upon. It ain't gonna be me.

I haul my bundle up in the tree and sit there watching the railroad tracks along the river, thinking on what to do—where to go. I wish I knew something about my mother. Where she came from. Who her people were. The nuns use that as their measuring stick: who your people are. Well, what if you don't have any people? Or any you know of? What then? Are you doomed?

I need a plan. The railroad could take me out, but there's the problem of money, which I have none. So I could walk the tracks, but there's always bums along the railroad, and I know enough of bums coming to the back door of the convent begging for a handout and looking at you like they're starved for female companionship. One of the novices snuck out with a bum one time and wasn't never heard from again. Besides, I don't know anything about what's where, so I couldn't decide where I was going if I wanted to. I just need to get out of Johnstown and figure out who I am.

I look down and see something caught between the tree roots on the river bank. A book! It's all damp and stuck together and smells like the river, but it's a book, and I figure to own it. I climb down and pick it up and sound out the title: *Deadwood Dick in Leadville; or, a Strange Stroke for Liberty.* The picture on the cover shows Calamity Jane standing tall and holding two six-guns at the ready, defending a wronged man. It's a cowboy book—got pictures and everything. I ain't never seen no book about the west before. Only the Bible, like I said, and it's mostly about shepherds wandering around in the desert, and wars with the Philistines, and sinners getting their comeuppance. Well, this here book is too good to put down, and I start in to reading it, damp and muddy though it is. It's hard to make out the words, but I'm caught up in it by the first page and I just keep reading and reading, even though I know I should get going.

It's about Calamity Jane, a western cowgirl of the first magnitude (I learned that word from reading the book), a real woman of the world, and a crack shot. She ain't afraid of nothing, as she demonstrates time and again when in a tight spot. She and Deadwood Dick, a fine specimen (another new word) of a man, fight all manner of outlaw to save the weak from predators (you guessed it). Evildoers shudder at the mention of her name.

I'm deeply engrossed (uh huh) in reading when I hear a commotion coming down the river. A rowboat drifts into view, close to the shore. Three young fellows in it, standing up in the boat, pissing over the side, laughing real loud and hollering for fare thee well. Yep. It's them. The tormenters. Roddie Yon and his friends. Drunk as lords, singing and bellering like it's Saturday night. They drift by under my tree, cussing and shoving each other, rocking the boat to beat the band.

"You son of a bitch, Yon! You drank it all! God damn! Why didn't you save some fer me?" It's the one with the mean laugh.

"Go to hell, Frank. Why should I save any fer you? You're drunk!"

"Hey, you guys! Stop rocking the boat! I feel a little discomforted." That's the fat, pudgy one. He turns around and vomits out the back into the river.

Roddie stands up and takes one of the oars in hand. He leans real deep, using it as a pole, and gives the boat a shot toward shore. The bow rams into the muddy bank, knocking the fat one out the back. He screams and hollers how he can't swim, and I hold my hand over my mouth to keep the laugh in. Roddie crawls out over the front of the boat and staggers a few feet up the bank before he falls down on his face in the grass. The other one throws out the anchor and lifts up the empty jug, holding it up to his eye to see if there might be a drop left.

"Help! Frank! I can't swim!" The screams from the river would be sorrowful if the water was more than three feet deep.

"Get up, you dumb shit," Frank growls. "It ain't deep." He starts to make his way out of the boat but trips over the rower's seat and sprawls headlong into the bow. Ouch! His head makes a sickening thud as it hits the wood. I don't think this is funny anymore.

The fat pudgy one finally figures out he can stand up, so he wades drunkenly toward the shore, but it's pretty steep where he wants to get out, so he falls on his wide butt, gets up sputtering, wades on down a ways and pulls himself out by a tree root.

Everything is quiet now. The afternoon light is waning, and as soon as the sun goes down, I know I'll be cold. I need to get out of here, but I'm afraid to move for fear these rapscallions'll wake up and do something awful to me. I'm hungry. I can't spend the whole night in this here tree. I'd fall out, sure as Ned.

After about a hour of waiting and watching, I decide I have to chance it. There's no staying the night in this tree. I drop my bundle and climb down quiet as I can, one branch at a time. On the ground, I pick up my stuff and look around.

Roddie is sound asleep on his stomach, head on his arm like a innocent little boy. Only the stink gives him away. I look at the one in the boat. He could be dead for all I know. Then the fat one. He's lying on his back, mouth wide open, snoring like thunder. A fly buzzes around and lands on his lip. Normally, I'd hang around to see if he eats it, but I've got business.

I turn back to the boat, toss my bundle in back and step in beside Frank. His head's bleeding and all swole up. I can't lift him, that's for sure, so I get down beside him and roll him up the side of the boat. I brace my feet and push with all my might. I'm half afraid he'll wake up, half afraid he won't. One more mighty heave and he topples over the side into the water.

He floats. Face down. Damn! Now what do I do? Let him float? I should, to pay him back for all the tormenting, but something makes me get out of the darn boat, wade in up above my knees and drag him out on the bank. He groans when I turn him over. I leave him there, feet still in the water, and climb back over the side of the boat. I put the oars back in place and pull up the anchor. Just as I push off from the shore, Roddie Yon sits up.

"Hey! Where you goin' with my boat?"

Chapter 3

The afternoon shadows are long, and Roddie is still drunk, so I doubt he'll be much inclined at pursuit. I keep rowing as fast as I can out to the middle of the current. Roddie's head must feel about as big as a pumpkin right now, so he ain't no-wise interested in chasing me down, 'specially if he has to swim to do it.

The current pulls me along toward the railroad bridge, where the most horror of the flood happened. All the debris dammed up against the bridge, and then it caught fire. Me and the nuns and the rest of the orphans was all up on Green Hill in the pouring rain with most of the town, watching and listening to the roaring and the screaming. The houses and such was jammed in there so tight they used dynamite to blow it up after a couple months. Couldn't get rid of it no other way. People was crazy with the dynamite. Hated the terrible noise and knowing their loved ones would never be found now.

The river carries me under the bridge, gentle as you please. Hard to remember how it was. Guess the Pennsylvania Railroad can be proud of that bridge. Held up better than the South Fork Dam.

I used to wonder if my mother was killed in the flood, but I decided no. She wouldn't have stayed in Johnstown with me there. Wouldn't have wanted to look at me. I guessed she'd moved on as soon as she dropped me off. Probably came in on the railroad in the fall of '75 and went out the same way.

My dress is wet up to my thighs. As evening progresses, I start to get cold, and I know it'll be a long night if I stay in this boat. Still, I need to get on downriver past Cambria City, at least. That's a rough town, full of saloons and immigrants. Saturday night ain't no night to be a girl out alone in Cambria City. I use the oars to keep to midstream and float on by in the gathering dusk.

It's full dark when I see the lights of a town on the right bank. I'm so hungry I could eat worms, so I pull in to the bank a little below the town. I creep through the woods along the river to a backyard hen house. Maybe there'll be a egg or two if I'm lucky, but a dog starts in to barking, and I skedaddle back to the boat. Then I see a lone light a few rods downstream, and I let the boat drift down to it. It's a little fishing shack with a dock out in the water, built out of slab wood since the flood. A big old hairy black dog is laying on the dock, and he into thumping his tail when he sees me. I put a finger to my lips to keep him from barking. Glory! It works.

I tie up at the dock and pet the dog. He like to knocks me over wagging his tail. Then I creep up to the fishing shack and peer in the window. A man sits asleep, leaning back in a straight chair by a table with a oil lamp on it. I can smell the whiskey from here. Thank God for Demon Rum! I go to the door and ease it open, but it still creaks. The man leans forward and rests his head on his arms on the table. I wait a few minutes for him to get cozy again. Then I tiptoe over to the stove. The supper fire is out, but the stove still gives off a comforting warmth. On top is a frying pan with half a fish still in it.

I grab it and eat it, standing right there beside the sleeping man, picking out the bones. Then I look around for what I can steal. Some flour, a little salt, sugar, coffee, three fishhooks, some string, a pan of biscuits and, wonder of wonders, a jar of jam. I gather up the stuff in my skirt and tiptoe back out to the dock. Whoa, Nellie! The frying pan! I'll need that, for sure. One more trip and I'm done. As I gently place my haul into the boat, I look up and see the black dog sitting on the back seat, an expectant look on his face. Thump, thump goes the tail. I don't want to cause a ruckus pushing him out, so I untie the boat, sit down and row.

He's about the friendliest dog I ever met, and I can't say I mind him for company. Better'n being alone. After a while I lie down in the bottom of the boat—good thing it don't leak—cover myself with my flimsy shawl and go to sleep. Before long I feel a wet tongue licking my face and the dog curls up beside me. I'm grateful for the warmth.

Morning finds us drifting down the Conemaugh with little idea of our destiny. It's still cold, and mist rises off the water. I wake up stiff and hungry. There ain't a town in sight, nothing but woods rising up on both sides of the river. Something moving catches my eye, and I look to shore and see some people, a man and two women, shouting and waving at me. I row in close enough to hear them.

"Give us a lift!" they yell. "Just as far as Blairsville. Our horse died."

My first thought is that they're maybe a family on their way to church, they're so dressed up. Then I see that they're anything but church goers. There's dressed up and there's *dressed up*. These are dressed up all right. Painted ladies. Ladies of the evening. When I get close enough to see, I'm all for laying on the oars in the opposite direction, but it's the man with them that stops me. He's near about the prettiest man I ever saw. Tall, slim, delicate—like one of them Greek statues they had a picture of in the library before the flood. I'm struck dumb by his beauty.

So I land the boat and they commence to pile in. Don't ask, mind you. Just pile in. The women head right for the back seat, and, being well nourished, they weigh the boat down considerable. I watch the water rise almost to the top of the sides. Just what I need—a swamped boat. They're kind of particular, too, if you ask me, making faces about the muddy boat floor and lifting their skirts to get past me to the back seat. The dog lies between me and the back, and one of them steps on his paw. He puts up a terrible yelping and whining, startles the woman, and she loses her balance and near about capsizes us.

"Can we put him out?" one of the whores asks.

"Who?" I says, looking at the handsome devil who is now balancing himself over me like to take his place on the rower's seat.

"The dog, of course," she says, snotty as you please, like I should know what she's talking about.

"The dog? No." I almost say, "If he goes, I go," but I think better of that. They're kind of brassy, but then, I guess whores need some brass to survive. "He's my dog, and he stays," I tell them.

Mr. Handsome is standing astride the rower's seat now with me in it staring full bore at his crotch. I blink my eyes and tilt my head up to look at him. He's younger than I thought. Maybe twenty or so. He looks down at me and smiles a nice, friendly smile. "Mind if I row?"

"No. That's okay." I move off the rower's seat to the bow, and he sits down to take the oars. Just that quick, I'm tooken over. I make a resolve right then to be more careful who I take up with.

"Phew! This dog stinks! Move him up there with you, Sweetie," one of the whores directs.

"C'mere, Soot!" I call him and he comes bounding over the seat, almost knocking pretty boy off. "Good boy, Soot. Now sit." You can bet I'm surprised when the dog obeys like he's been mine all his life, knows his name and is used to me giving orders right and left. I put my arm around him and hunker down in the bow, studying the handsome one's back. Presently he takes off his coat and folds it up real neat on the seat beside him. It's warming up considerable.

He sits facing the two ladies and they carry on a private conversation like I'm not even there. He talks fancy, like he's got rich relatives or something. It's plain I don't make no never mind to them. Seems they was run out of the town we just passed. The Temperance League didn't think whores was wholesome enough. Fancy that! My mind is churning ideas about how to get rid of them. I wonder how far it is to Blairsville.

You might ask how I know just from looking at them that these are ladies of the evening. Well I had some experience with that kind in the convent. They'd stop over for a dose of religion and repentance now and then. Most of the time it was temporary.

They'd do a little penance, which means they'd give up drinking and whoring for a month or so, but pretty soon it'd get the better of them, and they'd disappear in the middle of the night. One or two was regulars at the convent. They'd come around about once a year, hang around for about a month, and then be gone again. Kind of like a retreat, but without serious religious intentions. More like a rest from their labors. The nuns was nice to 'em, mostly—Sisters of Charity, you know—but they always tried to keep 'em out of the Mother's way. Her charity could be a little thin.

I'd always ask them their names, thinking maybe one of them was named Jane and I'd find my long lost mother, but they always had flower names, like Rose or Violet or Daisy. I don't know if it was required for a whore to have a flower name, but they always did. So I ask these two their names.

"Susan," says the blonde one on the right.

"Camille," says the redhead on the left.

There goes that idea, says I. Unless you think Susan is short for Black-eyed Susan, and Camille is short for camellia. That'd work. They don't ask me my name, which is all right with me, 'cause I don't intend on telling nobody my name or nothing else about me. I sit in the bow with my back against my stores, planning how to get rid of them.

After they get tired of talking to each other like I don't exist, one of them looks past Mr. Handsome and asks, "How come you talk funny, girl?"

It's a nosy question, and it makes me mad. I don't ask them how come they're whores, do I? I shut my mouth up real tight and turn to look downriver.

Then the handsome one up and talks to me, and I turn soft as butter on a summer day. "Jeremy Chatterfield, at your service." He aims the nicest smile at me and even offers his hand. I take it and shake it, polite as I can muster, considering the hand I offer him is dirty with river slime. His talk sounds real proper, like one of them there Shakespeare guys that come and put on a show for us after the flood. Kind of uppity, like, but nice. Dressed like a dandy. First time I ever seen a man wear stri-ped pants, but they go real good with his silk waistcoat and yaller coat. I wish I had a rag to tie around my head to keep my mouth from falling open every time I look at him.

Then one of the "ladies" says to him, "You better land us here. Blairsville is right around the next bend, and we can't just float up to the landing and traipse into town like we own it."

Mr. Jeremy Chatterfield pulls on the left oar and heads for the bank. I'm relieved at my luck in getting rid of them so quick, even if the one does look like one of those Greek guys. I don't have a plan in my head for where I'm going, but I don't see no advantage to taking up with whores even if Mr. Jeremy Chatterfield *is* part of the bargain.

"You know where this here river goes?" I ask.

"Pittsburgh, eventually," Camille says.

"Pittsburgh? Does it stop there?"

"Goes all the way to New Orleans if you're of a mind to follow it," Miss Susan informs me.

"New Orleans? What's that?"

Miss Camille makes the tsk sound. No matter. I'm used to that.

"It's a city," she says, real snotty, like I should know it. "Way down south at the end of the Mississippi River, near the Gulf of Mexico."

I wonder how *she* knows so much about where things are at and what they're next to. It ain't long before I find out.

"Now there's a city, New Orleans," Camille enraptures. "In my younger days, I was a queen, there." Looks to me like her younger days is long gone.

"A queen? A real queen? With a castle and all?" I'd heard about queens and knights and castles and such. "And knights?"

"Oh, honey, lots of knights. A few knights every night to keep me according to my tastes. Oh, yes, I *was* a queen!" She smiles at the memory.

Jeremy's looking over his shoulder, eyeing a good place to land. I look, too, but all I see is steep banks and tree roots. He eases the boat to the bank and lets her drift a ways. The ladies are getting anxious.

"Here. Here. This is good. Let's get out here." Miss Susan starts climbing over Jeremy before the boat is even against the bank. I duck down, holding onto Soot, and Miss Susan crawls right over both of us and grabs a tree root, bringing us to an abrupt stop that almost jerks her arm out of joint. "Ouch! Oooo! That hurts! Tarnation!"

"Hush, Susan. You'll wake the dead and have the law on us. Get your bustle out of this damn boat." Miss Camille climbs after her, knocking me in the head with her carpet bag. The two of them scramble up the bank like otters and turn to look for Jeremy. He sits tight in the rower's seat, watching them muddy theirselves up.

He smiles them the sweetest smile you ever saw and says, "Think I'll wait for a little nicer exit. Nobody's looking for *me*." He pulls on the left oar to head us back out into the current.

Chapter 4

Once we're far out in the middle, floating free, he turns and gives me a wide grin, like we have a secret or something. The other two stand on the bank, watching, but there's no yelling now. They just stand there, hands on their hips, mad as a couple of passed over old maids. Jeremy lifts the dripping oars and props them, letting the boat drift.

"What'd you do that for?" I ask.

"I needed to get rid of them. They were slowing me down."

"Slowing you down from what?"

He turns and motions me to climb over to the back seat. "From going places and doing things. I travel light."

I make the trip to the back seat, but tell Soot to stay put. No sense turning the boat over for a dog. Jeremy watches and takes up the oars again once I'm set.

As we float, I feel him studying me. I ain't used to being looked at. "Who are you and what are you running away from?" he asks.

I'm still almost struck dumb by his beauty—blue eyes the color of a chambray shirt, sandy brown hair thick like a wheat field in summer—so I start to jabber away about myself—like he'd even be interested. "I run away from a convent in Johnstown. Stole this here boat and some provisions. The dog adopted me, but I kinda like him. Who are you?"

"Jeremy Chatterfield, formerly of Suffolk, England. Bury St. Edmunds. Now of wherever I can find sustenance."

"England? You related to one of them kings or something?"

"I wish. T'would make my existence much simpler. No. Common folk, I'm afraid. And you? Did you enter the convent on your own, or did your folks make you?"

"Foundling. Been there all my life. Never knowed my ma or pa. Thought I better get out though, since they was planning on shoving me off on some hairy old fat farmer."

Jeremy nods.

"And I ain't got no roof in my mouth is why I talk funny, case you're interested."

He nods again. "I thought as much. I've known others with a similar affliction."

"You have?" That revelation strikes me dumb again. I thought I was the only one.

"Surely. Several. It's not unheard of, you know."

I turn and look back over the water at the retreating whores, now nothing more than two swatches of color ranging in and out of sight in the woods. This is a lot to chew on.

"Don't worry about them. There's a road close by. They're a couple of well seasoned old hens. They can take care of themselves."

"What was you doing with them? Was you a customer?"

"No. Nothing like that. Ours was more an arrangement of convenience." He sniffs. "A temporary association until something better comes along."

"Oh." It's a puzzle to me, but I keep my peace. Figure we'll be parting ways pretty soon, anyway. No need to trouble my head about this one, beautiful though he is.

We float in silence for a mile or so. The river is peaceful in the morning light. I turn and watch the rocky bottom pass beneath us. I like rivers. They promise to take you places you ain't never dreamed of. Besides, if you got troubles? Just slip into a river and let the current carry them away. That's what I think when I'm in a river.

Before long we pass the thriving metropolis of Blairsville without seeing a soul. It's about ten o'clock on Sunday morning, and my stomach is growling. "You hungry? I got some biscuits and jam."

He stops rowing and smiles at me like I'm pretty or something. "My dear girl. You are a dream come true."

I crawl over him again and scrounge in my bundle for the biscuits. They're dry and a bit crumbly, but the jam makes them go down just fine. I put it on with my fingers, two at a time. I hand the jar to Jeremy and he does the same. We lounge and float, watching the scenery go by, sucking jam off our fingers.

"How far's Pittsburgh?" I ask.

"My geographic knowledge of the area is quite limited. I've only been in your lovely country for two years, and this is my first trip west of New York." He turns his gaze downriver. "We'll know it when we see it, I'll wager."

Come lunch time we haul in to shore by a tiny town and Jeremy steps out to go see about finding something to eat. I sit on the bank with Soot and watch the river go by. It's warm and getting warmer, and I lie back and look up at the blue sky and study the clouds passing by. He's gone more than a half hour, and I'm thinking to move on without him when he comes back with a picnic basket on his arm and a grin on his face.

"What you got there?" I ask.

"Lunch," he replies.

"Looks like somebody packed it up real nice for you."

The grin widens. He sets the basket down on the riverbank and takes out some fried chicken, a bowl of potato salad, and a jug of cold apple cider.

"Where'd you get this stuff?" I ask digging into the potato salad with a spoon Jeremy hands me.

"I found a very nice lady who lives alone and had more Sunday dinner than she knew what to do with. I just relieved her of some of it."

"You didn't steal it, did you?" I'm beginning to have some doubts about this one's morals.

"Of course not. I didn't have to. She gave it willingly."

There's even a cloth to spread on the ground, and two white napkins. "What'd you tell her?"

"That we were missionaries traveling downriver and that we lost our provisions when our boat tipped over. She was more than happy to help God-fearing folk."

"I guess lying ain't as bad as stealing. I don't think so, anyway."

We sit on the riverbank and fill our stomachs to bursting. There's even enough for Soot to eat his fill of chicken. Then Jeremy gets up and stows the leftovers under the front seat of the boat. He puts the folded cloth, plates and silverware back in the basket and salutes me.

"See you in a short while," he promises, and heads up the path to the town.

I pick up my book, which is dry now and not too smelly, and commence reading about Calamity Jane again, while Soot snaps at flies and thumps his tail on the grassy bank.

When he gets back, Jeremy's all smiles again. Mighty pleased with himself. "Had to submit to a little Bible reading and a pretty long prayer, but it's a cheap price for a good lunch," he tells me.

We're floating aimlessly down the Conemaugh, talking idly and watching the trees go by, when, around four o'clock in the afternoon, there is a halloo from the bank. We look over and see our former friends, the two ladies of the Ivening, smiling and waving as though we're their favorite long lost relatives. Behind them on the shore sits a wagon with a mean-looking man in it, a shotgun across his knees.

"Damn!" says Jeremy, pulling hard on the right oar toward the bank.

Miss Susan and Miss Camille pile back into the boat, looking a little the worse for wear. Their clothes are muddy, their faces lined with dirt and sweat. Their hair frizzes out around their faces like that there light they show around Jesus and his mother in all the pictures. I pull Soot in close so they won't step on him again on their way to the back seat. Jeremy waits until they get settled, then lays into the oars in an all-fired hurry to get out of there.

They flump theirselves down in the back and stare at Jeremy in clear displeasure, waiting to be asked, I guess, about their adventures. Jeremy calmly steers the boat out into the current before he opens up and questions them.

"Well? What was that all about?"

Susan hardly lets him get his question out before she starts in. "About? About? Like you'd ever even care what it was about! You was gonna abandon us, you cur! After all we done for you! Put us ashore and leave us to the dogs, will you? If I could row this boat or swim, either one, I'd knock your pretty ass into the river this minute."

"Now, Susan," Jeremy says, "you misunderstand!"

"Misunderstand, my derriere! I know when I been abandoned. That constable could have raped and killed us!"

Jeremy raises an eyebrow. "Killed, maybe, but I don't know about the rape part."

Now Miss Camille starts in on him. "You're all nice and friendly when you need us, but you'll drop us and skitter off with this ugly girl like we was maggots first chance you get. What's she got? Money? Sure as hell ain't looks."

"Now, ladies, calm down. It wasn't what you thought at all. I intended to stop at Blairsville and be there to escort you when needed, but Blairsville was crawling with churchgoers and the like when we passed, so I had to use my good judgment. I was just about to turn the boat around and start rowing upstream to meet you when I was made aware of your plight."

"You're the lyingest puddle of pond scum I ever laid eyes on!" Miss Susan growls. "But keep rowing. There ain't no business to be had in that town. Just a constable with indigestion and a mean-looking shotgun."

"Yeah," adds Miss Camille. "Get us to Pittsburgh, where a lady can make a living."

We row along in silence for a far piece, nobody talking about nothing. I'm getting hungry again and tired of sitting in the boat, so I suggest we find a place to stop and camp for the night. All four of us would never be able to sleep in that boat and Soot, too. We find a flat, grassy place and pull up to the shore. Jeremy gathers firewood and Miss Camille produces a coffeepot out of her carpet bag. I take out the fish hooks and line and turn over a couple of rocks, looking for worms, which I give to Jeremy so he can catch us some fish to go with the leftovers from lunch. Then I measure out the flour and salt for Miss Susan to make the biscuits. I make the coffee, but I don't tell them about the jam. That's me and Jeremy's secret. We cook the fish on a stick over the fire and bake the biscuits in the frying pan. They're a little dark on the bottom—but passing fair. The smell of cooking fish and baking biscuits fills the air. We end the evening with full stomachs and middling warmth by snuggling together and covering up with all the clothes we have. I'm on the outside with Soot. The whores didn't want to snuggle with a dog, but I ain't proud. Warm is warm.

For the next two days we float on down the river, which gets bigger with every crick and branch that flows into it. I make up a game of trying to guess what's around every bend. Sometimes it's more woods. Sometimes it's a farm. Sometimes it's a railroad bridge. You never know. The Conemaugh joins a bigger river and ends up flowing into a really big one that the ladies call the Allegheny, and it carries us full bore down to Pittsburgh without nary even rowing. Pennsylvania sure is pretty, and I get all giddy inside when I think about how I'm exploring it.

All the way down the river the whores is nattering about how hard their life is and how they're gonna give up whoring and find respectable work. But we ain't barely bumped the riverbank in Pittsburgh when they're out of the boat and up the street plying their wares.

Now, Pittsburgh is a big city with lots of houses and factories and shops and all. I'm set on looking around and even think on staying there for a while. But the next day I'm wandering down the sidewalk near the railroad, where there's lots of stores and boarding houses, when I see them: The tormenters, big as life, walking down the other side of the street like they know where they're going. I juke behind a building and peer out to see if they saw me. Guess not. Looks like they been drinking since Saturday. All rumpled and dusty. Not too steady on their feet. Must've come up on the train looking for work. I step into a store and pretend to be real interested in some pots they got in the window, but I'm ready to tear out the back way if the tormenters make a move to cross the street. They just mosey on by, looking in store windows, shoving and punching each other like they always do. That's enough to tell me Pittsburgh ain't far enough away from Johnstown, and I light out for the boat, which is hid in a little inlet below town with Soot guarding it.

Jeremy and the whores haven't formally said good-bye, but I'm thinking they'll probably want to stay here, with all the business possibilities and such. But I need to keep moving. When I get to the rowboat I pet the dog and give him some meat scraps I found in an alley behind a butcher shop. Once he's done, I step into the boat, whistle for him, and shove off. I let her drift a few hundred feet before I hear a shout. I turn and see Jeremy stumble into the clearing, his face and the front of him all bloody. I turn the boat and row back.

"Jeremy! What happened?"

"Never mind, Nell. Get out into the current and start rowing. We've got to get out of this town."

Chapter 5

I **don't ask no more questions.** I help Jeremy to the back seat
and wait for him to get settled, then I start rowing. This river
makes the other ones look like cricks. Below Pittsburgh it is the Ohio
River, and it flows, deep and wide, to the northwest. I get us out in
the current and keep a watch for boats' cause there's some big ones
on this water, and they'd swamp us as soon as turn aside. It is just
about dusk, and I don't want to be overrun by some big steamer, so
once we get downriver a ways, I steer in close to the shore and let her
drift.

Jeremy's curled up on the back seat, facing away from me. Once
in a while he pulls up some water to wipe the blood off his face, but
mostly he just lies there, real still. I look for a place to tie up for the
night 'cause he needs nursing. I find a farmer's field on the north
bank a couple miles downstream and drift in. I go into the evening
routine of building a fire, catching a fish, making biscuits and coffee.
I'm grateful to those two whores for leaving their stuff in the boat. It
affords me a coffeepot and some clothes to cover us up at night.

I help Jeremy out and lay him down on the ground. Then I heat a
little water and tear up one of the whores' petticoats to get a wash rag
to clean him up. His beautiful face looks like somebody dragged him
behind a wagon. I help him out of his yaller coat and beat the dust
out of it against a tree. Then I look to the front of him. His shirt and
waistcoat are all bloody, so I take them and wash them in the river.
They come mostly clean, and I spread them over a couple of bushes
to dry. Jeremy still hasn't talked, except to groan when I try to move
him.

I get him sat up, leaning against a tree, and give him a cup of
coffee and a biscuit. It ain't much of a biscuit. The whores was better
cooks than me, but I smear some of the jam on it, and Jeremy
manages to swaller it down. He smiles at me through a swollen face
and bloody lips.

"What the hell happened, Jeremy?"

"Nothing much. I got caught stealing, is all. Happens now and again. I make my way by petty theft. Mostly it's easy, but once in a while. .."

"What the hell you stealing for?" I'm mad at him for getting his pretty face all busted up.

"Do *you* have any money?"

I shake my head.

"Well, then, how do you think we're going to get on without money?"

"We could get honest work." It passes through my mind that he's calling us *we*. Him and me. Like we're a pair or something.

He snorts. "Honest work! Now there's a joke. Honest work that would break your back in two weeks? No, thank you. Thieving suits me very well, and the pay is better."

I turn back to my fish and biscuits and keep my peace. No sense talking to him when he's in such a state. I clean up the supper and go through the whores' carpet bags to see what's useful. Mostly nothing but frills and under things. Maybe we could sell them. They smell all flowery, like Susan and Camille, and I feel a little bit guilty about leaving and taking their stuff. Just a little, though. They wasn't all that nice to me. I pile some of the clothes on top of Jeremy, and pretty soon he's snoring. Poor boy.

It's cool and damp along the river, and even though I fall asleep easily, I wake up in the middle of the night, chilled to the bone. I look over at Jeremy, sleeping soundly under a pile of ruffles and silks. Why should he be the only warm one? I wiggle gently under the clothes and feel the warmth of his body next to mine. Then I whistle softly for Soot, and he comes wagging up to me. I reach up and pull him down beside me, and there I lay, between man and dog, warm and cozy. Except for a strange uneasiness and the racing of my heart, I'm fine.

The next morning, Jeremy awakens stiff and sore. The swelling in his face is down, but the color from the bruises is rising. He looks like somebody beat him with a stick, which they did. Or their fists, maybe.

I think we should hide out here for a few days as long as we don't get run off. He needs time to heal up.

After breakfast I take stock and decide we need some provisions. Like everything. We ain't got a pot, so to speak.

"I think I'll float us down to the next town and see if I can get some work to earn a little money. We need just about anything you can think of."

Jeremy raises on his elbow with a groan. "I have money."

"Yeah. Stolen money. Shame on you, Jeremy. I don't want none of your stealings."

"Now, let's see," he says, with half a swollen smile. "We're floating the river in a stolen boat, eating stolen food, keeping a stolen dog. Keep your peace. It'll all look better to you the hungrier you get."

When I think about it, knocking on back doors will probably get me a day's worth of hard work and maybe one good meal, so I reconsider his offer. He holds out his hand and drops a ten-dollar gold piece into mine. I ain't never seen so much money in my life before.

"Get what we need, and don't let them cheat you," he says, rising painfully and making his way to the boat.

I stash our stuff and take my seat as the rower. Before long we spot a town off to the right with church spires and pretty houses rising among the trees, and I let us drift down a little below to tie up. I help Jeremy out and get him set under a tree, with Soot to look after him. Soot whines to come along, but I shoo him back. He looks from me to Jeremy, doubtful.

"How's my face?" I ask. "My hair? Do I look clean?"

Jeremy cocks an eyebrow. "Clean enough for a country girl."

I mosey up the road, which ain't much more than a lane, the ten-dollar gold piece in my pocket. Presently, I come to the town. It's called Sewickley. I read that on a sign. Reading is good to have. I go into the general store and buy us a pot for cooking, two blankets, flour, salt, coffee, bacon, beans, and a little sugar. Then I see the jar of stick candy and I pick out two peppermint sticks and lay them on the pile and four eggs. The store man counts it all up on the back of a paper sack and gives me the sum. I hand him the ten-dollar gold piece. He bites it, then looks at me suspicious-like.

"Where's a poor girl like you get a ten-dollar gold piece?" he asks.

"From my pa. He worked for it in Pittsburgh. Come home last night with it. Just got paid."

"Ain't nobody I ever heard of in Pittsburgh pays in gold, dearie. You're in Sewickley now. We ain't as small a town as you might think."

His remarks make me both scared and mad—not a good combination. "Money's money, dammit. You take your share and give me mine and I'll be gone. No need to quibble about where it come from."

He tilts back his head and looks long at me. "Best you keep moving. We don't need your kind around here. We got our own whores."

I pick up a iron stove poker from a rack and hold it aloft. "You give me my change and I'll go along. I ain't no whore, and you got no call to name me one. I come here to do my business, not fight with you. So give it over, right now."

"Now, now, Miss. No need to get in a lather. Put that thing down and we'll finish up here."

Well he gives me my money and quick about it. I take the change and put it in my pocket, load up the stores in a gunny sack he gives me and stalk out of there, ready to chew tacks. It's a heavy load to tote, and I stop pretty regular to catch my breath. By the time I get back to Jeremy and the boat I'm over being mad at the storekeeper, but telling Jeremy brings it all back.

He sits under the tree, listening to my tale, a smile playing around the corners of his puffy, mashed-up mouth. "Guess he figured you were no one to trifle with. Good thing, too. You might have thrashed him if it came to that."

"I would of, too. If it came to that."

After we eat lunch and sit under the shade of an old oak tree, I get to thinking about the Calamity Jane book. I ain't barely had a minute to read since I found it back in Johnstown, but it's been on my mind most of the time. I fetch the book out of the boat and show it to Jeremy. "This is real exciting to read. You wouldn't believe the scrapes she gets into, that Calamity Jane. I can't wait to get back and read it again. You ever read a book?"

"A few. My literary tastes lean to the English writers, though they tend to be a wordy and depressing lot. I think what you have there is a dime novel. Penny Dreadfuls, we call them. Mass produced for a mass readership. I should find you some of Dickens's work. You'd like it, I'm sure."

"This here suits me just fine," I say, turning the book over in my hands. "Who the dickens is Dickens?"

"Charles Dickens. I'm sure you've heard of him or his work at least."

"Nuns don't read nothing but the Bible and their little prayer books. This is the first real book I ever read."

He smiles a painful smile. "You know that Calamity Jane is a real woman."

I stop dead. "Huh? Who's real?"

"Calamity Jane. She lives out west. They say she was a scout for the army. Quite the colorful character."

"You mean her name's really Jane? How old a woman is she? How about Deadwood Dick? Is he real, too?"

Jeremy ducks to avoid the questions I'm throwing at him.

"I don't know much about it, but I think dime novels are mostly made up without any basis in truth."

An idea is forming itself in my head as I stash the provisions in the boat and push off from shore. I can't explain why I think it, but once it gets in my head it just sits there like a big ox, taking up all the room. Could it be that this Calamity Jane had a child back around '75? Could it be that she sent the child east to be cared for by a loving grandmother or someone? Could it be that loving grandmother was poverty stricken and had to drop the child at some convent against her will? Or that she was dead when the person got there, so they dropped the baby off at the convent? Could it be that this Jane, crack shot and mistress of the bull whip, is pining for her lost child in some wild and exciting western town like Deadwood or Laramie? I love those names.

I look at Jeremy, lying in the bottom of the boat and leaning against a pillow fashioned out of whores' petticoats. I think on telling him what I'm thinking, but I don't. Something stops me. This is too good a idea to get squashed first time out of my mouth. I keep it to myself. Where am I going? West. What am I going to do? Find her. Find Calamity Jane. Find my mother.

Chapter 6

When I finally decide to let Jeremy in on my notion, he listens to my outpouring with no change in his expression. He ain't nasty or nothing. He just listens, but I can tell he don't believe it. "I don't care if you believe it or not. I know it's true. My mama loved me and was sad to let me go, but she couldn't make a home for me out there in the west, no how. She gave me up, but she still cares about me, and I'm gonna find her."

"Nell, you don't have a shred of evidence to back this up. Wishing doesn't make it so." He talks to me real gentle, like I'm some sad little kid or something. It makes me mad.

"I do *too* have evidence!" I'm yelling at him now. "I got plenty of evidence. My mama's name was Jane, and I've got this!" I hold out a tiny locket. "Sister Helen Gethsemane give it to me when I was five years old, just before she left and never came back. Said it was wrapped up with me in my blanket when I was dropped off there at the convent."

Jeremy looks at it, opens it and studies the picture of a man inside and the lock of yaller hair. "So you think this would be your father, then?"

"Sure as hell. Don't I look just like him? Don't I?"

Jeremy turns the picture toward the light and looks from it to me. "Maybe. A trifle. Really, Nell, I still don't see how you think this makes the connection with Calamity Jane."

I grab the locket and stuff it down my dress. "Did you read the description of Deadwood Dick in that book? Huh? Did you? Well, this here is just what he looked like. You wait and see! I'll find her, and she'll see that there picture in that there locket, and she'll embrace me as her long lost babe."

Jeremy pulls himself up to a standing position. He winces like his gut really hurts and limps off to take a leak in the woods. I sit holding the locket, turning it this way and that, studying it for some trifle that will make it be so. It matters to know who I am. It really does. If not Calamity Jane, who? She's as good a bet as anyone, and I'd like it if she were my ma. Like to know she was somebody great who loved me but couldn't keep me. Brokenhearted and full of regret. Deep down inside is a little whisper that says I ain't really got a claim, but I push that down deeper. I got a purpose now, and a plan. Don't matter what nobody else thinks.

When Jeremy comes back, he's for going on down river, so we load up the boat and let her drift. It's such a big, wide, deep river, I wonder at it. You can't see the bottom much, except close to the shore, and it flows along real quiet, but fast, too. I feel like it is taking me right along on a big adventure. Me and Jeremy.

Sometimes I wonder why Jeremy Chatterfield stays with me. He don't seem to mind traveling with a ugly girl that talks funny. He even seems to like me. I don't get it, but I'm right glad he don't take the boat and float on downriver by himself. Now that he's hurt and needs me, I feel real special. Maybe it's wrong to feel good because of somebody else's misery, but I do.

He's trying not to let on, but I can tell he hurts real bad. I figure to let him rest a good long time, so I build him a sun shade in the back of the boat—out of some branches and one of the whore's petticoats. I keep the boat in close to shore, where the sun ain't so hot. He's short on conversation, but I don't mind. My head is set full bore on how to find my mother. I figure to stop at the next big town and get work so I can save up for a trip way out west. I ain't got no notion of where the west is—how far or how to get there, but I can tell this here river is going mainly west. A little north and a little south, but mainly west.

Me and Jeremy take to the river life real good. We float and talk and eat and sleep. That's about all, but it suits me fine. I ain't never had a friend like Jeremy—somebody to talk to and who likes talking back to you. We talk about all kinds of stuff, like how pretty the trees are and what kind they are. And the birds. Jeremy likes birds, and he knows just about every kind and what they do. Like Great Blue Herons. They're tall and skinny and they wade real slow in the shallows and catch fish in their beaks.

At night, he tells me all about the stars and what their names are and how they move across the sky. He says they don't really move, it's the earth that moves. He tells me about the constellations, which, as far as I can see, take a lot of imagination to see what they're supposed to be. But at least it gives me something to think about when I'm looking up on a clear night.

After five days of drifting all day and tying up and sleeping at night, we come to a pretty big city, the port of Cincinnati. Jeremy reckons himself better, and we're about out of stores, so I think to try and get work, but as I set out to leave the camp, Jeremy stops me. "Where are you going?"

"To try and find work, what else?"

"What kind of work?"

"Oh, I don't know. Cleaning, maybe. Odd jobs. Caring for the old folk."

"You stay here. I know how to work these towns. I'll be back by sundown with some money."

"You ain't in no condition to be goin' into town," I tell him.

He turns and smiles that smile at me. "Watch me," he says, cocky as a rooster.

I'm so glad to see the smile and the spunk come back, I elect not to argue. I sit down on the riverbank and watch him go. His face is almost better—just a little greenish yaller here and there. He can straighten up now, if he don't move too fast. His clothes is pretty mussed up, though. He don't look so much the dandy no more.

I ain't got nothing else to do, so I pick up my book and start to read it again for the fourth or maybe the fifth time. It's dried out, but it still stinks a lot like the river. I don't care, though. Every time I read it I'm surer and surer that Calamity Jane is my ma. She sure has spunk. My ma would have spunk. And she ain't afeard to take on any job, just like me. I get chills when I read about her getting the drop on a pack of outlaws 'cause that's just the way I'd deal them. I know I'd be a crack shot if ever I got my hands on a gun.

Good old Soot lies by me, watching the water. I think he must be a river dog, 'cause he's happiest when we're floating with the current. He whines and licks my face, like he wants to know when we're gonna get going. I scratch him behind the ears and tell him we gotta wait for Jeremy. That settles him down for a bit, but before long he's licking my face and sticking his snoot under my arm, like to say, "Hey! What're you doing reading again? Don't you ever get tired of reading?"

I get up, hungry, wishing I had something to make for a stew. I guess I could go find a farmhouse and try to barter an afternoon's work for some vegetables. So I set off down the path that winds along the river. Off to the north I can see a little unpainted house with a porch out front with honeysuckle vines growing all over it. Looks as likely as any, I think. Soot follows along after me, not happy to be led away from the water. The honeysuckle vines make a shade screen that keeps the porch cool and attracts every bee in the county. I step up on the porch, keeping a lookout. There ain't no barn, so I guess this is some old folks' cottage. Out here by the river where they won't be bothered by no one. I knock on the door.

I hear a rustling and scraping inside, like somebody's getting up and having a time of it. They take forever to get to the door. Then shows up a old lady with a face like a dried-up apple, all wrinkly and yellow and pink. She leans on a gnarled stick, peering at me from behind the half-open door. If I was of a mind to be afeard of scary-looking people, I'd be gone. She looks me up and down, like she's sizing me up for her oven. I heard a story about that once.

"Good afternoon, ma'am. I'm from just up the road. I thought maybe you might need some chores done today for a vegetable or two."

"Mary?"

"No, ma'am. I'm Nell. Can I cut you some wood or haul you some water?"

"Where you been all these days, Mary? I ain't seed nothing of you for so long, I thought you fell in the river and drowned."

"I'm sorry, Granny. I been busy taking care of the littl'uns. Ma said you might be needing something." I figure it's easier to be Mary than to try to explain Nell.

"Darn right! You don't care none about your Granny. No, sir. Leave me here to die by myself. Bet you just come down to see if I was dead yet!"

"Oh, no, Granny. I come down to put in a afternoon's work at anything you please."

The old woman reaches into the folds of her skirt and brings out a soiled rag. She wipes her nose and turns to lift a wooden bucket from a table beside the door. "Here. Fetch me some water and be quick about it."

I take the bucket and step off the porch in search of a well.

"And gather them eggs while you're at it," the boss lady yells.

I get my bearings pretty quick and come back with a bucket of water and three eggs from a makeshift nest along the fence. There's a garden out back, but it's too early for much of anything to be ready, except a little lettuce. The peas look like they're coming on though.

I lug the water inside and heft it up to the table. The house is only one room, dark except for the light that comes from the door and two little windows high on each side of the chimney. There's a bed in one corner, and a table, and two chairs. The stove is a big, old, black, cast-iron thing with a twisty wire handle for lifting the lids, like the one Sister Mary Patrick had in the convent. The old lady is back in her rocker, going on at a great rate about how abused she is.

"Anything else I can get for you, Granny?"

"Some kindling and a couple good logs to burn. The nights is still cold." Her tone is a little nicer, now that she's getting waited on.

I'm out the door before she's done giving the order. I fill the wood box and top it with kindling, then turn around to ask if she needs anything else. She's fallen asleep in the chair, her hands folded across her ample stomach, her head almost resting on her bosom. I figure I might as well take the opportunity to look around for something I can take as pay. It's a pretty cluttered room, with a lot of no-account junk piled high. Then I see them. Books! Stacked on top of and beside each other along the wall behind the stove. I go look them over. I've found gold! Dime novels. About twenty of them! I sort through the pile and find *five* that's about Calamity Jane. My reading's gettin' a lot better with all the practice, and I can't wait to get my nose into these.

I look at the old lady, snorin' there in her rocker. Don't look to me like she knows how much of anything she's got. Still, the work I've done don't match five dime novels, so I look around for more to do. I open the stove and see it needs the ashes cleaned out, so I start there. Then I go out and split more kindling and stack firewood on the porch so it's in easy reach. I look around and find another bucket on the step. I fill it with water and haul it to the table beside the first one. I'm getting tired, and I still don't have what I come for—food. I wonder how this old soul eats, way out here away from everybody, and I cuss out Mary, whoever she is, for neglecting her. I go out in the yard and look around.

There's a root cellar under the porch, so I let myself in. I find some potatoes, carrots, a turnip or two, some apples, and a moldy looking head of cabbage. I set these aside to carry up to the kitchen so the old soul won't have to duck in under the porch to get them. Back inside, I find a bag of dried corn and help myself to a goodly handful. There's a store of canned tomatoes, green beans, peaches and cucumber pickles on a shelf behind a curtain in the corner. I take a jar of each and set it outside to take with me when I leave.

Now I'm feeling like a thief. It didn't bother me those other times, 'cause I was stealing from drunks, and, if you ask me, drunks is askin' for trouble, is what. But this old lady, cantankerous as she is, is kind of poor and helpless. I can't think what else I can do for her, but then a idea pops into my head, and I stoke up the stove and start in to peeling the vegetables. I cut 'em all up and dump 'em in a big pot I found on a shelf behind the stove. I add water and a little salt, and before long the stew is smelling up the room something wonderful. Heating it up, too, but the old lady seems all right with it. She just keeps on snoring. It makes my neck hurt to look at her, so bent over on herself, but she don't seem to mind. Soot lets me know he's ready to go back to the riverbank. He's not happy more than five feet away from it. He whines and licks my hand, but I give him a pat and tell him we'll be going soon.

I sit down on the porch in an old hickory rocker to read. It's so exciting I hardly remember to get up and stir the stew. That Jane makes those outlaws pay dearly for their trespasses, and makes my scalp prickly doing it. I spend a lovely afternoon reading and stirring, feeling less guilty about stealing from a helpless old lady. When the stew is just about done the old lady wakes up. She frowns and peers around the house like she's in a strange place or something.

"What's this?" she asks. "Who are you?"

"My name's Nell, Missus. I was here talking to you before your nap. See? I brung in the firewood and the water, and I made us a fine stew."

I help her out of her rocker and guide her over to the table in the middle of the room. She eases herself down in front of a plate of stew and sets in to eating. "They's bread in the stove cupboard."

I get it down. It is old and dried up, but dipping it in the stew brings it back, and we share a tasty meal with little talk. She directs me to open a jar of canned peaches for dessert. Best meal I've had in many a day. When we finish, I get ready to go back to the boat.

"Ma'am? Can I borry these here books? I could read 'em in a day or so and bring 'em back."

The food has brightened her, and she even smiles at me. "Sure. They's my man's. He died a year or so gone, and I cain't read a lick. So you can have 'em if you want 'em. Pay for your work here today."

I feel better knowing the books are no use to her. I rise to go, but then I remember Jeremy is bound to be hungry. "Ma'am? Do you think I could have some of that stew to carry to my brother? He's by our boat down at the river, and he sure could use a good meal."

"Oh, yes. Do take some. There's more than I could eat in three days."

I fill one of the canning jars with the stew and cut a piece of dry bread to go with it. Then I wash up the dishes and set the kitchen to rights before I leave. The old lady is outside now, sitting on the porch, watching the sun go down, so I take the chance to put back the loot I was going to take with me. I feel kinda mean to steal from a helpless old lady. Once I've set the jars and the dried corn back in place, I step back out on the porch to bid her good night.

"You come back, girl. You're a right good cook. If you'd stay with me, I'd be obliged. I got grandchildren, but they don't pay me much mind."

"I won't be here long, I don't think. But if I stay a while, I'll come back regular to look after you."

She takes my hand in both of hers and smiles me a wrinkly smile. I feel all funny inside, like this is how it would feel to have a real grandmother. If I did, I'd take care of her, that's for sure. It's like turn about. They take care of you when you're a helpless baby, and you take care of them when they're a helpless old lady. Seems like a fair deal to me.

Soot sees me up and about and gets it in his head that we're going back to the boat. He bounds around and barks, wagging his tail as if to say, "It's about time!"

When I get there, Jeremy ain't nowhere around. I wonder about him, but Cincinnati is a big town, and I wouldn't know where to look for him, especially after dark. It's real late when he finally shows up. I've kept the stew warm over the fire all evening, and I've already finished one book and started the second.

He comes up all quiet, but I know it's him 'cause Soot is staring into the darkness, wagging his tail. Jeremy lowers himself to the ground beside me, looking a little guilty. I offer him some stew, and he takes it with a smile.

"How'd you manage this?" he asks.

"I got my ways."

He dives into the stew in the manner of a hungry man, and I'm proud to be the provider. When he's done, he lays out flat by the fire and looks up at the starry sky.

"You know, Nell, I'm thinking Cincinnati might be a good place to stay a while."

"Oh? Why's that?"

"Just a feeling I've got. Sometimes you know a place is going to be good for you." He reaches into his pocket and brings out a handful of paper money.

My eyes get big. "Where'd you get that?"

He grins. "I got my ways."

I sit on the bank, watching the reflection of the moon on the water. It bothers me how Jeremy gets money all the time. I don't want to know how he does it.

After a long quiet time, I ask him, "You know where this here river goes? Does it keep going west?"

"I hear tell it does. All the way to the Mississippi. That west enough for you?"

"Don't know. I need a map is what. I been reading these here dime novels, and I'd like to know where these places is."

I'll keep my idea under my bonnet for as long as I can. No sense getting into a argument and giving Jeremy cause to stay in Cincinnati and send me on down river. Besides, I'm getting used to traveling with him and I kind of like it.

Chapter 7

The next morning I can't wait to hear about Jeremy's adventures and tell him about mine. We breakfast on leftover stew, but before we're even done, Jeremy is all antsy, wanting to get back into town.

"What's so great about this town? What you want to stay here for?" I ask.

"Opportunity, my dear girl. Opportunity. I've noticed you Americans are easy prey for an English accent. You think we're all upper class and extremely intelligent just because our speech sounds that way to your unpracticed ear. A man could get rich just pretending to be rich around here."

I look at his soiled clothes and scuffed boots. "You don't look rich to me. No-wise."

"Give me a day or two under the tutelage of Mr. Henry Wattleman, Esquire, and I'll show you how rich I can look."

I cock an eyebrow. "Who's Mr. Henry Wattleman, Esquire?"

"A high-ranking, highly respected Presbyterian clergyman who doesn't buy the idea that wealth is sinful." He runs two fingers around his hat brim. "My kind of gentleman, I can tell you."

"So what's he to you?"

"A ticket to prosperity. He says I remind him of his dear son Wilfred, who went west five years ago and hasn't been heard from since. Says his dear wife pines for him every day. Wonders if I'd like to fill the void left by the dear boy. How can I refuse, Nell? There's money to be made here."

"You mean you're gonna pretend to be their long lost son?"

"Of course not. They already know I'm a nice young Englishman down on my luck. They think I'm headed west looking for my brother." He smiles that smile again. "But I *might* let them talk me out of that."

"Jeremy Chatterfield, you scalawag! I hope you ain't thinking on robbing those poor folks what lost their son already."

"Never fear, my dear. I do have a moral or two. I won't take anything that isn't given to me, but if they're in a giving mood, I'm in a receiving one."

He rises, tips his hat and steps off down the path toward Cincinnati.

Well, if Jeremy's gonna stay here and play these people, I might as well go to town myself and see if I can get some honest work so I can save up for my own trip west. After he goes I set the camp to rights, wash my face in the river and smooth out my dress. I washed it out a day or two ago, so it ain't too dirty. It's wrinkled, but at least it's halfway clean. My shoes are pretty dusty and scuffed up, but there's naught I can do for them, except dust 'em off. Anyway, they're getting too tight for me. I tell Soot to stay put and guard the camp. He lays down flump in the grass and puts his head on his paws, like I'm a real disappointment to him.

I'm walking to town, thinking about a lot of things. How Jeremy does, is one. He's nice to me, but it ain't the kind of nice you'd expect. I know a thing or two about men and women, and while I know I ain't no-wise a woman, or no-wise a pretty one, Jeremy is a man, and yet he don't always act like one. Never tries anything with me. Never acts brutish like the tormenters. Most ways treats me like a sister. I like that, but I still wonder what he wants with me if it ain't that.

Another thing to think on is that poor old lady all alone in her cottage by the river. Seems like her family should take better care of her and see to her needs. I wonder if they don't just want to leave her to die so they can get her money or what. Families is supposed to love each other and do right. I would if I had a family.

The last thing I'm thinking on is my mother. I know it's hasty judging Calamity Jane to be my ma, but it keeps gnawing at me, like, and I can't let go of it. I got one of them books tucked into my waistband, hoping maybe I'll get time to read today. I want to know all there is to know about her, like maybe if I read these here books enough, something will crop up to make me sure.

On the way to town I pass a couple walking the other way down the dusty track, "billing and cooing" at a great rate. Holding hands and walking real slow with her head on his shoulder. He says, "Oh, you are so beautiful," and gazes into her eyes like a sick cow. I'd like to be the object of such a look, but it ain't likely, being born ugly. I doubt anyone will ever see me as anything but an addled, imbecile of a girl. But Jeremy don't see me that way, not addled or an imbecile anyway. He may not see me as a beauty, but he keeps on hanging around. Ain't in no hurry to get shut of me. I smile at that. Makes me feel warm all over.

That girl is about my age. I'll bet it's that Mary one who's been neglecting her poor grandmother. Now I see why. She's besotted with that young man. I think of her poor old grandmother struggling to stay alive on her own, and her out here traipsing around with whosomever he is, like she don't have a care in the world.

It don't seem right to me, so I turn on my heel and head back down the track for the old lady's house. I pass them, Mary and her beau, 'cause they're just meandering anyway, and I turn off and follow my own path back to camp. Soot's so glad to see me back, he's beside himself. I tell him to come on, and we head off toward the old lady's place.

She's setting on the porch, dozing again. I rap on the post and she wakes up, smiling. "Why Nell, I was just dreaming about you!"

"Dreaming? About me?" I can't get that idea comfortable in my brain. Somebody dreaming about me.

"Yes. I dreamed you and I were caught in a winter storm, and you built us a fire and a lean to and kept the wolves away."

"Wolves, huh? Granny, you have some imagination."

"Oh, there's wolves all right. In winter they come across the river from the Kentucky side. Sometimes I hear them howling outside my door at night. Makes me think they've come for me."

I shiver. "Well, if I was here, I'd beat 'em with a barrel stave. You had breakfast yet?"

"Yes, dear. Leftover stew. It was even better this morning."

"Got any work for me today?"

"We could bake bread. I ain't had fresh bread in more than a week."

"I ain't never baked bread before, but I seen Sister Mary Patrick do it lots of times, so I guess I could figure it out."

The old lady rises stiffly out of her rocker and leans on her cane to get to the door. "Come on. Every girl should know how to bake bread. I'll show you."

So I get my first lesson in bread baking. It takes most of the day to mix it up and let the dough rise, and punch it down and let it rise again before you finally bake it. But I decide it's another good skill to have, so I pay particular attention. The old lady brightens up as we go and shows me the how and the why of it. I like her. I can't figure why that Mary girl don't take better care of her. Then I remember. Oh, yeah. That.

"Here. Punch it down like this." She tucks her stick under one arm and dives into the bread dough with both fists. She's kind of rough in her manner, but I'm getting used to that. "Didn't your ma ever teach you to bake bread?"

"No, ma'am. My ma had to give me up when I was just a baby. Sent me back east to be raised by the nuns."

"Nuns, is it? I mighta known." She gives the dough another good punch. "Popish. Them's the kind that begets children and lets 'em for somebody else to raise."

"Do you have any children, Missus?" I figure she does, what with her calling me Mary yesterday, so I nose around a little. Don't hurt to know how things set.

"I did, but I lost them. They was five at one time. The two gals up and married and run off west somewheres. The one boy got the typhus and died when he was but fourteen. The second went off to the war and never come back, and the last one lives around here someplace, but he don't come around but maybe once a year." She says it all matter of fact, like she's reading it out of a book. I look at her eyes for a tear or two, but they's so deep set, it would take a tear a coon's age to find its way out through the wrinkles.

I guess her eyesight ain't so good, 'cause she never says nothing about how homely I am. And maybe she don't hear so good, either, 'cause she don't ask why I talk funny. The only time she seems sad is when she talks about her Thomas. That was her husband, Thomas Hubbard, a good man and a fine provider. "But he's gone and left me. I get a bit lonely, 'specially in the winter. I can't get around so good, so I don't go neighboring."

I get so mad at that son of hers I could spit a nail at him. But then I get over it. His neglect gives me a chance to pretend I have a grandmother to teach me all the things a girl needs to know.

"Here, child. Sit down to this here quilt. I bet they never taught you to quilt, those nuns."

"No, ma'am, they didn't." While the bread rises, we sit over a quilting frame and she teaches me another great skill. I'm clumsy with the needle at first, but she has everlasting patience. Not like the nuns who would rap you on the head over nothing.

"Now make your stitches tiny." She gets down real close and peers at my work. "There, like that. My, you have a way with a needle. Such fine work on your first try." As we work, she prattles on like I'm kin. "Back in Philadelphy, where I was born, we was Quakers. Come west across Pennsylvania over the years. My brothers'n sisters was all older'n me, so they was getting married right along." She moves her chair to a new part of the quilt. "Then Papa got it in his head to float on down the Ohio to Indiana. He fell off the flatboat and drowned a ways upriver from here. My mama and I was all that was left after all the marrying, so we settled in Cincinnati with some other Quakers. That's where I met Thomas Hubbard. He wasn't a Quaker. That vexed my mother, but I couldn't hear her."

I listen to her story like somebody was telling me a fairy tale. I love peoples' stories. Everyone has one, but most folks don't think theirs is so interesting. I do. Maybe because mine is so full of holes.

When the bread is done, she gives me a warm loaf to take back with me. She ain't asked me about my life beyond knowing that I'm an orphan. I'm glad. I don't know what I'd tell her. I let on like I'm traveling with my brother, but I don't mention no destination and she don't ask. Before I go I make sure she has everything she needs to get her to tomorrow and I promise to come back. I know I should get to town and try to find work, but something keeps pulling me back to that little cottage by the river.

Jeremy don't come home that night, nor the next one, neither. I'm mad because he's missed my homemade bread and some corn pone I made and some stewed chicken. Granny Hubbard and I are having a time, teaching me to cook and sew and even knit. She has all manner of cloth and yarn stowed here and there. Just when I think I know where things is at, she brings something out of another hidey hole. I start in to knit Jeremy a pair of stockings, which I hope to have done before winter, or before he off and leaves me, whichever. Winter's a long way off, but I'm not that quick with my fingers. I don't let on to Granny that Jeremy ain't coming home nights. I don't want her to worry about me.

When Jeremy don't come home I read by the firelight. I'm done with all five of them books already, and the fire in my belly to find Jane has just growed. I sure do like Granny, and I'd hate to up and leave Jeremy, but I'm dying to get along. Still, he don't come home, and I keep going to Granny's ever' day.

Inside of a week she's taught me to cook, bake, quilt, knit and embroider. I like it, too. I could settle right in here and take care of her for the rest of her days, if it wasn't for Jane. It looks like Jeremy's never coming back. It'd hurt a lot more if it wasn't for Granny. But you never know. He might turn up any day yet.

One afternoon I go out and pick us a pail of raspberries for a cobbler. The berry patch is along the fence row out near the track. Berries as big as your thumb, and sweet. Granny shows me how to make the cobbler. She don't need no written down receipt. She knows it all in her head. We're just taking it out of the oven when a girl comes walking down the path from the road, looking like she owns the place.

"Who are you?" she asks. Demands, rather.

"My name's Nell. Who are you?"

"Mary Hubbard. This here is my granny's place. What you doing here, anyhow?"

It's the same Mary I saw on the road with her beau. I don't like her, right off. "Helping out," I say.

"Who asked you to?"

"Nobody. I could see she needed help, is all."

"Well, you can go along now. I'll take care of her from here."

Granny is sitting on the porch listening. "Leave off of her, Mary. She's been a Godsend to me."

"Looks to me like you're a Godsend to her. Bet she's been stealing you blind."

"No, I ain't."

Granny gets up and waves her stick at her granddaughter. "Off with you now! You ain't got time for me, and now you're jealous because somebody else has."

Mary gets all huffy. "You better be careful how you talk, Granny. Once this ugly one gets through with you, you won't have nothing left, and you'll be glad to see me come a cold winter day." She turns to me. "Who are you? Why do you talk funny?"

"Told you, my name is Nell. I ain't done no harm. Your grandma is a right nice lady. I was just trying to help."

"Well, you skedaddle. She don't need your help. We take care of her."

That makes me mad. "Don't look like it to me. Looks to me like you're just waiting around 'til she dies. An old lady like her needs looking after. I been here a week and ain't seed hide nor hair of you, 'cept on the track mooning over some feller. Seems like if you cared for your granny you'd come by every day, not just when you ain't got naught else to do!"

She gets fire in her eye and comes at me like to pull my hair, but I juke out of the way and put up my fists. Next thing I know, Granny is between us, shaking her stick and hollering, "Stop that this minute, you girls! Mary, she's right and you know it. Get on home with you. And tell your pa I want to talk to him. I'm his load to carry, not yours. Nell, get in the house."

I go, and so does that Mary girl. I figure she'll go get her pa and he'll come down on both of us like a duck on a June bug. I don't want to cause no trouble.

"Think I'll be going, Granny. I don't want no unpleasantness. I'll go back to my boat and get your books. They was amazing fun to read."

"Don't trouble yourself, child. Mary'll be a long time getting home, if I know her. She's silly over that Ebersole boy. Has been for six months. We'll be having a wedding one of these days, like as not. She'll meet him at the schoolhouse and waste the rest of the day and then forget to tell her pa when she does get home. I've asked for him time and again, and never see him for weeks on end. Come on inside and let's have our cobbler."

That evening, I'm lying on the riverbank with my back against a tree, reading by firelight. The night sounds—frogs, crickets, a hooty owl now and then—keep me company. Soot gets up kind of slow and walks around stiff-legged, sniffing the air like he knows something. Then, a second later, Jeremy appears out of the dark. As he approaches the fire, I get that funny feeling in my gut that I got when I first laid eyes on him. He's so beautiful, he like to takes my breath away.

He stands there all proud, wearing a new suit and a hat and new shoes, all fancy and stylish. He's got parcels under both arms, and he sets them down by the fire and puts down a rag to sit on.

"Where you been?" I ask, trying control my fluttering heart. He's a sight to behold.

"In town. I told you."

"Didn't tell me you wasn't coming back for a week."

"Sorry. I didn't know that. But you must come into town with me, Nell. I can get you work in the Wattleman household, and we can both live in utter comfort."

I give him a look. "I ain't comfortable with taking advantage of people."

Jeremy brushes a bit of lint off his pants. "I'm not taking advantage, really. I'm just meeting their needs. They need another son, and I need a comfortable life. It works just fine."

"How long you gonna keep this up?"

"I don't know. As long as it feels right."

Now I'm vexed at him, but I can't say why. "Well, I ain't got time to be hanging around Cincinnati playing on folks' needs. I gotta be on my way. I need to be out west before the summer is gone."

"You still hanging on to that Calamity Jane make-believe? Come on, Nell. It's a fantasy, if ever I heard one. I don't know why you feel such a need to prove she's your mother. You could probably find out who your mother was if you'd just write a letter to the convent and ask."

"They don't know. Sister Mary Gethsemane told me that before she left. Told me all she knew was my mother's name was Jane. That's all."

"Well, if you wrote and asked, maybe somebody would remember something. It'd be better than pursuing this hopeless pipe dream."

"It ain't no pipe dream. It's real. And why I need to prove it is, I ain't got nobody, Jeremy. I don't belong nowhere. I ain't important to no one. If I was, they'd have told me. Just wait. You'll be sorry you didn't believe me when I find her and she reaches out to me with love in her eyes."

Jeremy turns his head to hide a grin. This ain't one of his beautiful grins. It's a "making-fun-of-a-addle-brained girl" kind of grin. I stand up.

"You can stay here and steal from these folk if you want to, but I've a mind to move on. I gotta say good-bye to Granny and see that she's got what she needs, but after that, I'm leaving."

"Guess you won't want the presents I brought you, then, huh?"

"What presents?"

He rises and unwraps the first of three bundles. It's a brand new green and white gingham dress with a sunbonnet to match. "I ain't never had a new dress before," I tell him. He opens the second bundle, a shiny new pair of black leather high-button shoes. I'm speechless. The third bundle contains under things that I wonder how Jeremy even knows they exist.

"Joanna picked them out for you." He's back to the grin again.

"Joanna? Who's Joanna?"

"Mr. Wattleman's daughter. She's nineteen. My—ah—sister, you might say."

I'm so full of feelings, I can't sort them out. Jeremy's nice to get me these beautiful clothes, but he's rotten for laughing at my dream, and who's this Joanna? Sister, my granny's petticoat.

Chapter 8

The next morning I get up before dawn, feed the fire, and haul kindling and water. I put on the coffee pot and heat up the iron skillet. Jeremy is awake, but he lies still, wrapped up in his blanket, watching me. I don't want to talk to him. I wish he'd just go back to town. But I don't want him to go back to town. I want him to stay. I want things between us to go back to the way they were.

"So, are you going to dress up in your new finery and go to town with me?" He's lying on his back now, arms behind his head, yawning.

I don't want to answer that one for a while, so I make a job out of poking up the fire and rearranging the coffee pot.

"No."

"No? Why no?"

"'Cause I gotta get west is why. You think I'm crazy for thinking it, but I gotta go find her. Find out who I am."

"What if you find her and she's never heard of you? Thinks you've escaped from bedlam and sends you packing? What then, Nell?"

"She won't. I know she won't. She'll be so glad to see me she'll never let me go again."

"Just what do you think your life is going to be like when you do find her—if she should, by the wildest of possibilities, be your mother?"

"I don't know. Maybe I'll keep house for her while she goes on her adventures. Maybe she's getting tired of the wild life and wants to settle down with her daughter. Maybe she owns a nice little house in some town in the west where there's cowboys and lawmen and gunfights. How would I know? I just want to meet her, is all. Meet her and have a place in this world."

He rolls over with his back to the fire. I crack the eggs on the edge of the pan and set them to fry. When they're done, I divide

51

them up and put some on one of Granny's plates I've been using, along with a goodly slice of bread. I put the plate on the ground beside him, sit on a rock, and commence to eat my eggs out of the fry pan. Neither of us says anything for a long time.

"You can stay here if you want to," I tell him. "I ain't got no claim to you, and I don't blame you for thinking I'm addled. This here sounds like a good life for you. I can see you married to that Joanna girl and living high in Cincinnati for the rest of your life, like Mr. and Mrs. Andrew Carnegie.

Jeremy screws up his nose. "Put that way, it sounds dull. I'm not ready to give myself over to the domestic life yet."

"Well, then you better get in that boat and haul off with me, cause if you stay here another month, it'll be all over but the wedding vows."

He sighs and rolls out of his blanket. His new clothes are already dusty and wrinkled. He pouts and snorts as he dusts himself off. "Sometimes I think you're the most trying woman I ever hope to meet."

"Well, you ain't no joy in the mornin' yourself. I told you you could stay or go, no matter. Now what's eating you?"

"I can't let you go out there all by yourself on a hopeless quest. It's a dangerous world. Come on, Nell. We could be very comfortable here."

"Yeah. A couple of house servants, you and me. That's what it'd be, Jeremy. Voluntary slavery, for both of us. I want to see the world and learn its ways. I want to test my mettle and come up proud. I could survive in lots of ways, but that ain't enough. I want more. I want to know who I am."

"Okay. Okay. We'll keep going. But I need a few days to ease out of this situation. Then we'll say our good-byes and move on." He don't even eat breakfast. He just slings his coat over his shoulder and walks off without another word.

I'm standing alone in the clearing, the river flowing silently by. I watch it for a while, thinking I could just up and float on down without him, but I know I won't. Soot comes up and whines. I pat his head and give him a scratch behind the ears. I'm getting what I want, so why do I feel so empty?

I wash up the breakfast things in the river and look around at the new clothes Jeremy brought. Granny gave me some homemade soap to bring back with me, so I have my next task all laid out. I decide to clean myself up, so I slip off to a sheltered spot a little farther along and take off my dress. I give myself a good scrubbing and wash the leaves and twigs out of my hair. As I'm drying off with one of the whores' petticoats, I remember seeing a comb in the bottom of the carpetbag, so I slip into the new under things and go look for it. I sit on a rock and comb my hair for about a hour, till it's dry. Then I put on the new gingham dress and the black lace-up shoes. I tear a strip off the whores' petticoat for a ribbon and tie my hair back.

There. I'm ready. Soot and I set out for Grandma Hubbard's. I've got her books under one arm and her plate under the other. I rehearse how to tell her I'll be going soon. I know she'll be sad for that. I will, too, but Jane keeps beckoning me. Anyway, I've got to get Jeremy away from this Joanna girl before he does something stupid that we'll both regret.

Something's afoot when I get to Granny's cottage. There's a wagon pulled up to the front, and a man and a strapping big boy are loading stuff into it. I am near about up to the door when that Mary girl steps off the porch and comes at me fierce.

"You! I'm surprised you have the nerve to show your face around here." Her words make the spit fly and she comes at me fit for a scrap.

I take a step backwards and nearly trip over Granny's watering can. "Where's Granny?" I ask, recovering my balance.

"Gone from the likes of you." Mary moves toward me again, her hands in fists.

"I never done nothing to her. She's my friend."

The man comes off the porch and stands by Mary. I guess it's her pa, 'cause I see a resemblance right off. I nod a greeting to him, but he stands next to her aglaring at me like I should know why. Mary grabs the plate from my hand and her pa takes the dime novels. "I'm surprised you'd bring anything back," he growls.

"Bring 'em back? Of course I brung 'em back. Granny just loaned them to me. Where is she, anyway? Ask her. She'll tell you. I never took nothing she didn't give me."

"Oh yeah?"

Mary shoves her face about two inches from mine. Her eyes are brown, flecked with gold. I ain't never seen eyes like that before. Mine are brown, too, but not like that. Just brown.

I feel myself starting to get mad. "Yeah." I sidestep Mary Hubbard and set my path for the porch. "Granny! Where are you, Granny?"

"She ain't here. Gone. We took her to our place. Too much trouble to look after her, what with trash like you leeching off her and her whining all the time about we don't pay her no mind." It's Mary's pa talking now. He takes a step to the right and blocks my way to the porch. Mary comes up behind me, and I feel real tight closed in.

"If you never took nothing, where'd you get the money for them fine clothes? Fancy new store bought dress and high-button shoes! Don't tell me she give you money, too! Never give me any money. I'm damned if I'll stand by and let you have what shoulda been mine!"

She reaches for my bonnet and rips it off and drops it in the dirt. Then she steps on it and wiggles her foot to mash the dirt in good.

That's it. I go for her. I ain't never been in a fight before, and it don't take me long to figure out that Miss Mary has. She grabs me by the shoulders and drops me to the ground with a grunt. Soot's into barking and growling, but Mary's pa grabs him by the scruff and holds him back. Next thing I know, Miss Mary's on top of me, with two fists full of my hair. I twist and turn to get away from her, but she keeps one hand ahold of my hair and smacks my face with the other. I wish I had my ma's know how. I'd give her a lesson or two.

Mary's pa pulls Soot around behind. "Get in there, girl. Slap her good. That's it! Get ahold of her arm and twist!"

All of a sudden I see my Ma, Calamity Jane, standing there with her arms crossed looking at me in disgust. I give a big heave of my hips and turn over, dumping Miss Mary onto the ground like a sack of meal. Then I struggle my way up and put up my fists.

"Come on, then. You want a fight, I'll give it to you. Nobody got no call to accuse me of stealing."

Miss Mary is sitting back on her butt, still looking mean at me, but I sense she's surprised at my spunk and in no mood to test me further. "You go on. Get outta here."

"No! Not till I say good-bye to Granny."

"I told you she ain't here. Pa took her to our place last night. We just come to get the rest of her stuff. Now get on with you."

I pick up my bonnet and beat the dust from my dress. It's all dirty and torn loose at the waist. I have a notion to fly into her again because of my dress, but it could get torn worse, so I back off. "Well, tell her I said good-bye. Tell her thanks for all she done for me."

Miss Mary and her pa stand their ground. I turn and walk away, sure Granny's never going to hear one word about me. Soot follows me back down the path along the river and lies down with his face on his paws while I wash the worst of the dirt from my bonnet and new dress and wipe the dust from my shoes. They're scuffed. A fine muddle I got myself into. I ain't even got a needle and thread to fix the rip.

I don't think to see Jeremy for a couple of days, anyway, so I take me back to camp and start to pick things up a bit. I don't know what I'll eat, for I was counting on spending the day with Granny. I'm down to one book again, and I can almost recite that one, so I might as well go fishing. I'm sitting on the bank with a line in the water when Soot gets up and says a quiet woof and starts wagging his tail. I think it's Jeremy, but when I turn around, I see a big old plow horse plodding along the path. I stand up, wary of company.

"Don't fret, child. It's only me."

I jump at the sound of Granny's voice. "Granny! How'd you get here? Whose horse is that?"

"My own. Or used to be before they up and took it. Here. Give me a hand down."

I stand beside so she can lean on my shoulder while she slides down the wide flank a handful of mane to steady her. "You better get gone from here," I tell her. "They'd thrash both of us if they knew."

She stands beside me, a frumpy old lady, her hair flying out in wisps, her skirt spattered with mud. I put my arms around her. "Granny, ain't there no place else you can go? How can they just up and move you out of your own house like that?"

"I ain't never going back there. Never. They's an old Quaker couple in Cincinnati that'll take me in. Distant cousins. Don't you worry, child. Once you hoist me back up on that horse, they'll never see me again."

The horse looks near about as old as Granny, and I doubt he can get her into town without collapsing in the street. "Let me lead you. I ain't got naught else to do today, anyway."

For the next hour we plod along the road to Cincinnati, Granny aboard the horse and me leading with Soot following behind. It ain't far, and Granny is sure she knows where her relatives live, so I just tramp along, trying not to think about the hole in my belly. Nothing to eat since breakfast. The road is never very far from the river, and we pass all manner of folk coming and going. I keep an eye out for Jeremy, but I don't really expect to see him. He's probably got a full belly and another new suit by now.

My dress is dry and it still looks nice in spite of the waist torn out along the side. I'll fix it soon as I get some thread. Granny's tired. She slumps over the horse's big neck, and I sidle up to him so's to be there if she starts to slide. We're in town now, clopping along brick streets.

"You sure you know where this is?" I ask her.

She nods toward the next alley, so I lead the horse in there until she stops me by a iron gate. I help her down and we tie up the horse and Soot to the fence and open the gate. The back yard is lovely, green and full of apple, pear and cherry trees. We pass the stable and make our way along a vegetable garden on one side and the fanciest flower patch I ever seen on the other. One knock at the back door brings a round-faced woman about Granny's age, dressed in Quaker gray, flushed with baking and cooking. She recognizes Granny right off and welcomes her with a big hug.

"Elizabeth! Praise be to God! How did you get here?"

"Oh, Martha. I've so much to tell you. Can you make room for a poor wayfarer? My home is no longer my own."

"Of course! You've a home here as long as you need it."

Granny collapses into a big old wooden rocker by the kitchen stove. "This here is my girl, Nell. A true friend and helpmeet. I couldn't have got here without her."

The woman notices me for the first time and fusses over me. "Oh, dear girl, you look hungry. Sit down. I'll be only a minute."

I sit at a long plank table covered with oil cloth. The kitchen smells of strawberries. She's making jam. It isn't a moment before she's set a huge slab of fresh-baked bread before me, next to a pot of new strawberry preserves. My mouth is watering so I can hardly taste.

Once I'm finished eating, I remember the horse and dog out back. "Ma'am? We got a horse needs tending. If you'll tell me where to put him, I'll..."

"Nonsense, girl. My grandson will take care of him." She goes to the hall door. "David! Come here a minute. We need a man."

I'm still distraught over my torn dress, so I venture to ask for a needle and thread. They are soon provided and I sit quietly on the bench mending while Cousin Martha bustles about, stirring her preserves, setting out jars and melting paraffin to seal them. The kitchen is big and bright, with a whole wall of windows on one side, a pump, and a sink under the windows with a pipe that carries the water to a barrel outside. There's a great big cook stove, bigger than Granny's, and this here table where I'm sitting could seat about eighteen. I stitch up my dress in no time, listening to Granny unfold her tale of woe. Martha's reaction is nothing but open arms and welcome. If I have to go off and leave her, at least I'll know Granny'll be taken care of here. It's getting on toward dusk, and I'm looking at a two-or-three-mile walk back to my boat, so I rise.

"I gotta go, now, Granny. Seems like you'll be fine here."

"She will!" Martha chimes in.

Granny pulls herself up, a tear already glistening in her eye. "I got something for you," she says, reaching deep into her skirt pocket and bringing out a little satin reticule like they had back in the war days. She opens the drawstrings and reaches in, brings out three big gold coins and turns to Martha. "Here. These is for my keep." She drops them into Martha's hand.

"Now, Elizabeth. There's no call for you to pay for anything."

"Keep it for me, then. I don't want my no-account son and his young'uns to get at it. That's what they was looking for at my house. Like to turned the place upside down trying to find them gold coins. My man had 'em saved from before the war."

She reaches into the purse again and turns to me. "This here one's for you, Nell. I know you need it, so don't make no arguments. You just go on. I hope you find whatever it is you're looking for. You been good to me."

I take the coin, a twenty-dollar gold piece, without protest. A double eagle! I know I need it, too, but my eyes fill up. No one has ever treated me so before. My heart quickens, knowing this will help me get where I'm going a lot quicker.

Hold on, Mama Jane. I'm coming!

As I bid her good-bye, Granny clings to me like I'm her own. Whatever I find out about my ma, I know this: I have a grandmother right here in Cincinnati praying and watching out for me. I walk back to the boat trying to shake off the sadness. Soot keeps pace with me, his head ever within reach of my hand, like he knows I need a friend.

When I get back to camp, there sits Jeremy in the boat, all loaded up and ready to go. He looks as dejected as I feel.

"What're you doing? Trying to run off without me?"

"No. I figured you'd show up before dark. I'm in a bit of a hurry to be gone from here. My situation has changed."

"How so?"

"Remember young Wilfred Wattleman?"

"The one that went west and wasn't heard of again?"

"Right. Well, he showed up last night, very much alive, and that made me excess baggage. An interloper. Persona non grata"

"What about that girl? That Joanna? I thought you was courting her."

"So did she. That's another reason why I need to be gone."

He gives me a hand into the boat and whistles. Soot comes bounding in, tail awag, ears alert. Like to spill us over. The broad Ohio River pulls us in.

"Where was that Wilfred Wattleman, anyway? Why didn't he write home?"

"Out west. Place called Deadwood. I guess he was too busy adventuring."

My heart stops. "Deadwood! Did you say Deadwood? As in Dakota territory?"

Jeremy pulls on the oars to get us well into the current. "I guess so. Why?"

"Jeremy, turn this boat around. We gotta get back to Cincinnati. I need to talk to this Wilfred Wattleman."

He looks at me like I'm daft. "Hell, no, Nell. I'm not going back there. It's late. Besides, I don't think I'd be welcome now."

"Why? Did you steal something? Make off with Mr. Wattleman's watch or the family silver or something?"

"Never mind, Nell. I'm not going back, and that's that."

"Well, then, turn in to shore and let me out."

Chapter 9

I never thought of myself as stubborn, but Jeremy allows that I am, about as stubborn as a dog worrying a possum in a woodpile. He don't actually say that, but he says a lot of other things while he's rowing us in to shore, which he hits so hard I almost topple out backwards.

"I don't know what you're so put out about. You was the one that wanted to hang around Cincinnati for a while. What's the matter? Wore out your welcome already?" I feel mean. I grab a tuft of grass to pull myself up out of the boat, but it gives way, and I almost fall into the river. Now I feel meaner. "Bet them folks seen through your pretty face shenanigans right off. Probably sent you packing even before their precious boy come home."

Jeremy sits in the rower's seat giving me a look that would stop a clock. I can't tell what he's thinking, but I can bet it ain't nothing nice about me.

He snorts, scornful-like. "I ought to just put you out and go on my way. I swear, you are a trial with your silly fantasy life."

I suck in my breath. But what did I expect? I *am* a trial. Like Sister Mary Patrick used to say, I could drive a priest to drink. 'Course, in my experience, lots of them drank anyway, and it didn't have nothing to do with me. So I guess nothing's changed in the three weeks I been out here on my own.

I turn away and reach for another tuft of grass. This one holds, and I haul myself out of the boat. Up on the bank, I look back at him. "You ought to be the one that's out here, not me. It's my boat. You ought to be the one walking."

"Now, Nell, don't be illogical." He's standing now, reaching for the anchor chain. There's an old flatiron hooked onto it, and he swings that for the shore, aiming it a few feet from where I stand.

Then he pulls the boat in close and reaches up for a hand. I stand still, hands on my hips. Wouldn't give him a hand if he was drowning.

He looks up at me, shamefaced. "I'm sorry. Here, give me a hand up so I can apologize like a man." He balances himself holding onto one oar, his hand extended.

I look down at him from the grassy bank. Oh, he's handsome all right. Fancy clothes and boots a little past their prime, but still a fine figure of a man standing there in that grimy rowboat. Irks me how he can be so fine looking and so vexing all at once. "I ain't of a mind for apologies. You can get out and start walking."

Soot sits in the back of the boat, whining. It's a high jump for him, so he stays put, but he's edgy all the same. I turn on my heel and head back for Cincinnati, with no idea how to find this here Wilfred Wattleman. Guess I'll just ask around 'til I do.

I step along at a fast pace, not really sure how far I'll go this evening. It's getting dark fast, and I haven't thought this out. Next thing I know, Jeremy is beside me, hurrying to catch up, still apologizing.

"Honestly, Nell. You *are* a trial. You have to grant me that. You can't say I haven't been patient. Anyway, how are you going to find the Wattleman house without me? It's dark already! Do you want to be alone out here on the road at night?"

I stop. "I can find it without you. You need to get on downriver and leave me alone. And don't take my boat. Or my dog. Just get on with you."

He reaches out and grabs my arm, spins me around to look right in his face. He looks like he might could cry. "Nell, it's a fantasy. A dream. A fairy tale you made up for yourself. Wilfred Wattleman won't know anything about her. He'll just think you're a lunatic."

I wrench my arm free and back off as if to hit him, but he steps up and puts his arms around me, holding me so tight I can't get loose. I struggle, but not too much. He tucks my head under his chin and rocks me back and forth.

"There, there, girl. It's all right. I am sorry, you know. Let's just get past this, okay?"

"Why does everything have to be a big run-in? You know you're going to go back and help me find that Wilfred What's-his-name. Why don't you just do it and not have a set-to about it?"

"One, in case it's escaped your notice, it's dark night, so we can't go until morning, anyway. Two, you don't know what kind of people you might run into. Three. .. Well, three is, I don't really want to face Joanna Wattleman again."

"Nasty breakup, huh?"

"In a manner of speaking, yes. She had high hopes for a permanent relationship."

I look at his face, trying to read his feelings. Is he sorry or relieved to be leaving this girl? I can't tell for sure.

"You can probably get in and out without even seeing her if you go early in the morning."

"Oh, all right. I'll go, but I want you to know, it's a sacrifice."

I nod. "Now, let's go back and get Soot and make a camp." I'm back to myself pretty quick, but the memory of him holding me lingers, and I take it to bed with me to warm me in the night.

Me and Jeremy sleep in our clothes, snuggled up like spoons, with the whores' wardrobe for a comforter. Good old Soot adds his warmth to the mix. Morning has barely dawned when I'm up and groomed for the walk back to Cincinnati. Jeremy groans as he rolls out, but he ties Soot up by the boat, leaves him some water and a bone to gnaw and we start walking before the mist has lifted.

We're in town by eight o'clock, and Jeremy goes into a bake shop and buys us each a roll. We munch on them, walking along a street by the river, dodging the boatmen as they load, unload and launch the steamboats. I'm fascinated by steamboats. They're real big—and some are pretty fancy. I always wave when they pass us on the river. Sometimes the folk wave back. I'd love to take a ride on one, just once.

We turn away from the river and come to a little park, kind of like a town square, with a band shell surrounded by big leafy maple trees, but this town is too big for this little square to be all. Jeremy nods toward a bench, and we sit down.

"It's only a few blocks from here. I'll go see if I can get Wilfred to come down and talk to you. You wait here." He's up and gone before I can form a protest.

I yell after him. "Don't tell him why I want to talk to him. I don't want nothing made up."

I figure he don't want to take me with him 'cause he don't want to be seen with a ugly girl, or maybe he don't want to flaunt me in front of this Joanna. I don't care, long as I get to talk to someone who's actually been to Deadwood. He's probably seen my ma. Maybe he knows her real good. I sit in the morning sun letting myself run with the dream.

In about a hour I see them coming more than a block away. Wilfred Wattleman is a skinny little slip of a man. He walks kind of bent over, looks old before his time. When they get up close I see his eyes are real close together, like God pinched his forehead. He don't appear real glad to be rousted away from his comfortable breakfast on a fine June morning to come down here and talk to me.

Jeremy makes the introductions. "Go on, Nell, ask him. You were so anxious to talk to him. Now here he is."

I turn a little pale and my mouth feels dry. I talk funny anyway, but when my mouth is dry, my voice sounds like a chicken getting its neck wrung. "Um. Do you. .. Er. .. Did you ever hear of Calamity Jane?"

"Of course. Everyone in Deadwood knows about her." He answers like he's already bored with the conversation.

"Did you ever meet her?"

"No. She doesn't live in Deadwood any more. I heard she'd gone off and got married or something. Hard to tell where she is now."

I feel the need to account for my interest. "I read all about her in them books."

He nods, inspecting his fingernails. "Lots of people have. It's hard to know the truth about her, though. She makes up stories about herself, and the dime novelists make them up, too. So you can't count on the truth of anything you've read about her."

He stands in front of the bench where I'm sitting, hands behind his back—like a lawyer—looking around like he's nervous or something. Like he'd rather not be seen talking to the likes of me.

I look from him to Jeremy, trying to get a purchase on this feller. He's a puzzle. "Did you ever hear about her having any kin?"

"Something about her family all being dead. Long time ago. "

"Did you hear anything else?"

"There's a million stories about Calamity Jane, but, never having met the woman, I can't be a reliable source."

"Was she really a scout for the army?"

"So I've heard. It's how she got her reputation, but again, even that might be an exaggeration. Local folks don't set much store by anything she says."

I stop for a second and work up this picture of my mother leading the army away from a tribe of screaming Indians bent on slaughter. My heart beats with pride.

"What about kids of her own?"

"There's talk that she had a daughter, but you never know what's true and what's not. Nobody's seen hide nor hair of a child, but then, you can't prove anything by me." He dusts his fingers with his thumbs when he talks, like he has powder on them and wants it off. He smells awful good for a man.

My ears are ringing. My face must be white as granny's underwear on a clothesline. I can hardly breathe. I look at Jeremy, and he lowers his eyes, like he hopes this is enough talk so he can be gone from here right quick. I don't guess there's much more this Wilfred can tell me. I can hardly keep still, though. I want to yell at Jeremy. "See? What'd I tell you? See?"

"Thank you, Mr. Wattleman. You've been very helpful." I say it formal-like, so he knows we're done. I get up and start walking back down toward the river. Jeremy stumbles through his thank yous and good-byes and follows after me.

We've turned the corner, with the river on our left side heading downstream, before I say anything.

"Well, what do you think of that? Huh? If you was Jane and you got this child without any roof in her mouth, wouldn't you send her someplace where she'd be taken care of? Wouldn't you think the Wild West was maybe too wild for a poor, deformed child? I would. I'd send her back east to live with a grandmother or a aunt or somebody, or someplace she could grow up and read about me then come back and find me when she was all growed."

Jeremy walks along beside me, biting his lip. "It still isn't real evidence, Nell. Just because she might have had a daughter around your age, doesn't mean it's you."

"Now, Jeremy, that's just why I get so vexed with you. You ain't got a ounce of imagination. You can't see something that's sitting there staring at you, like a ox in a outhouse. Of course it's me. I *know* it's me."

He walks beside me, staring straight ahead. I can't resist one more jab at him. "And don't go telling me what a trial I am. Good thing I made you turn around and come back here."

Jeremy's discomfort at being back in this town is plain visible. He looks around kind of nervous and quickens his stride. I hurry to keep up with him, lost in the joy of being the daughter of Calamity Jane.

We get back to the boat and Soot just in time to see a big steamer passing, headed upriver. I wait for the waves to settle down before I row out into the current. The whole time, Jeremy is crabbing at me about how silly I am to think what I think, and I'm crabbing at him because he refuses to think it. Finally, I fall silent. I've heard enough about how dumb it is to think Jane's my ma. But when I entertain the notion that I might be wrong, I get a creepy feeling in the back of my neck that goes all the way down to my butt.

I feel all lost and alone, like everbody else has some place to be. Somebody to care about them, some purpose for their life. My heart gets to pounding like I'm being chased by wolves, and I can't run because the snow is too deep. I turn away from Jeremy and study downriver like there's something real interesting down there. I can't let him see me cry.

A few minutes later, I turn to him. "Jeremy?"

"Yes, Nell."

"Why do you stay with me, anyway? I know I ain't pretty, and I ain't got no money, so why didn't you just stay back there in Cincinnati, or go someplace else?"

He stops rowing and looks me in the eye. "Sometimes I wonder that myself. I guess it's the need for adventure. Right now my funds are low, and this is cheap transportation. But, it's more than that. You're a vulnerable girl out on a dangerous quest. You need me, whether you know it or not. I can't just leave you and go on my way until I know you'll be safe. Besides, I'm always up for adventure, and being with you is that."

I listen, studying the bottom of the boat. I feel the urge to get riled at him for thinking I'm so weak and needy, but I don't. The feeling passes. "What you gonna do once you decide I'm safe to leave?"

"I don't know. Keep going I guess. These American towns are a fascination to me. Like St. Louis, or New Orleans, or even your precious Deadwood. I'd like to see Denver and San Francisco, maybe even Seattle. After that, who knows? Hawaii? Australia?"

"What's so fine about those places? I mean, don't you ever want to settle down in one place and make a home? Get married? Start a family?"

He raises his head and looks me in the eye again, but don't say nothing. Then he looks out at the river going by. "No. No, none of that for me." There's a little tinge of sadness in his voice.

I can't figure him out. Not a bit. Handsome as he is, and charming. He could have any girl he ever wanted, and he's just as happy to be floating down the Ohio in a boat with about the homeliest girl you'd ever want to meet.

Chapter 10

We leave Cincinnati and float along without talking much for several days. Every time I look in his direction, Jeremy's looking someplace else, so I leave him to hisself, but I'm still wary that he'll make fun of my dream, and it's a sure thing he's just about run out of patience with me. Every town we pass, I pray he won't take it in his head to leave me, because the thought of it brings on a deep down feeling of loneliness.

It's rainy and dull—kind of like how I feel—but we float along in a quiet standoff until we come to this place called Magnet, Indiana. A good name for it, if you ask me. 'Specially with some preacher man holding a revival there. We hear the hollering and chanting from way upriver, so when we find the place, our curiosity—or Jeremy's, anyway—makes us stop. It's like a great big camp with tents and cook fires and mud everywhere. There's people wandering around arm in arm, some of them holding Bibles that they wave at each other to make a point. Jeremy is just plain taken in by it all. I ain't. To me it seems like a lot of play acting, but Jeremy ain't never seen such carrying on, so he makes out that we have to stop and stay a while.

If ever there was a body you'd never forget, it'd be that preacher man, Valoreous Cates. He runs this tent meeting, and it don't take long to see shy. He ain't very tall, and he ain't very handsome, but there's something about him. Charismatic is what they say, but I don't rightly know what that means. Except if it means he can make folk do and say what they wouldn't never have done nor said, then I guess that's what he is. Charismatic. I'll never see the like of him in this life, I can tell you.

"What do you think you're going to get by hanging around here?" I ask Jeremy, anxious to keep floating.

But he's already stepping off through the camp, dodging children and dogs and all manner of people singing hymns and talking real loud about Jesus. I ain't never heard such as this before either, but I can tell a fool when I see one, and I see a whole lot of them right here.

First thing, Jeremy runs into Mr. Valoreous Cates, striding through the mud, followed by a little crowd, mostly women, hanging on every word he says. Jeremy steps right up and introduces hisself. Seems like he's caught up already. I shake my head. How can one man be such a dolt? I turn back to the boat, figuring to let him have a hour or so to settle his mind, then go.

I'm slogging back toward the river bank when a seedy-looking young girl grabs my arm, stares into my face and asks, "Are you saved? Is your soul going to heaven?"

I give her a look and try to pull my arm away, but she's got a right strong grip. Her face is real white, like she's just seen a apparition or something. She looks at me with searching pale blue eyes, like she's got to save me before it's too late.

"Yes, ma' am, I'm saved," I tell her gentle-like. She seems too fragile to let her down hard. "I'm a Catholic."

She pulls back in horror. "Popish! God, help her. She's *Popish!*" She makes a lot of fuss, and pretty soon there's a crowd gathered as she holds onto my arm and looks into my eyes like she expects to find the devil himself camping there with a tent and a bunk.

I try to yank my arm free, but she goes on. "Oh, Jesus, thank you for sending this soul to me. I am ready, Jesus! Ready to cast out the devil and save this soul for you!"

She goes on like all possessed while I pull back into myself. I figure talking ain't going to get me out of this. Things is getting out of hand when the crowd parts and out steps Valoreous Cates himself, followed by—you guessed it—Jeremy Chatterfield.

"Unhand her, Alice. This calls for a man's judgment." The reverend stands broad shouldered and bent over, like he knows the heft of a sack of grain. His long, gray hair hangs loose from under a wide brim hat, kind of like what the cowboys wear but droopy. He has a big mustache that almost covers up his whole mouth, and beady little eyes that look out at you from under bushy brows and give you the shivers. I look over his shoulder to Jeremy, kind of pleading-like.

He steps forward. "I know this girl, Reverend, Sir. She's with me. No need to concern yourself with her salvation. I take that as my responsibility."

My mouth drops open. What'd he say? My salvation? Honestly, Jeremy, where do you get such notions?

The girl lets go of my arm, and I stand there on a muddy slope trying to steady myself.

"Yeah. I'm with him." I nod toward Jeremy.

I need to get us out of here before this salvation thing takes hold of him and ruins our progress west. Heck, Jane could die of old age before ever I even get there.

Mr. Valoreous Cates nods to Jeremy and dismisses the crowd with a wave of his hand. "Take care of it and stop by my tent when you're done. We can talk." He winks at Jeremy and slogs off through the mud in leather moccasins that lace all the way up to his knees.

"Come on, Jeremy. We need to get going."

The deranged Mr. Chatterfield slip-slides after me down the river bank. I step into the back seat of the boat, and he sits down like to take up the oars. But he don't. He sits there looking at me like he's sizing up how mad I'm going to be when I find out he wants to stay. He gauges it right. Pretty mad. Mad enough to chew nails and spit tacks.

"You ain't thinking on staying *here*, are you? Jeremy! Why would you? These people is all addled. You want to be like that?"

"I see an opportunity, Nell. I could make some good money here. Enough to take us all the way to St. Louis."

I finger the twenty-dollar gold piece I have tied up in a rag in my pocket. I ain't told Jeremy about it. I don't know why. But I ain't impressed with his plan. Addled or not, they don't deserve to be duped out of their money, if they have any.

"Why're you always so set on stealing? Can't you think of any honest ways of getting money?"

He sighs and leans back in the rower's seat, looking up at a leaden sky that looks like it might open up and dump gallons on this soggy little campground any minute. "Let's just stay this one night. I'm curious about how these itinerant preachers operate. Anyway, we can eat here and maybe even sleep in a tent. That's better than being out in the river in the rain."

I see he's bent on staying, so I nod, but I think to hide out in the boat with Soot and keep out of the way. Jeremy's up the bank and out of sight in the crowd of people and children and dogs and campfires before I can whistle. I sit there alone in the boat and hug Soot. He whines a little. Must be hungry. The smells of cooking fill the air and make my stomach growl. Guess I better see what I can beg or borrow to eat.

I make my way to a small campfire away from the busy part of the camp. Just a few people are standing around, and I don't even have to ask. As soon as I stop for a minute, somebody shoves a spatter gray enamel mug of hot coffee into my hands. It warms me and smells good, so I hang around the kettle waiting for the food to be dished out. Folks smile at me like they know who I am and why I'm here. They don't seem to be related or nothing, just a lot of people come from around to hear the preaching.

I try to make myself small so they won't pay me no mind. This salvation stuff is confusing. One thing, I might have worried over my sinful soul at the convent, but I never guessed being a *Catholic* could be anywise wrong. Just that I couldn't measure up. Here these people are, full of vinegar about what's right to believe, and I wonder how they can be so sure.

Pretty soon you can hear somebody playing the piano in the big tent, and I wonder how they got *that* out here, and the people reach for the lanterns that hang from about every tree and they move in one big mass toward the tent. I take the chance to grab some food and tuck it between the folds of my skirt and head off to give it to Soot. He's a patient dog, that one. Then I join the others, mostly because I'm curious, but also because I wonder what's become of Jeremy, and I figure to meet back up with him there.

The big tent is alight with hundreds of lanterns, and the piano playing gets louder and faster. Some of them knows the song and they clap and take it up. "When the roll is called up yonder I'll be there!" One lady right next to me sings real loud and shrill, like she's pushing to make sure God hears her. Another lady looks at her, kind of haughty, and moves away. Once everybody is in the tent and pretty well settled on the wooden benches set down in rows, the music stops and everything gets quiet. Not a murmur.

Then Mr. Valoreous Cates steps out on the stage—it's like a big, wide, wooden box, there in the front of the tent—and starts in to preaching real slow and quiet-like. He talks so low you have to strain to hear him, but then he speeds it up and loudens it just a little. He's talking about sin and sinners and how God is going to punish them and send them to hell. He slaps his Bible with his fist. "It's all right here in the book," he shouts. "Right here, every word of it!"

Then he goes off and talks about faith and how if you have it, God will forgive you and save you and heal you. Next thing, he's going on all possessed about the sick and the halt and the lame, and he's getting louder and the spit starts to fly. The crowd is right there with him, nodding and murmuring "Yes!" "Yea, Lord!" and "Amen."

Then comes a girl, wandering up the aisle, bumping into things, like she's blind. It's that pale one that had ahold of my arm a while ago, so I know she ain't blind. But nobody else seems to notice. She stumbles up to the front and cries, "Reverend Brother Cates! I'm blind! Blind since birth. I know you can heal me! I know you can. Just lay your hands on my head, sir, and God will do the rest."

Well you never did hear such carrying on when the reverend leans over and puts hands on her head, real vigorous, and yells for God to heal her, and she pulls away and looks up at the ceiling and screams, "I can see! I can see! What a beautiful world! Praise the Lord!"

Then the people into hollering and stomping, and out comes a guy with a tambourine, and he's beating out a rhythm and shouting. The Reverend Valoreous Cates takes up the chant and before I know it people all around me are stomping and hollering. Then some lady gets out of her seat and wrestles her way into the aisle, babbling in some language I ain't never heard before, and she falls down on the ground—in the mud—and wiggles around like she's got the itch and can't scratch.

The reverend comes down off the stage and lays hands on her in some private places and shouts up to heaven, and she immediately stops jerking and wiggling and sits up like she's just woke up from a dream. Then he helps her up and she goes back and sits down, tears streaming down her face.

The reverend is standing in the aisle now, looking toward the back of the tent where a man stumbles toward him, dragging his left foot. He's a pathetic sight, limping along, his arms flailing. Then I get a good look. It's Jeremy!

"Reverend Cates," he goes on in his best English accent. "A word with you, sir. You see I am afflicted. My foot was crushed in a mining accident. I've been to the finest physicians in the world. No one can help me. You are my last hope."

The reverend takes Jeremy by the shoulders and shakes him like a bed pillow. Jeremy falls to his knees in the muddy aisle while the reverend prays. Then he reaches out and grabs Jeremy by the scruff of his neck and jerks him up. Jeremy flops like a rag doll and rises to his feet, turns and walks out the back of the tent with nary a hitch.

Then the reverend gets back up on his wooden stage and hollers for the people to dig deep in their pockets to help with God's work. The music starts, and the tambourine man beats out a rhythm while four big fellows wade in among the crowd with hats upside down to collect the money. Valoreous Cates stands up there a-clapping and singing, dancing around on the stage like a show star. When they're done, they bring the hats up front and dump the money into a box on the stage.

I can hardly stand to watch, thinking about these poor people giving to a faker like Valoreous Cates when they have so little. But I don't have time to think on it, because the reverend is working the crowd up into a frenzy. There's weeping and wailing and moaning and screaming. People are hugging and kissing and shaking hands, and moving around like ants that their anthill's been poked with a stick. They into jumping and shaking and falling down and all manner of rapture until I get real uncomfortable.

I need to get out of there and quick. My throat's real tight and my palms are cold and my heart's pounding. It feels like the ants are biting my butt, and I look around for a quick way out. I push my way to the side and lift the canvas. Outside, the night air feels cool and fresh. I move away from the tent and slog my way through the empty camp to the boat. I'd rather sleep there than with these poor sad souls getting tooken in by the likes of Valoreous Cates.

I'm walking away toward the river with my back to the tent when I hear a great roar. I turn to see the tattered old tent aflame and the people screaming and running helter-skelter in every direction. Then there's a bolt of lightening and a huge clap of thunder, and the sky opens up. I stand there, dumbfounded, watching the tent burn in the rain. I'm scared for Jeremy, but I can't make my way back against all the running, screaming people.

"Help! Oh, Lord help us!" they cry.

The rain comes down and the tent crashes to the ground, some of the poles still stand like the twelve apostles in a circle, and others fall into the burning mass.

People scatter, hollering for the reverend to save them, but he ain't nowhere to be seen. Then a man steps up and yells, "He's gone! I seen him run out the back when the tent caught fire. Took the money box and run!"

It takes about five minutes for the tent to burn, and then nothing. It's a smoldering ruin with the rain pouring down. I wander back with everybody else and stand watching for about a half hour while they stumble around trying to find their folks and treat the injured. The excitement dies down. The mood has changed to tears and quiet prayer. It's hard to tell how many are hurt and how bad, but folks are feeling mean toward the reverend. Someone goes back to his tent, but he's gone for sure. I move through the crowd looking for Jeremy. I can't find him, so I make my way back to the boat. Maybe he's there already, waiting for me.

When I get to the river bank, I see a mound covered up on the floor of the boat between the rower's seat and the back. As I go to step in, Jeremy appears from the trees by the shore and takes my hand. "Come on, Nell. We've got to get out of here."

"That ain't news to me," I tell him, stepping into the boat and over the rower's seat. Soot is in his place in front. I nearly trip over whatever Jeremy has loaded into the boat and plunk myself down in back. The back of the boat rides low in the water. Jeremy is at the oars before I can regain my balance.

He lifts a finger to his lips to shush me and pulls on the oars with all his might. We are out in midstream, carried along with the current before he slows down rowing to look at me. He nods to the mound on the floor.

"You can come out now, Reverend."

Chapter 11

Since me and Jeremy wasn't getting along all that well before Valoreous Cates came along, I can't say things are any better between us. He's still grouchy with me, giving out orders and ignoring me otherwise. I ain't much better with him, since his taking up with Valoreous gives me the jeebies.

Sometimes I swear Jeremy Chatterfield ain't got the sense the Lord give a louse. He takes up with the lowest scum he can find, and he don't even apologize or promise to do better when I take him to task about it. Well, I try to, at least, but Jeremy gets pretty slick at avoiding me. He and Valoreous Cates got their heads together under that tarp in the back half of the boat for the next day or so, and I'm lucky they let me come along, fetch the provisions and bail out the boat. It's still raining, and I feel put upon, since they don't even offer me a corner of their tarp. Nobody rows. We just let her drift, and if we get in too close to the bank or out too far in the current, I give Jeremy's back a nudge and he rights her.

Soot don't like Valoreous Cates, so I grab him by the scruff of the neck to keep him in tow. I'm bothered how Valoreous looks mean at him every time he gets in or out of the boat. We float on downriver till around noon the next day, when Valoreous directs Jeremy to put in on the Kentucky side below a town called Owensboro. Valoreous likes big towns better than small ones. Says it's easy to escape notice in a big town. This one ain't huge, but we need provisions, so it'll have to do.

When we hit shore, Valoreous lifts the oil cloth tarp and takes out a tin box with a lock on the front. I figure it's the collection box, and Valoreous carries it off with him into the woods while he attends to his personal needs. I wonder if he's going to carry it everywhere he goes, but he comes back without it and says to Jeremy, "Come on. Let's get what we need and move on. This country's getting uncomfortable."

Jeremy is up and following after him like A follows B while I just stand there by the boat, holding Soot back from growling at Valoreous. They don't say nothing to me—not "Come along," or "Stay here," or "Jump in the river," so I elect to wait.

It's a long wait because they don't even come back that night. Soot and I sleep under the whores' petticoats and that oil cloth to keep off the dews and damps. I go berry picking in the morning and mix up some raspberry biscuits. I use the last honey we got, but they sure taste good with a cup of hot coffee. I am about to give up on them two rapscallions when here they come marching in about dusk like the conquerors of yore. I read that line in a book. I don't know where Yore is, but it must be of some account if its conquerors are so proud. I hold onto Soot so he won't make Valoreous mad with his barking and growling.

Anyway, they've been transformed—at least Valoreous has. No fringed buckskin shirt, floppy hat and lace-up moccasins. No sir! He's had a haircut and a shave, and probably a bath. His mustache is trimmed real neat and fine, and he's wearing a brand new broadcloth suit and a string tie. He looks almost handsome—and certainly trustworthy. Funny how little it takes to make a scalawag look like a honest man. Jeremy's had a bath and a shave, and his suit has been brushed and his shoes shined. He's wearing a new hat. They parade into the campsite and look around at the lowly state of things, and immediately Valoreous turns on his heel and declares he's heading back for town. Ain't about to ruin his new clothes with sleeping on the ground.

Jeremy hands me a sack of provisions and gives me a look like I should take care of them. Then he turns around, too, and off they go again without even asking how I am or if I need anything. I think on it a while and then I load the provisions in the boat and whistle for Soot. If that's how they're going to be, I might as well teach them a lesson.

I untie the rope and the boat drifts out into the current. I let her drift for about a mile and then row in and tie up again. This place is right along a road that skirts the river, so I won't be too hard to find. Then Soot and I snuggle up for another night under the stars. I really don't mind the sleeping out. I'm used to it. What I mind is being treated like I ain't nobody. Maybe I ain't, but I don't like being treated like it. I miss the special way I used to feel about me and Jeremy—like we was friends, but more than friends—fellow travelers on the road of life. I miss that.

'Round about noon the next day I'm lying on a pile of petticoats reading my dime novel again when Soot starts growling, and here they come, down the road. When they see me, Valoreous into berating me for leaving them. "Who you think you are, gal, to up and leave like that?"

"Can if I want. It's my boat."

"I could have you arrested for stealing our provisions!"

"Yeah, but you won't, 'cause if any constable came to arrest me, I'd tell him about your doings upriver, and then maybe they'd have a few more questions for you."

He shuts right up.

I look at Jeremy, hanging back, looking sheepish. He should.

Valoreous throws the tin box into the boat. He must have dug it up this morning at the old camp. He's got a new carpetbag, too, and he throws that in and motions to Jeremy to get in, and he takes up the oars, pulling away from the bank before Soot and I have a chance to get in. Soot jumps for it and lands smack in the middle of Valoreous's back, knocking the wind out of him. I'd laugh, but I'm too busy stretching one leg in the boat and one on the shore. I'd be doing the splits if Jeremy didn't grab the oars and force Valoreous to back oar so I can get in.

We float on in silence. Sullen silence. I am about fed up with the Reverend Mr. Valoreous Cates, and I hope Jeremy is, too, but I can't get him alone to talk to him. The day goes by mostly floating along in silence. Once in a while, Valoreous says something private to Jeremy, but he keeps it low so I can't hear. I'm like a intruder in my own boat. I just keep staring at the river, thinking on how I'm going to get out of this. By evening, we float past Evansville on the Indiana shore, a bigger town than Owensboro, and Valoreous directs Jeremy to let him off at the dock and he'll find them a place to sleep in town while I take the boat on down river.

Jeremy obeys, but when it's time for him to get out, he declines to go with Valoreous. "I think I'll stay with Nell tonight," he says.

Valoreous gives him one of them looks like he knows why Jeremy wants to stay with me. A leering, smiling, knowing look.

"Glad to hear you got it in you, boy. I was beginning to wonder. Guess you favor the ugly ones for some reason."

Jeremy looks all washed out, but he don't say nothing. I'd throw a clamshell at Valoreous's Smart Alec face if I had one handy.

He stands up and rearranges his suit. Then he hauls out the cash box and shoves it into his carpetbag and steps out onto the dock. "I'll meet you downriver in the morning. Don't go too far. These new shoes are giving me a blister."

Jeremy nods and the reverend turns and walks up the street like a drummer on a mission.

As soon as we're out of earshot I start in on Jeremy, but he ain't in a mood to listen.

"Just be quiet, Nell. I saved your bacon more than once today."

"My bacon! My bacon! Yours is the bacon needs to be saved. Have you lost your senses or didn't you ever have any? That man is mean to the core. Can't you see that?"

"You're just mad because he treats *you* badly. There's a lot to be learned from him."

"Yeah. How to get yourself arrested and thrown in jail. How to cheat people and lie and playact your way through life."

He pulls on the oars and the boat skips away from the bank. I sit in the back seat, now that Valoreous has given it up, looking at Jeremy like I can't figure what he's thinking or why he can't see what a good-for-nothing Valoreous is. We drift downstream less than a mile to the mouth of a crick, where Jeremy pulls in and we make camp in silence. I feel all discombobulated. I can't make Jeremy see what's plain to me, and he's tired of hearing me go on. We spread that oil cloth out on the damp ground and cover up with the blankets, of which I get one, since Valoreous ain't here, and go to sleep. Morning don't ease the tension. I'm all for piling in the boat and pulling out before his majesty gets back, but Jeremy won't hear of it. I give serious consideration to going on by myself, but the prospect of leaving Jeremy stops me. The handsome Mr. Chatterfield has a hold on me, damn him.

Valoreous don't show up until about two o'clock, carrying a heavy sack that clinks together as he walks. He sets down the sack and wipes his brow. "Busy morning," he tells Jeremy. He opens his sack and brings out a empty square bottom glass bottle. "Got a sack full of 'em. Some tins, too, and these." He pulls out another bottle, this one round with a skinny neck.

Jeremy nods like he knows just what Valoreous has in mind, but I bet he don't. This brotherhood of theirs makes me want to retch. I take hold of Soot and we go off to drop a line for fish. Valoreous and Jeremy have their heads together the whole afternoon. Around five o'clock, Valoreous allows as he has to attend to his personal needs and goes off into the woods. I fry up some fish for supper and Jeremy pretends to be taking a nap. It's a long time before Valoreous comes back, but when he does, he's full of excitement.

"Come see what I found! The perfect place to set up business!" He picks up his carpetbag and leads the way.

Jeremy jumps up and follows him into the woods. I go too, invited or not, never mind the fish. What he wants to show us is a old abandoned settler's cabin about a quarter mile inland on the bank of the crick. It's log, about twenty feet square, with a big, old, stone fireplace across one end. In the other end is a double-decker bunk built into the wall. There ain't no mattress on it, but there's still ropes strung across. The floor is dirt and there ain't no windows. Just the door for light, and there's precious little of that.

"The roof is sound. This will do quite nicely," Valoreous crows, dropping his carpetbag on the floor. Then he turns and addresses me directly for one of the few times ever. "Go back and get the boat and provisions."

Then to Jeremy, "I'll see about some lumber for a door tomorrow, and some ticks and straw for mattresses."

It takes me close to a hour to pack up the boat and row up the shallow crick. Soot goes with me, so I reward him with some of the fried fish. Back at the cabin, Valoreous stands in the middle of the room directing me where to put stuff. He's claimed the bottom bunk for himself.

"Nell and I will share the top," Jeremy says. I wonder that he didn't say I could sleep on the floor.

The next day is all abustle with cleaning out the cabin and the two of them running to town for stuff. I stick to cooking and berry picking and thinking about how I'm going to get away from this place. Too much stuff is going on that I don't like, and none of it is getting me any closer to my mother. Jeremy ain't available, so I think to bide my time for a while, but only for a while.

The day after that, Valoreous comes back from town with two cotton ticks and Jeremy carries in straw to fill them with. That turns out to be my itchy job, but I make good use of it. I stuff a couple forkfuls of nettles into Valoreous's tick. Figure he's got it coming.

Next, Valoreous shows up with a big iron kettle to hang over the fire and some boards cut to length and some nails for Jeremy to build a door. He even brings iron hinges for it. This all looks mighty permanent to me, and I ain't interested in permanent.

He pulls a bunch of paper labels out of his coat pockets. "Dr. Cates' Elixir," and "Dr. Cates' Liniment," and little round ones that say "Dr. Cates' Miracle Ointment." I begin to see what the reverend, or the doctor, if you please, is up to.

He and Jeremy start concocting stuff that smells vile and makes my eyes water when I go near the kettle. Jeremy rows over to the Kentucky side and comes back with a keg of corn whiskey which they pour liberally into the kettle. They add stuff they bought from a horse doctor in Evansville and more stuff they bought at a drug store. When Valoreous declares it ready, Jeremy starts to fill the bottles, square ones and round ones the same. Then he passes them to me, hands me a glue pot and a stack of labels and tells me to fix them.

"Which labels go on which bottles?" I ask.

"No matter," Valoreous counters. "It's all the same."

I feel dirty and low down doing this. I know they're going to sell it to poor, ignorant country folk who'll believe any lie they tell, and when the heat gets on, they'll head on down river to find another bunch of poor souls. I don't say nothing, though. I don't want no trouble with Valoreous. I can read mean, and he's mean.

When all the liniment and elixir is out of the kettle, Valoreous brings in a tub of lard and tells me to scoop it in. I do, but the lard is rancid and it stinks up the whole place. Valoreous produces a little bottle of camphorated oil and dumps it in. That settles down the rancid smell and opens up both my nostrils wide. After a little mixing, Jeremy and I spoon it into the round tins and stick the labels. One day's work and we have a couple hundred bottles and tins to sell at twenty-five cents each.

The next day the reverend doctor starts complaining of the itch, and goes on about it for hours on end. He scratches everywhere and rants about how it's eating him alive.

"Why don't you try some of your miracle salve?" I ask him.

"Shut up, you ugly girl," he snarls.

I keep my peace, but it feels good to know he's getting some comeuppance. He's so put out he even sends Jeremy into town with the first batch of elixir, liniment and ointment to sell by himself.

He stays at the cabin, moaning and scratching and generally making a nuisance of himself. Then he grabs the lard bucket and smears that rancid stuff all over himself, head to toe, all the way down between his toes and the soles of his feet, pulls on a union suit and wool socks, even though it's hot summer and crawls into bed. He stays there for three days, sleeping and smelling up the place so bad I stay outside just to breathe the fresh air. After the third day, he gets up, takes a bath in the crick, gets dressed and heads for town with another batch of his wares, completely cured of the itch. I guess the nettles wore out.

Between him and Jeremy, they sell about half of the medicinals and sit around on Sunday right pleased with themselves. They count out their money and share it, eighty-twenty, 'cause Valoreous put up the cost of the ingredients and bottles and such. Nobody suggests that I should get any. That's all right. I don't want none of their dirty money.

I am so ready to be gone, I even think some more on leaving Jeremy behind, 'cause he's so caught up with Valoreous, he can't think straight. Money makes him like that. I never saw anyone that loved money so much. I swear he'd do anything to get more. Well, almost anything, and I'm wondering where the limits might be—'cause I ain't seen 'em yet.

Then, come Tuesday afternoon, the two of them come back down the track from town, stepping lively and talking about moving on. Seems the constable in town suggested that. But Valoreous is in a snit about how much money he's sunk in this here cabin. New door, bed ticks, iron kettle. We can't take none of that in the boat, and he can't let himself just walk away from it. So we stay one more night and the next morning Valoreous allows he needs to go to town one more time. I look at Jeremy with a question on my face and hope in my heart. Maybe the constable will catch up with him and throw him in jail. No such luck. Just after noon, out from town he comes with a poor immigrant in tow, who can't hardly speak English. I have to put my hand over my mouth to keep from yelling at this poor bugger to run away while he still has money in his pants.

Valoreous takes one look at me, reads my intention, and moves to grab my wrist. I don't struggle, 'cause I know what's good for me. He gives the man an oily smile and introduces me as his daughter. Then he shows the feller all around the place and fast talks all of its advantages, which, outside of what you can see, he is making up as he goes along. The poor immigrant smiles and nods, beside himself with joy at his good fortune. One hundred dollars changes hands, and we are loaded in the boat and floating down the crick toward the river before the sun sets.

By now I've had enough of both of these fools. If I could have warned that poor soul, I would have, but Valoreous kept a tight hold of my wrist while he talked the man out of his money. I'm afraid of him, what he'll do next, and what'll happen to me if I defy him. And Jeremy can't see past the next dollar. I lay low for the next town.

Chapter 12

We float on down the Ohio in the gloomiest weather you ever saw. Rain, rain and more rain. But it don't bother the two of them a bit. They got important business to discuss under the oil cloth again. Me and Soot huddle together in the bow under a scrap of old canvas I found on the riverbank. It stinks, but it keeps us sort of dry.

By the time we get to Paducah, Kentucky, the rain is about over and I'm for stopping for a few days to dry out and get my bearings. I still don't know which way to go after this here Ohio River meets the Mississippi, which I know it will soon. I'm sure I don't want to go to New Orleans, like the whores said. That's south, but I ain't got no notion of how to go west except by the railroad, and my twenty-dollar gold piece probably won't take me that far.

We pull up to the south shore and find a place to camp a mile or so below Paducah. The days are warm, but humid, so it'll take a while to get everything dry and stock up on what we need. I get up in the morning and start up the fire, put on the coffee, and get out my frying pan. I wish I had some eggs, but I'm too hungry to go out looking for them. I settle for biscuits.

The reverend doctor don't care much for my cooking. He takes a bite from a biscuit and puts it down. He takes a swig of coffee and rises to his feet. "Let's wander into town and find ourselves a boarding house," he says to Jeremy, like I'm a rock on the riverbank. The reverend stuffs his money box into the carpetbag and heads off down the track.

Jeremy looks my way, shrugs his shoulders in a gesture of apology—the first I've seen in more than a week—and brushes off his pants. Then he picks up his hat and sets it on his head like he's ready for adventure and walks away without so much as a by-your-leave. I watch them go, the bile rising in me as fast as a horse can trot.

I have to ask myself why I get so riled at Jeremy. He has a right to choose his own friends. It's not that I worry about him getting in trouble. He's been in and out of that often enough. No, it's something else. I don't like Valoreous because I feel like he's snatching Jeremy away. Turning his head. Making him forget about me. It feels like I've got a pain burning in my chest—kind of like the epizootics you get from eating too much sugar candy. All I know is, I ain't happy when Jeremy's off paying attention to someone else, and I *am* happy when he's here with me, even if we're on the outs.

I spend the morning spreading all our stuff over the bushes to dry. I even try to clean out the bottom of the boat—wash the mud out, at least. Then I look to our stores. There ain't much. About a pound of flour, a little piece of bacon, a handful of beans and enough coffee to make one more pot.

I decide to take advantage of the chance to clean myself up, so I even wash the dress I'm wearing and rub the mud off my shoes. They don't look new no more. Neither does the dress. Jeremy carries an ivory comb in his rucksack, and I dig it out and go to work on my hair. It ain't been attended to in so long, it takes me about an hour to get all the tangles out. I rig up the oil cloth for shade and sit under it in my shift, reading my dime novel again. I wish I had something else to read. I lost track of how many times I read it, but I still get goose bumps when I read about my mother's exploits. I know there's more books about her, and I wish I owned every one of them. I stop reading and watch the boats coming and going for a while, but it ain't long before I'm bored with that.

I'm restless, like a leaf that's fluttering and can't decide whether to let go and fall or hang on for a while longer. I wish I could talk to Jeremy alone and private. Get him to see this groaty old man for what he is—a cheat and a charlatan. But Jeremy can't see nothing but money.

It's noon, and my stomach reminds me that breakfast was sparse. Soot comes up, licks my hand and whines. He's hungry, too. In a burst of generosity, I fry up the last of the bacon and make up one more batch of biscuits. Soot and I share the bounty for lunch. Around one o'clock I begin to realize that it might be some time before I see my two traveling companions again, if ever, and I tie up Soot and wander off in the direction of town, hoping to find some odd job to do in return for dinner.

Paducah's a pretty little town, lots of shade trees and neat houses with white fences and gardens in the back. The beans are ready, so I go along an alley until I see a backyard garden with a bounty of beans, and I go up to the kitchen door and knock.

The door is opened by a black woman wearing a flour sack dress, rag wound around her head and a ready smile.

"'Scuse me, ma'am. I was wondering if I could pick your beans in return for my supper."

"Ain't my beans. I ain't the lady 'o the house, but I kin ask her." She swings the door wide and I enter a big, open kitchen with a steel cook stove and a sink with real running water. It's richer than any kitchen I've ever seen in my life.

"You kin set here. Want a piece of cherry pie? I just made it this mornin.'"

I am amazed at her generosity, especially if it ain't even her house, but the pie smells too good to pass up. She cuts me a slice and leaves through another door. I eat in silence, looking around in wonder at this kitchen. There's a cabinet with a white enamel top and a flour bin with the sifter built right in. Sister Mary Patrick would say a hundred "Hail Marys" over that. And the cupboards have glass doors so you can see all the dishes without even opening them. I ain't never seen such pretty dishes. And the teapots! There must be twelve of them, all lined up on a shelf over the sink, all with pretty flowers painted on them, all different.

The black woman is back in a few minutes. "Missus say yes, you kin pick beans for your supper."

"Thank you. Or thank her. Whichever. Do you have a basket I can use?"

She leads me out to the back porch, where she hands me a basket and a sunbonnet, which I am glad to get.

"My name's Nell." I stick out my hand to shake.

She smiles but doesn't offer her hand. "You ain't from around here, is you?"

"No, ma'am. I come from Pennsylvania. Johnstown. Ever hear of it?"

"Don't call me ma'am, and don't shake my hand, less'n you want to get us both in a heap of trouble. I got a good job here, and I 'spect to keep it."

"Yes'm. What should I call you?"

"Lizzie. You can call me Lizzie."

I carry the basket out to the garden and start picking beans. It's hot and tiring, but I keep at it 'cause a bargain is a bargain. I fill the basket and take it in to Lizzie, who empties it into a pan and puts it in the ice box. I go back for more. By five o'clock I've picked three baskets of beans, and my back is aching.

The smells coming from the back door set my mouth to watering. I knock, and Lizzie opens the door to the kitchen wonderland for me. I sit at the table and she brings me a plate of pot roast and vegetables. I eat quietly, watching her prepare the plates. Then comes a little bell ring from the other room, and Lizzie picks up four plates of fresh fruit salad decorated with mint leaves and carries them through the door, which swings on its hinges both ways. She's back in a flash, and out again, carrying plates of fresh bread and butter. Coffee, tea and ice water go in next. Then the pot roast and a salad of greens she's cut from the garden. She's quick and neat about her work, and the kitchen shows that. Everything is washed and put in its place as soon as she's done with it. The door shuts out any noise from the other side, but there don't seem to be any. Just Lizzie bustling in and out, fetching, carrying, cleaning up.

I sit watching her in wonder, looking for a chance to talk to her again. Finally, she returns with the empty dessert plates. The cherry pie is almost gone. I rise to help her do the dishes, but she takes me gently by the shoulders and sits me down at the table again. "What missus think if she come in here and see you doing my work? Huh? You gonna lose me my job yet."

It's getting dark outside, and I think I should get back to the boat. But I like this dark-skinned, efficient, no nonsense woman. I don't want to go yet. She sets about getting the kitchen ready for breakfast. Sets the table out in the dining room and mixes up the dry ingredients for biscuits. Sets out corn meal for grits. Just as she is taking off her apron and putting on her hat, there's a knock at the back door.

"That be Tobias." She goes to the door and opens it for a tall, angular black man about her age. Thirty, I'd say. They smile at each other and she hands him the last piece of pie. He nods at me and sits down at the table to eat.

"Who you?" he asks.

"Nell. I just stopped to pick beans. I'm passing through."

"Where to?"

"West. All the way to South Dakota. Looking for my mother."

"She come all the way from Pennsylvania. That far!" Lizzie tells him with a hint of pride.

He smiles a smile that lights up his face. Broad. Open. "What your mother doing all the way out there?"

"She lives there. She's famous. Maybe you've heard of her. Calamity Jane."

He laughs a big laugh that doesn't feel like he's making fun of me—just enjoying me. "I sure 'nough *have* heard of Calamity Jane. How you gonna get all the way to South Dakota? Better hurry up, gal. Winter come early to South Dakota."

"I don't know the way exactly. Once I get to the Mississippi I don't know how to go."

"Well, first you wanta get to St. Louis. That's north, upriver. Once you get there, you'll wanta go up the Big Muddy. I know. I used to work the river boats. You been floatin' downstream so far, but the rest of your way is against the current. Tough swimming."

"Big Muddy?"

"Missouri River. Goes west and north from the Mississippi. Full of sand bars and river demons, I can tell you. But if you follows it far enough, it take you to the Dakotas."

I rise and thank Tobias for his help. At least I know where I'm going now. All I have to do is pry Jeremy loose from the clutches of Valoreous Cates, and I'll be fine. As I head out the back door, Lizzie hands me a glass jar full of pot roast and vegetables.

"Missus don't like no leftovers," she tells me.

I thank her and go down through the yard to the back alley. It's dark, but still warm. I walk along the river and in ten minutes I'm back at the boat, sharing my bounty with Soot.

No Jeremy. No Valoreous.

I figured there wouldn't be.

I sit down on the grass of the riverbank and think about how I'm going to get to South Dakota. Tobias's words ring in my ears. "Winter come early to South Dakota." June is already past, and July is near about half gone. I got to keep moving, or I'll never make it to South Dakota before winter. I might be another month tagging along after Valoreous and Jeremy. I can't afford it.

I rise and pick up everything from around the camp except what rightfully belongs to Jeremy and Valoreous and stow it in the boat, then I step in and sit down in the rower's seat. I wonder where Jeremy is. Wish he'd come back by himself and be ready to go with me. Wish everything could go back to the way it was before Valoreous Cates came along. Then I start to puzzle over this whole idea of Calamity Jane. I want to believe it, even though I know it might not be true. Why? 'Cause I ain't got nothing else to believe in, I guess. No place else to go. Deadwood, South Dakota, is as good a place as any. Soot sits on the shore whining until I whistle for him. With a heavy heart, I let her drift out into the current. I know I got to get shut of Valoreous, but. ..

Jeremy.. .. Aww, Jeremy.

Chapter 13

When the morning fog lifts, I see a town off to the right bank, so I make for it. The Ohio River is real wide here, and swift, like it has some place to go in a hurry. I beach the boat above the town and tie Soot to a tree root. It's a fair-sized town, and I wander up what looks to be the main street. I hate to part with my double eagle, but it's that or work my way for food, one.

The other thing I'm thinking about is Jeremy—where he is and if he knows I'm gone yet. I picture him distraught, telling Valoreous he's leaving and coming after me, hell bent. That's what I picture, but it ain't what I see.

Coming the other way I meet a woman pushing a wheelbarrow full of sacks of flour and sugar and bags of apples with a basket of eggs perched on top. She's thin and angular, and her arms look like there's ropes running through them, under the skin. She pushes that barrow along behind horses waiting at their hitching posts and stops in front of a store.

"'Scuse me, ma'am, but could you tell me what town this is?" I ask.

"Why, Cairo, Illinois," she replies like I ought to know. She says it *Kay-Row*. I recognize that name from my talk with Tobias.

"Well, then this ain't far from the Mississippi, is it?"

She looks at me like I'm daft and motions over her shoulder. "That's it, right there, behind me."

I look over her shoulder and see a river to remark on—bigger, wider, deeper and muddier than the Ohio. No wonder the Ohio was in such a hurry to join up with it. Cairo sits on a little neck of land between the two rivers. You can get out of your boat on the Ohio side and walk right across to the Mississippi side without wearing hardly any leather off your shoes. "Where do you go to get on a steamboat for St. Louis?" I ask.

"You can come with me, I guess. My man and I run a boat between here and St. Louis. I'm shopping for stores. You can come along and spell me on this here wheelbarry, if you've a mind."

"Yes'm. Do you need any help on that boat of yours? I'm a hard worker, and I need to get to St. Louis quick as I can."

"We heave to tomorrow at dawn. Can't say as to the work. I could use some kitchen help, but my man's got the last word on that."

I fall into step beside her and take the basket of eggs off the top of the load. "You live here or there?"

She gives me that daft look.

"Kay-Row or St. Louis?" I say.

"We live on the river. That's what river folk do. Come winter, we find someplace to hole up cheap until the ice melts. River people. That's what."

She directs me to stand watch over the barrow while she goes into the store for some yard goods. I do as I'm told, but I'm tested almost immediately. Three local boys, barefoot and scruffy, come wandering up the street bent on mischief. When they see me, one of them calls the other two aside to make a plan. I know that's what they're doing, just like the tormenters, so I keep a good eye on them. They're only about twelve, so I guess I can handle them.

They saunter up close, and then one of them gets a good look at me and starts into laughing. He points in my direction and makes a cross-eyed, buck-tooth face. The other two into laughing too, at him or me, one. I stand my ground and look them straight on. I have to guard the barrow or I know they'll make off with everything in it.

"Hey, homely miss, can I buy a apple?" one of them asks, nice as you please.

"These here apples ain't for sale," I tell him, looking around for the boat lady.

The boys come in real close, and one of them reaches around me and grabs a apple. When I turn to smack his hand, the other two grab more. I turn and swat, and they duck and laugh like this is the best fun they've had in years. I wait. One dodges in close, and I reach out and grab his arm and take a step toward him, twisting his arm up behind his back. I give it a jerk.

"Now! Give over that apple!" I shout.

He hesitates, but I give his arm another good jerk, and he cries out in pain. He drops the apple on the ground and stomps on it with his clodhopper shoe. Now I'm mad. I give him a swift kick in the pants that sends him sprawling.

"You can give me a nickel for them apples, less'n you want more learning."

The boy on the ground is crying and wiping his nose on his shirt. The other two run off down the street but not far. A huge hulk of a man who's been leaning in the shade of the store roof, watching, steps out of the shadows and grabs the two of them by the arm. He drags them, struggling, back up to me.

"We don't want no trouble," one of them boys whines.

"Fine," I say. "Then give me back my apples and get on with you. I still need two cents for the one he squashed."

The man don't say nothing. He stands there with a squirming boy in each fist and lifts them off the ground. Then he shoves them out of the way just as the woman comes out of the store.

"Why, Al, I didn't know you was coming up town this morning," she greets him.

"Needed some parts for the engine," he replies. "Who's this you got with you?'

"Gal I picked up. Wants to know if we need any help to earn her passage to St. Louis."

He looks me up and down. "If she handles herself on a boat as good as she handles herself on land, we can find something for her."

"This here's Al Gilpin, a river man from bow to stern," the lady tells me. "Works for my husband, keeping the boat in the water."

Al takes over the wheelbarrow, and the lady falls in step beside him. I follow with the basket of eggs. Then I remember Soot.

"Could I go get my dog?"

"Dog?"

"Yeah. Soot. He's a good river dog. He won't bother none."

Al Gilpin nods, and I set the eggs back on top of the barrow and tear off toward the Ohio side. It's a quick good-bye to the little boat that's brought me all the way down the Conemaugh, the Allegheny and the Ohio. I was going to try to sell her, but there ain't no time. I grab my few belongings and give the little boat a pat. I leave the whores' petticoats—hope I won't need them anymore—take hold of Soot's rope and lead him through town. We get to the Mississippi side and I stand looking down the row of steamboats pulled up to the wharf. Then I see Al Gilpin leaning over the rail of one, waving to me.

The name of the boat is the Queen Marie, and it's seen better days. Peeling paint, rotting boards. Looks like it's been up and down the river more than a few times. Al Gilpin works around the clock to keep the boiler going and the stern wheel turning. They haul freight, mostly—logs down river and whatever they can get back up. It's just the man and his wife, Al, another young fellow, and an occasional passenger. This Al Gilpin is a nice man. Big and heavy—no stranger to hard work. He's got a soft side, though, and Soot isn't long discovering it. Hangs around the boiler room for handouts and stays close when Al's sitting, looking for his ears to be scratched. I like him, too, so I find reasons to hang around him when I can. Some folks are like that. Make you want to be with them no matter what.

Al's right curious about who I am and where I'm going. In the evening, after supper, I sit on a coil of rope and talk to him. He asks a few roundabout questions, trying to get to know me better. I like him, but I ain't of a mood to tell much about myself. Been laughed at too many times. Still we strike up a friendship right away. I got good sense about people. Like I can mark Valoreous for a rogue right off, and I can mark Al Gilpin for a good man. I just know.

The trip up the Mississippi to St. Louis is close to two hundred miles and takes a couple of days barring disasters, which according to Al are common. The lady of the boat, Mrs. Allison, shows me where I can sleep and put my stuff behind the stove in the galley—that's what they call the kitchen. Then she herds me off and hands me a apron. Puts me to work right quick, peeling potatoes for the noon meal.

A steamboat on the Mississippi is a right exciting place to be. The noise of the boilers and the turning of that big wheel that drives the boat could make you deaf before your time. Navigating is the hard part. That's what Captain Allison does. He don't pay me no mind. I might as well be cargo to him, but missus is okay. She don't yell at me or nothing. Just keeps me busy from the time I get on board until dark. That suits me, though. I still got that double eagle wrapped up in a rag in my pocket.

The second night out it's about nine o'clock before Mrs. Allison tells me I can go. I step out on the deck and take a little walk around. I seen so many of these big boats, it feels real good to be riding one up the Mississippi, even if it is on the far side of prime. The moonlight shows up all ripply on the black water, and off in the distance you can see the lights of a town. River towns all look better in the dark. Up near the bow I see the light of a cigarette and wander over by Al and Soot.

"Where you bound for, Missy?" It's the third time he's asked that question and got only "St. Louis" for an answer. I'm for loosening up a little, but I'm still wary about being laughed at. But Big Al is so kind, I feel myself wanting to trust him, so I let go a little of my story. Al nods and takes a puff on his cigarette. "Must be a hard road, not knowing who your people are."

Next thing I know, I'm blabbering my whole story out. I tell him all about my mother and where I'm going, never even worrying about how he's taking it. He listens, scratching Soot's neck and puffing away on that cigarette.

"Deadwood, eh? That's a helluva long way, Missy. What happens if you get there and your ma ain't there?"

That stops me dead in my tracks. "I don't know."

"And what if she ain't your ma?"

He leans back on a coiled rope, the smoke rising above his head. "Seems like you ain't thought this all the way through, Missy. Seems like you got all your eggs in one basket."

I sit quiet. He's right. I ain't got a plan for what to do if what I want to be turns out not to be.

"You want to know where to go or what to do *before* trouble befalls you. I'd hate to see you end up like one of them St. Louis street waifs, selling themselves for dinner and a bed."

That stuns me. I hadn't thought I could get that desperate, but that was because I had Jeremy, and he could think of a way to get money if his brain was addled, which it was, in my opinion, a lot of the time. Now I feel real bad about leaving him. Lonely and scared. I wonder where he is and if he's thinking of me. Wish I could let him know where I'm at and that I miss him.

"I guess that might be how it is, but I'll think of something. If Jane ain't there or she don't want me, I can always do what I'm doing here—kitchen work." I try to see his face in the glow of the cigarette, but it's too dark. This talk has me feeling all edgy.

"I hope so, Missy. I hope so." He crushes his cigarette and throws the butt into the river, then gets up. "Best I look in on the engine before I retire. See you in the morning, Missy."

I wander back to the galley and find my corner behind the big iron stove, where I lie down on a old, cotton mattress that smells like chicken feathers. I miss Jeremy, and my head aches, but sleep don't come easy. I'm woke up at 5 o'clock by Mrs. Allison banging the pans and shaking down the ashes. She carries the pan to the side and dumps them in the river. They hiss real loud. I get up and head for the privy. It's at the other end of the boat, near the boiler, and I make my shaky way along the side. Everything feels dipsy-doodle today. Kind of like how you feel when you been spinning around in circles till you fall down. I hold onto the rail for balance, use the privy and come back. Missus hands me a kettle and tells me to make the oatmeal while she tends to the rest.

I don't ever remember oatmeal smelling so awful. Standing there stirring it makes me want to retch. I back off from it to clear my head, but the smell won't go away. Missus slaps a couple of fish in the fry pan, gutted, but with their heads and tails still on. The smell of frying fish on top of the oatmeal gags me, and I run out, holding my mouth for the rail.

"You ain't with child are you?" Missus asks when I come back.

"No, ma'am. Not unless it's another Jesus."

She raises one eyebrow and gives me one of them "I don't believe you" looks and goes back to lifting breakfast. I choose to stay outside in the fresh air. My head aches, my neck aches, and so does my back and my arms and legs. I know I have to work to earn my way, but I don't seem able to navigate this morning.

I'm still holding onto the rail, looking at the water, when Al Gilpin comes along for breakfast. "What's bothering you, Missy? You look a little green around the gills."

"Don't know. Sick, I guess. They'll probably put me off at the next town. I can't do no more work."

He disappears into the galley and I don't see or hear from him again until noon. Missus is pretty nice all morning, waiting for me to get over whatever's wrong with me. I try to help with the dishes, but my head aches so bad I can't hardly stand up. She sees how it is and leads me back to the musty-smelling mattress. The whole place is spinning.

I drift in and out for the rest of the day and into the night. I feel the hum of the engine and the rocking of the boat, and it makes me sicker, but I'm too weak to even turn over, so I just lie there. Sometimes I hear talking, but it don't make no sense. I can't even tell whether it's day or night no more.

Then the rocking and rumbling stops and I slip into a really deep sleep. Jeremy's there, and he's holding my hand and crying, "Please forgive me, Nell. I didn't mean it."

"It's okay, Jeremy. I understand. It's all right. I love you anyway."

I'm sweating. Then I'm cold. I look for Jeremy. I want to talk to him some more. Then someone is there, talking to me, but it ain't Jeremy. It's Valoreous, berating me for running off. I scrunch up to get away from him. I hear Mrs. Allison banging around in the galley, getting a meal. It's quiet now. I hear breathing. Someone is sitting next to me, holding my hand.

I sleep for a long time before I'm woken up by strong arms lifting me and carrying me a long way. I try to stay awake, but it's too hard. I slip away again and then next time I come back, I'm in a room with beautiful flowered walls and a clean white bed with a stitched coverlet. There's a big fat white-haired man sitting beside me, holding a gold watch on a chain and touching my forehead.

"There you are, young lady," he says. "You gave us quite a scare."

"Who are you?" I try to sit up, but I'm too weak.

"Now, you just rest there, child. I'm Dr. Beckwith. I've been taking care of you."

I lay back and stare at the ceiling. It's near about the cleanest, neatest fanciest room I've ever been in. I want to study it, but I keep falling back asleep. The next time I wake, there's a round-faced fat lady there. She's all bubbly and happy, smiling and full of chuckles. I like her right off. She comes in like a whirlwind and fluffs my pillow and talks to me like we're old friends.

"How's it going today, Dearie? You feeling up to a little broth? Got to get some nourishment into you, you know. You'd like to starved when you got here."

"How'd that happen? The getting here, I mean."

"Oh, Al Gilpin brought you. Carried you in his arms like you was his own. Gave you over to Dr. Beckwith and paid for your keep." Her smile tells a lot about how she feels about Al Gilpin. "Now there's a man, that one. God only made one of him, you can bet. Too good he is. Too good for this world."

Dr. Beckwith stops by every evening after his rounds. He checks my fever and gives me medicine and talks to me like I'm a right and proper young lady. I don't know what to make of it, but right now I'm too weak to make anything. One evening I get up the energy to ask him.

"What's wrong with me?"

"Encephalitis," he replies. "You almost died."

Chapter 14

I can't rightly recall most of the next two weeks, I'm that muddle-headed. I stay in that fancy bed in that fancy room until I'm sick and tired of it. Then they let me get up and halfway carry me out to the upstairs porch. I sit there doing nothing but watching the river flow by about a block away for another week. "They" means Dr. Beckwith and Mrs. O'Shaunessy. That's the fat lady that likes Al Gilpin so much. She's the doctor's housekeeper. They keep me down for a lot longer than I think they need to, but when it comes to getting up I find out pretty quick that they know what they're about. I'm weak. Weedy. Sickly. Feeble. All of them.

I learn a new word from Mrs. O'Shaunessy: eggs-*hen*-trick. She says that's what Dr. Beckwith is. I don't know how hens can do tricks with their eggs, but I make out that she means Dr. Beckwith is odd, queer, different. She's right about that. See, he's not just a doctor, he teaches other people how to be doctors, and dentists, too. He's a professor of medicine at Washington University.

He works all the time, and don't care to do nothing else. He goes out on his rounds every morning and comes back around noon for lunch. He's so fat that when he eats, he has to sit back a ways from the table. This results in a lot of spots on his shirtfront and a lot of nagging from Mrs. O'Shaunessy.

He spends a couple afternoons a week seeing sick folk in his office, and a couple afternoons up at the university teaching medical students. Then supper, and he goes back out to his office and reads and writes 'til almost morning. Then he starts right over and does it again. On Sunday he's out there in that office all day long. He don't even go to church. He's got a machine that writes words on paper when he hits keys with letters on them. He's running that machine day and night.

One warm morning he comes in and sits down in a chair in my room. "I've got something for you, Nell. I need you to work with me on this. Open your mouth and let me see if this can help."

I shrink back. I don't like to open my mouth ever since the tormentors. I don't want nobody to see the hole in my head.

"Come, now, girl. I've seen a cleft palate before. This is going to make it some better."

He's a kindly looking man with a shock of white hair and a dimple in his chin. This morning he's fiddling with a little whitish disk, turning it this way and that, carving at it with a pocket knife, filing the edges ever so careful.

He puts the little disk in behind my upper teeth. It feels funny, but he don't leave it long. He takes it out and works on it some more with the little files he has in a leather case.

"What's that?" I ask, eying the disk with distrust.

"Whalebone, my dear. I'm making you a new roof for your mouth."

"Why?"

"Why not? You'll talk better and it will be easier to eat."

I watch his jowls lop over his shirt collar as he talks. He files and fits and files some more. After a little while, he sticks the thing in my mouth again, and after one or two more filings, it fits right in. It's even curved a little.

"This feels funny." I stop at the sound of my own voice. It sounds just like anybody's. It ain't hollow no more. Don't sound like it's echoing around inside my head. It scares me. Makes me want to go back to the way it was.

"You'll get used to it. You can take it out and put it in any time you want to. Clean it. Brush your teeth. But I have a feeling you'll want to leave it in most of the time." He stands, smiling down at me, proud of his work.

It takes a while to get used to the thing. It feels real awkward at first, but I got to admit I like the way it sounds. They won't make fun of the way I talk no more. That feels good.

Dr. Beckwith ain't done yet. One day he brings a strange man onto the upstairs porch where I'm reading, still in my nightgown. I been looking for my clothes, but I guess Mrs. O'Shaunessy took them to wash them. Anyway, I ain't comfortable with the doctor bringing this man around.

"Nell, this is Thomas Payton. He's an artist. An illustrator, actually. I want him to do some drawings of your face and your mouth."

"Huh? Why?" I'm mighty perplexed at this, but Dr. Beckwith ain't hearing none of it.

He sets the man up at a little table with pencils and paper and pens. "I need his drawings for a book I'm writing."

"You write books? About me?"

He sits down and looks direct into my eyes. "Nell, I can fix your face if you'll let me. It's simply a matter of changing your teeth. See, here, I've drawn a diagram after studying your face. If I remove these two teeth, and pull these four around straight, and put in a brace to widen your upper jaw, I can drastically change the way you look."

"Huh? What you talking about? How can you move teeth around? The nuns always said I looked like I looked. I'm used to that. Anyway, I got to be going. It'll be fall before I know it."

The artist man has his paper and pens ready. He gives Dr. Beckwith a nod.

"First, I need you to open your mouth for this man so he can draw an accurate picture of your deformity."

Deformity? I ain't sure I like that word. Makes me feel even more like a freak. Dr. Beckwith's all business, and I feel like I owe him for taking care of me and all, but I can hardly make myself open up for this stranger. I expect them both to have a good laugh over me.

Still, I open my mouth in spite of my bad feelings, and the man looks in and starts right in to drawing. He don't laugh at all. I ain't never seen the inside of my mouth, but I can feel it with my tongue. I guess I know what it looks like. He draws real careful while I sit there with my mouth opened up. Dr. Beckwith looks over his shoulder and points to things he wants changed. By the time he's finished, my jaw is aching.

"That's enough for today, Thomas," Dr. Beckwith says. "Come back tomorrow and we'll get another view."

Every day for the next week the artist man comes and draws pictures of my mouth with and without the disk, my teeth, my jaw, everything. He lets me look at the drawings after he's done. Yeah. That's me all right. Crooked teeth and all.

Dr. Beckwith don't let up on his plan to fix me. He keeps wheedling for me to give in. "Take some time to think about it. If we do it, it'll take six months or more, and you'll have some pain to contend with, but in the end it'll all be worth it."

"No. No. I don't want no teeth pulled. I can't stay here for six months. I got to get going if I'm ever going to find my mother."

I've been here almost a month already, and I still can't hardly get up on my own and get dressed, if I had any clothes, that is. Deep down I know I'm not ready to leave, but I still think I have to. I wish I knew where Jeremy is. Wish I'd never left him. Him and me could be halfway to Deadwood by now.

The next day, Mrs. O'Shaunessy brings me some new dresses—two of them! That's more than I've ever had before in my life. And two pairs of shoes and some under things.

"We had to burn everything you had, Dearie. Not that they was anything worth saving." Mrs. O'Shaunessy is given to honesty, I'll say that.

I dress and go out on the upstairs porch, but I ain't got the energy to do nothing much beyond sitting. I look out to the river, flowing past on its way to New Orleans, like the whores said. I sit there longing for Jeremy and wishing I was back on the water.

Turns out I ain't the only guest in the doctor's house, there's a young woman named Addie, a bit older than me. Mrs. O'Shaunessy brings her out to the upstairs porch and introduces us once I get up and around. Addie's real pretty—her mama was a Sioux Indian and her pa was a Irish buffalo hunter. Addie's husband dropped her off with Dr. Beckwith because she's with child, and they're afraid she's going to lose the baby. Her husband had business to do in the hinterlands of Missouri, and she's real anxious to get back to him and her people. Dr. Beckwith makes her sit most of the time and won't let her lift nothing, so we keep each other company on the upstairs porch.

One thing I like about Addie is, she don't make fun of my talk about my mother. "Indians are mystical people," she says. "They don't have to have proof to believe in something."

"Well, most of the white folk I've told about my mother won't have none of it. They say I'm a dreamer or addled, one."

"I hope you find her some day," she says, like it's a real possibility.

One morning, Mrs. O'Shaunessy comes out on the porch, making rounds with her feather duster. "My, my. Don't we sound fine? I guess doctor fitted that whalebone in just right, huh?"

I look away, embarrassed.

"Now, Dearie, don't take it any way but good. You sound right smart. And doctor says he can do wonders for your face, too, if you'll let him."

"I ain't got time," I mumble, looking in Addie's direction.

"Oh, surely you have time for this. It'll make everything ever so much better. You wait and see. You won't even know yourself."

"That's what scares me," I tell her.

Mrs. O'Shaunessy brushes my protests aside and hands me my books and needlework, and Addie and I spend the morning reading and sewing and talking. I remember the stitches Granny taught me, and Addie teaches me some new ones. I teach her how to knit, and she into knitting booties for her baby. I'm mighty glad for her. She's good company, and it ain't long before I'd call her my best friend. She settles me down when I get fretful about staying here so long, like I ain't even in charge of myself no more.

She's right sensible and thoughtful, like if you ask her about something, she'll think on it for a long time before she answers you, and when she does, you feel like she's making sense. I tell her about Dr. Beckwith's idea for rearranging my face, and she puzzles over it and asks me questions about how it feels to be different. Different, she says. Not ugly or deformed, just different.

"I don't know. I guess it hurts sometimes, if people are mean. I don't guess I can expect much more than that."

"Does it keep you from doing what you want?" she asks. She has a real gentle, quiet way of talking.

I mull that one over. "Well, I guess it does, some. I mean the nuns thought I wasn't worth sending to school. Thought I wasn't of no account. So if folks judge by what I look like, I guess it does."

"Is that why you want so much to find your mother? To be of some account?"

I look down at the embroidery hoop in my lap and pull a string of thread. "Uh huh."

"Well, then, if Dr. Beckwith could make you look different and people wouldn't be mean and would think you were of some account, maybe you should let him do it."

I pick up my needle again and finish a row of lazy daisy stitches before I make a reply. "I'll think on it."

Addie rises and stretches. "I wish Robert would come." Robert's her husband. He's on some kind of mission to save the Lakota Sioux. Not a church mission, mind you, but a mission of mercy, Addie calls it.

Now it's my turn to give the advice. "You want to watch out, Addie. You could die if you was out on the prairie and you lost your baby. Then what?"

"I know, but my people need so much, and Robert needs me to translate for him."

"How'd you two come to meet, anyway?"

She smiles every time she talks about Robert, which is a lot. "Robert was a soldier, but he felt so for the Sioux, especially after the buffalo were all killed off." She holds up a half-knit bootie she's working on, inspecting it for flaws.

"When his enlistment was up, he stayed in the Dakotas to do what he could for my tribe. Things are real bad for the Sioux these days." Her eyes cloud over when she talks about her people. "Now they're herded together on the Pine Ridge Reservation in South Dakota, but it's too dry to farm, and without the buffalo, their lives are ruined."

It's hard for me to know what to think about Indians. Around St. Louis, they're not much account. People treat them bad, even Addie when she goes out, which ain't often. But I like her, so I guess I'm a Indian lover, like they say—like it's a bad thing.

Al Gilpin comes to see me every time the Queen Marie is in town. I can hear him half a block away, hollering and laughing. He joshes Mrs. O'Shaunessy all the time, but it's clear she loves it. "Al, you prodigious fool! You'll flatter your way into heaven some day!"

"Not too soon, Mrs. O. Not too soon!" He bounds up the stairs and the porch shudders under his step. "Missy! How goes it with you? You up to a little walk?"

I welcome the chance to get out of prison, but I know my limits. "Maybe just down to the water, Al."

"That's all right, Missy. If'n you can't make it, I'll carry you. Done it before."

I nod to Addie, wishing she could come too, as he takes my arm and leads me down the hall to the stairway. We descend slowly, one step at a time, while Mrs. O'Shaunessy watches from below. "Careful, now, Al. Don't keep her up too long."

We step out into the sunshine of a dusty late August afternoon and turn toward the river. It only takes two steps for me to stop. Soot! Al has him tied to the front fence, and he's pulling on the rope, barking and whining to get at me. We go over careful, and I reach out and pet him and soothe him until he gets over being so anxious. Then I put my arms around him, bury my face in his curly black coat and cry. He licks my face and wiggles all over with joy.

"Al! Oh, thank you for taking care of him for me. I was afraid he was lost."

"No, Missy. I'da kept him myself, he's that good a dog, but I knew you'd want him back. Had to get the doctor's permission to bring him."

We take Soot around to the back yard and untie his rope. It's a big yard, with a picket fence and a lot of trees and flower beds, plenty of room for Soot to roam. He bounds around like he's just escaped the gallows, stopping every round or so to sit in front of me and lick my hand.

"Ready for that walk now, Missy?"

I nod and Al offers his arm. We go out the gate, leaving poor Soot to whine his confusion at being left so soon. Al lets me set the pace, slow, but joyous. Just being outside and walking again sets my spirit free. There's a park by the river not a block from Dr. Beckwith's, where we sit down on a bench and watch the boats churning upriver against the current.

"How's Mrs. Allison?" I ask.

"She's fine. Sends you her best. She felt bad that you took sick on her boat, like it was her fault or something."

"No. Now that I look back on it, I was feeling poorly before I ever got to Cairo."

He turns and looks curious at me. "You talk different," he says.

I smile. "Uh huh. Doctor put this here thing in my mouth. Made of whalebone. Covers up the hole."

Al shakes his head. "Ain't it a wonder what doctors can do? I hear tell he thinks he can rearrange your teeth a bit and fix up your mouth."

I look away. Why are they *always* talking about me? "He says so, but I can't wait around here that long. He says six months. How am I supposed to find my mother if I sit around St. Louis for six months? Anyway, in six months it'll be the dead of winter, so I'd still have to wait around for spring." I shake my head.

"If he knows what he's doing, and I think he does, it could change your life."

"I don't want my life changed! Leastways, not my face. I'm used to it. I know I ain't nothing to look at, but that's how I've always been. I wouldn't know how to *be* any other way."

I can't put words on it, but the whole idea scares me, even though everybody else seems taken with it.

Al senses my plight and changes the subject. "You know, ever since you were on the Queen Marie, I been asking around about this here Calamity Jane. Come across some that say they knew her once upon a time."

I jump at the mention of my mother. "Really! What'd they say about her?"

"Hear tell she was born right here in this here state—Missouri— up north in Mercer County. Her real name's Martha Cannary."

"Cannary? Well, then, my name's Nell Cannary. I always wanted a last name." I pause, searching his face for more. "What else did you find out?"

"Guess her folks took her west when she was just a mite. Local folk don't seem to know much more'n that."

I'm delighted at any information about my mother, and the last name is an unexpected prize. I sit looking out at the river, mulling over this new tidbit. As I watch a boat tied up at the wharf, passengers walk down a gangplank to the shore. Then something catches my eye. My heart jumps up into my throat and stays there.

Jeremy!

Chapter 15

I rise and start running for the boat, yelling, "Jeremy! Jeremy! It's me, Nell!"

He stops and looks at me like he's never seen me before, or like I'm a ghost, one. Then that beautiful smile crosses his face, and he steps off in my direction.

"Nell! Where've you been? I've looked all over for you!" He stops a few feet away and frowns. "You've lost weight. Have you been sick?"

I nod and turn to introduce him to Al Gilpin, who's followed me to the wharf. "This here is Al Gilpin. He saved my life. I was that sick."

Jeremy looks at Al and takes a step back. Al is so big, and he don't smile when he shakes Jeremy's hand. Jeremy looks a little unsteady, but he flashes that smile again. It works for him most of the time.

"This the one you was mumbling about in your sleep, Missy? The one you was crying out for?"

My face burns red at that. "No, Al. You must have him mixed up with somebody else. This here's Jeremy, my traveling friend."

Jeremy frowns like he don't know what to think. "Nell and I came all the way from Pittsburgh together," he tells Al.

"Then you left her," Al counters.

"Not at all, sir. She left me. Took the boat and left without even saying good-bye. I have no idea why."

That spites me. "No idea why! Jeremy, are you deaf and dumb or just stupid? You know why I left. I couldn't stand no more of you and Valoreous. And if you're still with him, you can just keep on walking, 'cause I still ain't got time for *him*."

Al steps back with a chuckle at the way I wade into Jeremy, but Jeremy don't see no humor in it. He stands there, all injured innocence, and looks at me like he don't know what I'm talking about.

"Where is that good-for-nothing pole cat?" I ask.

"He had some trouble in Paducah. Seems they have a law against selling snake oil, as they call it. They shut us down and told us to get out of town by dark. Valoreous lit out for New Orleans. I stayed on in Kentucky, living with a friend at his plantation outside of town. Beautiful place. Escaped the ravages of war. Then we had a falling out, so I came on to St. Louis."

"Falling out, huh? Guess he probably found out you wasn't who you said you was and cut off your allowance."

He winces at that remark. "Really, Nell, everything I do isn't a game. I'm capable of having an honest relationship."

"Not that I've ever seen," I remind him.

He looks over at Al, then back at me. "Where are you staying?"

"She's got a place with a doctor friend of mine. She ain't fully recovered yet." Al has stepped up to claim me back from Jeremy. Not like a beau, mind you. He's old enough to be my pa. Yeah. Kind of like that. Kind of like a pa or a nice uncle.

Jeremy gets it and backs off. "Well, then, I guess I'll take my leave. I wish you well." He tips his hat and turns to go, but I can't let that happen.

"Jeremy! That's the doctor's house, right up there, the white one with the upstairs porch. Maybe you could come by and visit me sometime."

He takes brief note of the house, nods and walks away. I watch him go, wishing I could run after him and we could get on a boat and keep going. Al leads me back to the doctor's without a single word about Jeremy on the way. When we get there, I'm all tired out from the walk, so we sit down for a glass of lemonade on the porch. Addie joins us.

"When's your baby coming?" Al asks her. Addie's been here for a couple of months, so Al knows her from before.

"Around Christmas."

"When's Doctor going to let you go?"

"Soon, I hope. We have to get to Pine Ridge before winter sets in."

"Pine Ridge? Ain't that a reservation in Dakota?"

She nods.

"Ain't it dangerous, going up there this time of year in your condition and all?"

That sad smile again. "Maybe. But Robert and I want to help. We left, right after we got married, to raise money to help my people. Now we go back as soon as Doctor says I can travel."

"I guess things are still pretty iffy among the Sioux." Being a river man, Al knows the west. North, south and east, too, for that matter.

She nods. "Hard to change. People try, but anger runs deep. They've lost so much, and they've nothing to work with. No buffalo. No good farmland. Besides, the Sioux aren't farmers. If we don't get there with food and supplies, I don't know how my people will make it through the winter."

"Not much the two of you can do. You'll need a lot more help than that," Al tells her.

"I know, but I can't just sit here and wait until spring. We've got to do what we can."

I like Addie. She's very serious, but fun loving, too. She understands why I feel smothered here. She does, too. When I talk about my mother, she never laughs—doesn't even smile. She just listens. "You might be right about this Calamity Jane. Great Spirit might be guiding you."

My heart leaps at that idea. "Yeah. Something's pushing me to find her, whatever you call it."

I like it at Dr. Beckwith's, but they keep a pretty good eye on me and the company I keep. I mean Jeremy. Al Gilpin tells the doctor and Mrs. O'Shaunessy about our meeting at the wharf, and I can tell they're afraid I'll run off with him before I'm all the way better. No such luck. I ain't seen anything of Mr. Chatterfield since then, and that was two weeks ago. Not that I think Mrs. O'Shaunessy would let him in if he did come calling.

I'm all better now, and dying to get back on the river to South Dakota, but everywhere I look they put up a stumbling block. "Winter's coming, you know." Or "I wouldn't want to get caught out on the plains in a fall snowstorm." Or "Anyone sick as you've been.

.." I don't want to be ungrateful, but I really want to leave. I would, too, if I could find Jeremy and talk him into going with me.

Turns out, finding Jeremy ain't as hard as I thought. He finds me, real late one night after the house is asleep. I wake up to the sense of somebody in my room. A hand over my mouth silences me.

"Hush, Nell. It's me."

"Jeremy! How'd you get in here?"

"Simple. Up the trellis to the upstairs porch and in the door. They leave that door open in the night all the time?"

"Just in the summer. Lets in the breeze from the river. Guess they don't expect low forms of humanity to try and get in." I sit up in bed and look at him in the darkened room. My heart quickens. Even in the dark, he's a joy to behold. "Where you been, anyhow?"

He pulls up a chair and sits on it backwards, facing me. "Around. St. Louis is a great town. A person could get rich here without half trying."

"*Jeremy.*" I swing my legs over the side of the bed and meet his eyes. "I want to get back on the river before winter comes. These here people are real nice, but they take too gooda care of me."

"No, Nell. We can't go out in the wilds now until spring, and I'm not promising to go then. I'm hoping you'll give up your hair-brained idea about Calamity Jane and decide to settle down someplace civilized."

The words *settle down* ring in my ears. What does he mean? Settle down—with *him?*

"I ain't gonna give it up. Not till I see her and she tells me I ain't hers or I am, whichever. Besides, where and why would I want to settle down? I ain't got no family, so what's to keep me?"

"These people here care a lot about you."

"That's another reason why I gotta get outa here. That Dr. Beckwith is always pestering me about how he could fix my face."

"Fix your face?"

"Pull some teeth and twist some others around and make my jaw wider. Make me look almost pretty. Says he can do it in six months."

"That sounds grand."

"Grand? It don't sound grand to me. He already fixed the roof of my mouth, but he ain't satisfied. Has to fuss with my face."

Jeremy stands and takes my hand, leads me to the door and down the hall to the porch. He climbs down the trellis and reaches up to help me. I don't mind Jeremy seeing me in my nightgown. He's seen me in less. We go around to the backyard and sit on a bench. Soot bounds across the yard, wagging his tail in delight at seeing Jeremy. I feel the same. I shiver a little in the nighttime damps, so Jeremy takes off his jacket and puts it around my shoulders. My heart quickens again.

"You should think about letting him do it."

"Why?"

"Why? Because it'll make your life better. You won't have to listen to the insults anymore. I can't figure out why you wouldn't want to."

"Cause it ain't me. I am who I am. I'm used to being me. It would turn me into somebody I don't even know." I reach out and pet Soot's head. Feels good to touch him when I feel myself getting wrought up.

"I thought you *didn't* know who you were. That's what you told me up on the Conemaugh. Maybe if he does this and it turns out well, you'll know who you are and won't have to go chasing off to South Dakota on a fool's errand."

I sit silent on the bench, Jeremy's jacket still around my shoulders. It feels right to be here with him. It don't feel right to be turned into somebody else. Then it hits me. Maybe he wants me to get fixed so he can marry me! Sure! That makes sense. I think on that for a while, and it feels real good. Jeremy wouldn't want a ugly wife, that's for sure. The whole idea takes on a new aspect. If Jane doesn't turn out to be my mother—not that I'm saying I doubt it—but if she doesn't, or even if she does, marrying Jeremy would be the answer to all of it. I wouldn't care about finding my mother. I'd have Jeremy, and him and me could have a family of our own. If there's even a tiny chance of that, I've got to do everything I can to help it along.

"Well, maybe I should let him see what he can do. But I don't like spending six months here, I can tell you."

"There's my girl. Six months will go by in no time. I'll stick around and come to see you now and then. Help the time go faster. In the meantime, take advantage of the opportunities that come your way. I certainly intend to."

He rises from the bench and plants a kiss on my forehead. "You can get back up the trellis on your own, can't you? I'll see you in a couple of weeks." He walks around to the front of the house, puts a hand on the gatepost, jumps the fence and is gone. I'm still reeling from the kiss.

Dr. Beckwith don't waste no time after I tell him I'll let him work on my teeth. He uses some stuff called sweet air to put me to sleep while he pulls out what he calls my eye teeth. See, they're all crooked and they overlap the other teeth, so he says they've gotta come out. Then he fits me with a wire spring in the roof of my mouth. It's supposed to push my mouth wider.

"This is all experimental, mind you," he says. "I've read about these procedures, but I've never seen them done. We'll see how this works. If it doesn't work, we'll stop."

I nod. My mouth hurts. The pulled teeth and the spring pushing against the sides give me the misery, but I keep telling myself Jeremy will like it. It's for Jeremy.

Al Gilpin don't let no more'n a week go by without a visit. Mrs. O'Shaunessy is sweet on him, I can tell. I think he likes her, too, if complimenting her cooking at every turn is a sign. One day in mid-September he comes in the kitchen door and plops his sea bag on the floor.

"That's it for this year. Allisons sold their boat. Truth to tell, I don't know if I'll be ready for more come spring or not."

Mrs. O'Shaunessy wipes her hands on her apron. "What else would you do, Al? You're a river man, body and soul."

"Been thinking about opening up a repair shop. Work on boat engines in port. They's plenty of call for that. This coming and going gets me in the back of my neck."

I listen, wondering what he's leading up to. He turns to me.

"How's your business coming, Missy? You look better'n the last time."

The last time, my face was swollen from pulling my teeth and my jaw ached from the spring. "I'm doing better now."

It still hurts, but there's no use complaining. Dr. Beckwith has these wires around my teeth, and just when I get to feeling okay, he comes around and pulls them tighter. Ouch! He's pleased with what's happening, and he makes me sit still for that artist guy at least once a week.

Al turns back to Mrs. O'Shaunessy. "Come for a walk, Mary?"

They're gone about a half hour, leaving me and Addie to wonder what they're about, and when they come back, it's clear something's afoot. Al is grinning all over his face and Mrs. O keeps smoothing back her hair and glancing in the mirror she keeps above the sink. Her face is red and her hands keep fluttering to her mouth and down her neck. Addie and I wait. They'll tell us soon enough, like we don't already know.

When Dr. Beckwith comes in from his rounds, Mrs. O'Shaunessy puts lunch on the kitchen table. We always have breakfast and lunch in the kitchen and supper in the dining room. Dr. Beckwith ain't as mindful of the comings and goings of people as Addie and I are. He sits down and starts into eating without taking note of the tension in the air. Mrs. O'Shaunessy and Al Gilpin stand on their side of the table, looking at him. Looking silly at him, I might add.

He glances up and waves his hand at them to sit, but they just stand there. "What's going on here?" the doctor finally asks. I could tell him.

"Well, sir," Al stammers, "We—ah, Mrs. O'Shaunessy and me— we was thinking it might suit us to get married."

"Married! Why would you want to do that?"

I let out a giggle. Dr. Beckwith ain't never been married, or even entertained the notion, if I know him.

Mrs. O'Shaunessy is more flustered than ever. "Oh, Doctor, it would make us ever so happy, and with your permission, I'd stay on." Her face gets even redder, and her hands flutter so that Al takes ahold of them and presses them to his ample chest.

"Of course, you'll stay on. Why would you do anything else? I won't brook any disruption in my routine." Dr. Beckwith talks to them like they're his kids. I giggle again. Al is almost as old as the doctor, and Mrs. O'Shaunessy ain't much younger.

Al turns to me. "What're you so giggly about?" he asks.

"Nothing. I'm glad for you is all."

Mrs. O'Shaunessy comes around to my side of the table and takes my hand. "We've been thinking on all of this for quite a while, but you brought us to the decision, Dearie."

"Me? What'd I do?"

"You're the missing piece. We wanted a family. A real family," she goes on. "Al and I would like you to stay on, too, and be our daughter."

Boom! It goes off in my head like a bomb. Their daughter! "No. No. I've got to find my real mother. Sorry, but I'm off as soon as spring comes. I like you both, and I'm flattered that you want me, but no. I can't stay here. I gotta find her." The words come tumbling out, helter-skelter. I'm so flummoxed; I couldn't stop them or polish them up if I tried.

"Now, Missy," Al soothes. "You know you ain't got nothing real that says she's your mother. It's just the dream of a child without a family. We can fix that for you. We can be your family. It would pleasure us no end."

I look over at Addie. She understands what I'm thinking. These people are as nice as I could ever want. I could stay here and live in a fancy house and get schooling and finish growing up. But it don't fit. It don't fit with my plan.

Jeremy would say I don't have a plan. He's right. I don't. But this ain't part of it, I know that much.

Al and Mrs. O'Shaunessy get married on the first Saturday in October and settle into the doctor's place. They got their own part of the house, downstairs, beside the kitchen. Got a bedroom and a little parlor, with their own door leading out on the porch. For a little while, Mrs. Al is so caught up with having a husband, she leaves off acting the mother hen to Addie and me.

I like them both just fine, but, like Jeremy, they keep telling me how silly I am to keep talking about my mother. They're nice about it, but you can tell they're frustrated with me, so I make them a promise

I'm not sure I can keep. I tell them if I ever find Jane and I'm not hers, I'll come back to St. Louis to stay with them. That settles them down, for a while, at least, 'cause they're sure I'll be back. Maybe they're right, but I have to see for myself.

Chapter 16

Me and Addie spend so much time together, it feels like
we're sisters. I tell her about Jeremy's nighttime visit, and she
smiles that gentle smile of hers.

"See? He cares about you. He'll be back, you can be sure of it.
And every time he comes, he'll see a world of difference. I see a big
change in your face already. Spring seems a long way off, but it will
be here before you can blink."

Addie can counsel me to be patient, but she sure is anxious to get
back to Robert and her people. She hasn't heard from him since early
August, and she's all wrought up about it. Then one day in early
October about a week after Al and Mrs. Al got married, like a ghost
out of the fog, he shows up.

He steps into the parlor where we're reading on a fall afternoon
and when Addie sees him, she jumps from her chair and runs to his
arms. I feel real strange, sitting there watching their reunion, but
they're blocking the doorway and there's no escape.

Addie is beside herself. "Robert! Where have you been so long?
I've almost died of worry!"

"I've come for you, Addie. I hope you're well enough to travel.
We've got to go. There's no time to waste."

He's all full of hurry up and excitement. "I've had a windfall. A
man I was working for upriver died, and his family gave me a wagon
and a horse!" He talks real fast, like if he don't, it'll all go away.

Addie's so happy to see him, she glows. "Oh, Robert, how fine!"

"That's not all. One of the churches took up a collection. Loaded
the whole wagon with blankets and provisions to take. We can go
now, Addie. We can go back in comfort."

He's a tall, hatchet-faced young man, skinny and intense—hard to
change the course of. Addie's so delighted to be with him again,
she'd shave her head if he asked her to. That'd be a job, with her

long, shining, black hair. I'm doubtful she's in a condition to go, but there's no heading either of them off.

Addie's joy knows no bounds, and she rushes out to tell Mrs. Al to set another plate for dinner. Mrs. Al saw Robert come in, so she's way ahead of Addie.

"Hope he likes pot roast and vegetables." She's almost as happy to see Robert as Addie is. "I think I recall that he does."

I go out into the kitchen to help Mrs. Al and to give Addie and Robert time to catch up. I'm glad for Addie, but not too glad, because I'm pretty sure this means she'll be leaving.

After dinner, we spend the evening in the parlor, Dr. Beckwith, Al and Mrs. Al, all trying to talk Robert out of taking Addie out on the plains in her condition, but he ain't hearing none of it.

"Just stay through the winter," Mrs. Al pleads. "You can take the provisions when spring comes and your baby's big enough to travel."

"You don't even know where you're taking her. What you'll encounter." Dr. Beckwith sputters. He don't deal with mulishness very good. He turns to Addie. "This is suicide, child. Suicide."

Robert takes offense at that. "God will provide, Dr. Beckwith."

"Humph!" The doctor snorts and shakes his head. "God will provide a grave, maybe."

Al stands up, hands on hips and hollers at Robert. "I'm of a mind to stop you any way I can. *Beat* some sense into you if I have to."

Addie covers her ears with both hands. "Please. Please. We'll be all right. When we get to Pine Ridge, my mother will care for me."

"*If* you get to Pine Ridge." That's Dr. Beckwith.

Robert puts an arm around Addie. "I understand how you feel, but things with the Lakotas are going from bad to worse. They need us *now*. I feel helpless hundreds of miles away."

Addie nods, leaning into Robert's arm.

I understand how she feels. She needs to get back to her people. Robert, too. But Dr. Beckwith and the others ain't wrong about the dangers. I'm scared for Addie.

We go off to bed, Addie and Robert down the hall from me. Everybody else sleeps downstairs, so they don't hear what I hear in the night. A door opening. Footsteps down the hall past my room.

The door to the upstairs porch opening and closing. I get out of bed and peek out the window. Robert has brought the wagon around. The horse gives his harness a shake, as I watch Robert help Addie up into the seat. I want to run out and say good-bye, but I'd wake the whole house. I stay at the window until the wagon creaks around the corner into the shadows. I lie awake for the rest of the night, feeling lonely and friendless. Addie was the first real friend I ever had. Like a sister, I'd guess. I'm worried about her and her baby, that's sure. I turn and go back to my bed, but I don't go back to sleep. I hear every sound of the night. Soot out back giving a low bark, at a cat, probably. The leaves rustling in the breeze, sounding dry, like they ain't got long to stay. The low, mournful sound of a train whistle coming up along the river. Addie's leaving makes me want to go, too.

In the morning, Mrs. Al waits until almost ten o'clock, out of respect for their reunion, before she knocks, opens their door and finds them gone.

I get up early, eat breakfast and spend the morning trying to read, but the books don't interest me today. I'm sorry I didn't even get to say good-bye. I turn to my needlework. Addie and I were crocheting doilies and antimacassar sets to sell in the shops before she left. Addie wanted to make some money to take with her, and I just wanted to pass the time. I keep wondering how far they got in the night and how long it will take them to get to Pine Ridge. I ain't got a notion of how far it is, but if Dr. Beckwith is any judge, it's a long, long way. When Dr. Beckwith comes back from his morning rounds to the news, he mutters something about fools, shakes his head, and sits down to lunch.

"I think she'll be all right," I tell him. "People been having babies forever. Her folks'll know how to take care of her."

"We can hope," he replies. "Meanwhile, young lady, it's time for an adjustment."

That means a torture session. He tightens the wires around my teeth and sets that spring wider. I'll have a headache tonight. I miss Jeremy when I'm feeling down. I want him to see how this treatment is working. It *is* working. I look in Mrs. Al's mirror above the kitchen sink about every day, and I already can't remember what I used to look like. The girl in the mirror ain't exactly what you'd call a beauty, but she ain't ugly, either.

Soot still knows me, though. His tail pounds the floor every time I come into the kitchen. Dr. Beckwith says he has to stay in the kitchen, so I resist the temptation to call him upstairs to my room. Dr. Beckwith is so nice, I try not to vex him.

Time drags with Addie gone. I try to keep busy helping Mrs. Al with the household chores and working on my needlework, but what I really want is for Jeremy to turn up at the door. He don't show through the whole month of October. It's getting colder, and I wonder where he is and if he's all right. I don't talk about Jeremy to Mrs. Al. She already thinks she don't approve of him.

Chapter 17

It's into November before I see Jeremy again. He wanders down to the park below Doctor's and stands around looking up at the house. I see him from the upstairs porch, make an excuse to go out and hurry down to meet him. I'm so happy I want to run and shout, but I don't. Soon as I get there I realize he ain't alone. There's a man with him, standing off to the side while we talk.

"Nell! How've you been? Sorry I haven't been around much lately, but I've been frightfully busy." He looks fine, all dressed up in fancy clothes. Jeremy always finds a way to get him some fancy clothes. I wonder at how he always manages to get his hands on money and turns it right into clothes.

He motions for his friend to come forward. "Nell, I'd like you to meet Ethan Banks. We have rooms downtown—just a few blocks from here."

Ethan Banks ain't as handsome as Jeremy, or as nice, I can tell that already. My guess is he's a lot older—like maybe thirty or so. It don't take me long to figure out who's boss of this pair, and it ain't Jeremy. I already know I don't like this Ethan Banks any better than the last fool Jeremy took up with, but I push aside my doubts and try to be friendly. Ethan Banks barely looks at me when I offer my hand; he gives it a weak shake, like touching me would give him the itch or something. I swear, I don't know why Jeremy takes up with such no accounts.

Jeremy is oohing and aahing about how fine I look.

"The doctor ain't done yet," I tell him. "He says it'll take another couple months to get my teeth all straightened out."

"I can't get over how different you look already." Jeremy seems real pleased with my changeover. That makes me feel real good.

Ethan Banks wanders off to the far side of the park, away from the river, glancing over his shoulder at us now and then. I'm glad he's gone so I can talk to Jeremy in private.

"*Jeremy!* Where have you been? I thought you was gonna come visit me."

"Oh, Nell, I haven't forgotten you. You know how life goes. You get caught up in things. Anyway, I'm learning a trade. Ethan's a riverboat gambler. The off season is coming up, so he'll be working some of the local hotels for the winter, but he's teaching me all I need to know about cards. By spring I'll be ready to go off on my own and make a fortune."

I put my hands up to my face and sigh. "A trade? Huh! You mean he's teaching you to cheat, don't you? Teaching you to get your pretty face beat up or worse. Jeremy, when will you ever learn?"

He smiles, like I'm just a little girl that don't know nothing. "This is different, Nell. It's a great opportunity to learn from a master."

I look at Mr. Banks, fine clothes and all, standing now looking out at the river with his hands behind his back, fidgeting like he's in a all-fired hurry to be someplace else. "He sure don't look like no master to me. Looks to me like trouble. You gotta learn to stay away from trouble."

Jeremy ain't in no mood for preaching. He steps back and pulls on a pair of fine leather gloves. "I'll come see you soon, Nell. I promise. I've got to run now." And then he walks away, just as happy as if he had good sense. Goes back to his friend, and they turn upriver, heading for the busy part of town.

As I walk back up the hill I notice two old men, regulars at the park. River men, too old and feeble for real work but still living on the river in their minds. One of them leans over to the other, and says, real loud, 'cause they're both probably hard of hearing, "Couple 'a Nancy Boys."

I've heard that phrase before, but I'm not really sure what it means. I just know he's talking about Jeremy, and it ain't nice.

I walk back to the doctor's house real slow, with a low feeling in my heart. Guess I'll just have to settle in and get along without Jeremy. He's got things on his mind, and I ain't one of them. I still hope he'll be around come spring when I get ready to head out for Deadwood.

With Addie gone there ain't much that interests me at Dr. Beckwith's except Soot. I take him out for a walk about every day. Mr. and Mrs. Al are all wrapped up in each other, and Doctor works all the time. I'm at loose ends. Nothing to do but read or do needle work. Nobody to talk to but Mrs. Al. Then Dr. Beckwith brings in a young medical student from the university and things take a turn.

His name is Andrew Clark Morgan, and he's a shy, quiet fellow, given to books and study, handsome enough in a boyish sort of way. He's tall and fit, with brown hair that has a mind of its own, and steady gray eyes that never waver. He comes from way up north in Wisconsin where he was raised on a farm. At first he looks at me like a study—watching Dr. Beckwith tighten my wires and widen that infernal spring. He makes notes about how to do it—move teeth around, I mean. He don't talk much, even at table when we all sit down together and eat. I'm not sure if I like him or not, but it's clear Dr. Beckwith does. It's all "My boy" and "Son" and talk like that.

One day in late November, Mrs. Al and I bake pumpkin pies for Thanksgiving and Andrew comes in the kitchen. "I love the smell of pumpkin pie," he says. "Reminds me of home."

Mrs. Al gives him a smile. "The first one'll be cool enough to eat pretty soon."

"What was home like?" I'm bored and want to make conversation. It don't matter to me what home was like. I just want something different to happen.

He lights up. "Home's a place called Bear Valley, on the banks of Bear Creek, that flows into the Wisconsin River. We have a tight little community there—centered around the Brown Church and Dixon school. The Brown Church was founded on the principle of tolerance. Any faith can worship there."

"Even Catholics?" I ask, mindful that the nuns I knew would never even go into another kind of church.

He smiles. "Well, there's a Catholic church nearby, so there hasn't been a need, but, yes. Even Catholics would be welcome."

He opens up real easy when he gets to talking about Bear Valley, like it's a real special place. His face lights up and he smiles a lot -- even laughs when he talks about his friends and all.

121

"Everyone there is a farmer—dairy mostly. Lots of hard work, but plenty of social events, too. Corn husking contests, strawberry festivals, skating parties. The county fair every year. There's a mill pond that freezes in the winter, and we have a swell time showing off our skating skills for the girls." His face gets a little red at that.

"You going back there when you're done here?" I'm interested even though I don't care to be. This Bear Valley, Wisconsin, sounds like a real fine place.

"I hope so, but I don't know. My folks are gone. I was raised by my grandparents, and they're pretty feeble now. If they last long enough for me to finish here, I should go back and look after them."

"What if they don't? Last, I mean."

I guess I'm too direct for him. He ain't used to girls that speak right up. He clams up at that one, like he never heard it, and starts in on the piece of pumpkin pie Mrs. Al has set out for him. When he's done, he pushes his chair back, thanks Mrs. Al for the pie, and goes off looking for the doctor.

I turn to Mrs. Al. "What's wrong with him?"

She shakes her head. "Too forward, Dearie. Men don't take to girls who ask too many questions."

I'm puzzled at that. I never knowed that there was a certain way you should talk to a man that's different from the way you talk to a woman. I resolve to hang back and watch for a while. Maybe I'll learn something that'll help me with Jeremy, if I ever see him again. But then again, I doubt it, 'cause it's just the way I am. If I want to know something, I ask.

Between Andrew being unforthcoming and me being unsteady in my conversation, we don't warm up to each other very quick. Thanksgiving comes and goes. Andrew follows Dr. Beckwith around like a baby duck. There ain't hardly a chance to get acquainted except when they make my "adjustments." Andrew's real interested in that. He gets out all the drawings that Thomas Payton made and studies them and asks the doctor lots of questions about the how and the why of it. Asks me how it feels to chew and if I have any pain here or there. I don't mind, because it gives me a chance to understand what they're doing better. After all, it's my face.

Then one day, a couple weeks before Christmas, without so much as a 'by-your-leave,' Andrew asks me to walk downtown with him. I'm befuddled, but I go anyway. Anything to get out of the house and think about something besides Jeremy.

"I want you to help me pick out a Christmas gift, Nell." He holds back from telling me any more, and by now I know not to press him.

We walk along Washington Avenue toward Fourth Street looking in the shop windows. I'm wearing a new wool coat that Mrs. Al helped me pick out. Dr. Beckwith paid for it. See what I mean about being beholden? Sometimes I wonder if I'll ever be able to pull free from these people, kind as they are.

Andrew takes my arm and steers me across the street to a lady's shop. "Here. This is what I was thinking of getting." He points to a delicate lace collar in the window. I wouldn't know what to do with such a fine thing, but maybe his lady friend would.

"Who's it for?" I have to ask. How can I help him decide if it's right if I don't know if it's for a countess or a country girl?

"My sister."

"Your sister? Well, what's she like? How old is she? Where's she live?" I bite my tongue. Too many questions.

But he's in a talkative mood, so it don't seem to matter. "She's twenty-five, and she lives in a town called Lone Rock—it's right at the foot of Bear Valley—with her husband and two children. She loves nice things, but she doesn't have many. Her husband has a drug store there."

"Well, then, I think she'd like it. Do you plan to send it to her?"

"Take it to her," he corrects me. "I'm going home for Christmas."

I'm let down at that. He's not all excitement, but him being around makes life in the Beckwith house a little more interesting. 'Specially since Jeremy ain't showing his face around there. "Oh, well, I hope you have a nice trip. I'm sure she'll be thrilled with your present. You taking any presents for those children?"

"Of course. That's the next stop. And I thought maybe some fine cigars for her husband."

We go into the shop and Andrew buys the scarf. Then it's on to the toy shop, where we pick out a nice wooden train for the little boy and a lovely doll with a porcelain face for the girl. I know I'd have loved a doll like that when I was little.

The tobacconist has several recommendations for the cigars, and he and Andrew engage in a long discussion of the merits of each. I'd be getting tired of the whole thing, except that it feels kind of good because the store keepers treat me like I'm Andrew's wife, and even if I have no interest in that at all, it still feels good to be treated like I might be, anyway. They look to me about every choice and look to Andrew to pay. He seems all right with the arrangement, and I like to play act myself, once in a while.

On the way home, he asks if I'd like to stop for a cup of tea. That feels way too fancy to me, but I don't want to hurt his feelings, so I agree. We go into a little corner tea room and sit down. The inside is all dark walnut paneling and quiet little booths with glass on the tabletops and curtains at the windows. A young woman in a white eyelet apron comes up and asks for our order. This is the first time I've ever been in a place like this—and with a young man. I sit up tall and try real hard to act like a lady.

Andrew seems to feel right at home. I decide Bear Valley, Wisconsin, must be a fancy place where people are refined and used to being polite and drinking tea. I sit quiet until the lady brings ours, but the need to fill the silence moves me to start up my questions again.

"You coming back after Christmas?"

"Oh, certainly. I wouldn't miss a chance to study under Dr. Beckwith. He's famous. Known all over the country for his pioneering techniques. Do you have any idea how lucky you are that he's treating you?"

He says that like I should kiss the floor at the doctor's feet or something. Well, I guess I should. Not that I ain't grateful. Just that I want to be gone, and I miss Jeremy and I don't even recognize that girl in the mirror any more.

"Uh huh." I wonder what he'd think if he knew I didn't want no part of this whole face fixing thing if it wasn't for Jeremy.

Andrew opens up, asks about me, like where I come from and who my people are. That gets me right away, and I sit quiet for a while before I answer. "I ain't got no people," I tell him. "Leastways, none that I know of. But I'm looking for my mother."

Just then the door to the tea room opens and who should walk in with a gust of wind but Jeremy, all decked out in a new long overcoat, new hat and gloves. If he don't always look the dandy. Jeremy. He's alone, and he don't see me at first. I keep my eyes on him as he makes his way back in our direction. He passes our booth without looking down, but I can't stop myself. I reach out and tug his sleeve. He turns and looks down for a second, studying me.

"Nell! You're so changed!"

"It's me, all right. Jeremy, this here is Andrew Morgan. He's from Wisconsin."

Jeremy don't wait for me to say *his* name. He bows and shakes hands with Andrew. "Jeremy Chatterfield. A friend of Nell's."

He talks to us as though we're old friends. We are, except that it don't feel that way anymore. I can tell he wonders who Andrew is, but I just let him wonder. Do him good to wonder once in a while. After a few minutes of talking pleasantries, he moves on to a back booth, takes off his coat and hangs it on a hook at the end of the booth, and sits down like he's waiting for somebody. My back is to him now, and I've a notion to get up and go talk to him some more, but Andrew is such a proper gentleman, I don't see how I can.

I drink my tea and fight the urge to keep looking back over my shoulder. Then in walks Mr. Ethan Banks himself, dressed up even finer than the last time I saw him. He's even got a gold stick pin in his tie. I try to avoid his eye, but I know he sees me as he passes back and sits down across from Jeremy.

I guess Andrew can see I'm bothered, 'cause he drinks his tea and asks for the check without talking anymore. When we get up to leave, I steal a glance back at Jeremy. There he is, bold as brass, smiling at me as Andrew helps me with my coat. Okay, Mr. Chatterfield. Here's to you.

I take Andrew Morgan's arm and we walk out of the tearoom just like we was a twosome. I even smile up into Andrew's eyes, just to make Mr. Chatterfield know he ain't the only man in the world.

Chapter 18

Before I know it, Andrew's boarded the train north to Wisconsin and I'm feeling low with nobody to talk to but the Gilpins and Dr. Beckwith. It's almost Christmas and it's cold. The air has an edge to it. Snow flurries flit along the streets, promising to stick, but too light and airy to keep the promise.

Two days before Christmas, I take the money I've saved from making doilies and antimacassar sets and go downtown to buy Christmas gifts. The snow is sticking now, and I trudge along, pull up my collar, and keep my eyes on the sidewalk so I don't slip. The snow quiets the city. Horses clop along, the sounds of their hoofs muffled and soft.

Now that Andrew's gone and I ain't got nothing to distract me, I can't get my mind off Jeremy—wonder where he is and if he's all right and if he ever even thinks of me at all. I'd like to get him something for Christmas, but I doubt that I'll see him. The handsome Mr. Chatterfield has more important things to do than visit me. Suddenly I'm crying and I don't know why. Yes, I do. I'm crying because it's Christmas, and I want more than the kindness of strangers. I want my own place, my own family, my own people. Thinking back on the past six months makes me wonder where I'm going, really. To find my mother, yes. But what if I *am* just an addle-brained girl with a silly dream? What then? I wade through the snow, head down, wondering if they're right.

Christmas is a nice day with the Gilpins and the doctor, full of presents and cooking and good smells. The only Christmases I remember was in the convent, and, even though some of the nuns tried to make it nice for us, it wasn't anything like this. I get a whole lot of presents—clothes and books and whatnot. Mrs. Al has had fun shopping for all of us, but I don't rightly think I deserve all this, knowing how, deep down, I want to leave. I miss Jeremy. I miss

Addie. I even miss Andrew, quiet as he is. I wonder what my mother is doing this very day—if she's thinking at all about me.

On Christmas night, we sit down in the parlor and crack nuts and drink cider. Mrs. Al takes great pride in her ginger cookies, so everyone has to eat at least one. She's happy and flushed with the effort of making a happy Christmas for everyone. Sometimes I think I should just stay here and let her mother me. She's so keen on it.

Dr. Beckwith has joined us for the evening, a rare exception to being holed up in his study. "You're not still thinking about going on west, I hope," he tells me.

I look down at my hands, feeling guilty and ungrateful. "Well, yes, sir, I am."

"Humph. Fool's errand, if you ask me."

Al and Mrs. Al jump right in. "Yes, Nell. You have a home here. You could go to school. Maybe get a teaching certificate. Meet a nice young man."

I nod, but it's plain I ain't about to give up my dream. "I know. I guess it would be a good life, but I'd still be wondering who I was all the time. Where I come from—who my people are."

"What are you going to do if your dream turns out not to be what you hope?" That's Dr. Beckwith again, always the rational thinker.

"I don't know." It always comes back to that.

Al and Mrs. Al spend the next five or ten minutes trying to get me to give up on my dream of finding Jane, but I don't budge. I know they're getting frustrated with me, but I can't deceive them. "I'm going, first chance I get," I tell them, "and that's that."

Then before I know it, it's January. One cold day I'm out doing the shopping and I stop in a stationery store to pick up some paper for the doctor. I see a rack of postcards—lots of them—showing scenes from some Wild West extravaganza, so I stop to look, and there it is, right in front of me, like God put it there: a picture postcard of my mother, Calamity Jane. She's dressed like a man—I knowed she would be. Couldn't be a scout for the army in skirts—and she's holding a rifle. Her jacket and pants are all fringy, and she's wearing a belt made of bullets. She's got a kind face, though. And underneath it says, *Calamity Jane, Gen. Crook's Scout.*

I'm so touched I stand there, my hands shaking, and let the tears roll. My mother. How sweet to look on that dear face. I am taken by the need to reach her—to rush to her side and hear her tell me how much she's missed me. I don't even know if she's in Deadwood or where to look for her, but I know there'll be someone there who can steer me right. I double my resolve to get back on the trail. Alone if I have to. At least I have Soot.

I buy the postcard and slip it into my coat pocket. All the way home, I keep my hand there, holding on to my mother. In my room, I put the picture in the drawer with my scented hankies and a lavender sachet to make everything smell good. I think my ma likes lavender.

From that day on, it's even harder to stick around. I haven't seen hide nor hair of Jeremy since before Christmas, and the urge is in me to just leave. Go. Take off upriver for Deadwood. But the river is frozen, travel is hard, and I know my gold piece won't take me far. Besides, the doctor ain't done with me yet. There's still these here wires around my teeth, and they ain't all the way straight and pulled together.

When Andrew comes back from Wisconsin, we sit together in the parlor of an evening. Mr. and Mrs. Al usually stay in their own little parlor, and Dr. Beckwith is always clacking on that typewriter of his, so that leaves me and Andrew to play draughts or read by the fire. Sometimes we make popcorn and he gets talkative. When that happens, I sit quiet and let him go on, mostly about Bear Valley and what a fine place it is.

"I can tell you're homesick, Andrew."

He nods. "I brought back some pictures a neighbor took of our farm, and my grandparents."

He shows me a picture of this old couple sitting out on the porch of a big farmhouse. It's extra fancy for a country house. Pillars and turrets and even a widow's walk. I don't know what you'd need one for in Wisconsin. Maybe to see if the farmers was working in the fields or taking a nap.

"It's a nice house," I say. I can't think of aught else.

"Here's one of my sister and her husband and their children, taken in a photographer's salon."

He seems right proud of his family, and it makes me wish I had someone to brag on, too. I don't know what possesses me, but I tell him I have a picture of my mother.

"Really? May I see it?"

I hesitate. "You might laugh," I say. "You might think I'm foolish."

"I'd never think that of you, Nell. You're one of the most sensible people I know."

I blush at the compliment. "Well, it's just that nobody but me thinks she's my mother, but I know it. I know it in my bones, and I'm going to find her just as soon as the weather breaks."

"Where do you have to go?"

"South Dakota. Deadwood. My mother's Calamity Jane. Ever hear of her?"

He nods. "Of course. Everybody's heard of her. She's your mother?"

"Uh-huh. I'm sure of it."

I lay out all my evidence for him. Her name's Jane, the locket, the stories about her having a daughter. It's starting to appear a little thin to me, but he don't seem to notice.

"I wish you well, and I envy you the adventure," he says, real kindly, like he thinks it's a sensible thing to do, go looking for her. That makes me feel so good I excuse myself to go upstairs. I open the drawer and take out the picture postcard. It looks real nice in the lamplight. I tuck it into my dress pocket and take it downstairs and show it to Andrew. He looks at it with interest and don't say nothing about her wearing men's clothes or toting a gun. For the first time since he showed up here, I kind of like him.

I pray for an early spring, and by the first of March I take to wandering around the wharfs on the Missouri side, watching the crews get the steamboats ready for the ice breakup. I ask which ones are bound upriver, and keep a special eye on them. It's nigh time for me to go. I can feel it in my bones.

I ponder how to break away from Dr. Beckwith and the Gilpins with the least pain. They've done so much for me, and it ain't that I ain't grateful. But every time I bring up leaving, they into lecturing me about the dangers and the folly of it. Dr. Beckwith even offers to pay my train fare all the way to Deadwood, just so I can see for myself how silly my thinking is. I can't let him do that, and I can't think of nothing but getting away.

April comes, and every day I get up earlier and earlier with the sun. I plan what I'll take with me and how I'll make my way upriver by working for my passage on the steamboats. It's still pretty cold, and I know being on the river this early with the spring thaw flooding most everything will be dangerous. I just can't seem to get shut of my need to go. I look for a kindly way to break out, but there don't seem to be none, so I write a long letter to Dr. Beckwith and the Gilpins, thanking them for all they've done for me. I slip out of the house at dawn one morning, get hold of Soot and head for the river. One of the boats I've been watching is firing up its boilers, so I step aboard and ask for the captain. He's a burly fellow, wiping his greasy hands on a rag.

"What is it?" he asks, giving me a good looking over. I don't look so poor no more, so he probably thinks I'm a paying passenger.

"I'm looking to work my passage up the Missouri," I tell him.

"How far?"

"As far as you go."

"I go to Kansas City. That far enough?"

"It's a good start," I say. "I can cook and clean and look out for myself."

"What about that dog?"

"Soot? Oh, he won't be no trouble. He's a river dog."

"Well, it's a long way to Kansas City, but if ya work out, I'll let ya stay. If not, I'll set ya off at the first town."

"Fair enough." I pick up my bag and Soot's rope and follow him along the promenade to a little cubby hole just back of the engine room. There's a bunk in there, and that's about all. It's noisy, being so close to the engines.

"You'll work in the scullery, for Mrs. Boykin. She's been with me for years. A good cook, but a hard lady, so don't cross her." The captain closes the door and is gone before I can even ask directions to the galley.

I stow my bag under the bunk, which ain't made up, and go in search of Mrs. Boykin. I tie Soot to the railing, and he finds himself a place to lie just out of the way of the gangplank. There's a world of activity going on. Last minute cargo loading—a bunch of stuff in crates with writing on them. Two big black men wrestle the crates from here to there and tie them down. The load is heavy and the boat rides low in the water.

Mrs. Boykin does prove to be a hard lady. She don't give much direction, and then yells at me for not doing things the way she wants them. She don't ever smile or laugh. Looks to me like she's had a hard life and wants to pass some of the meanness on so nobody gets slighted. I keep my distance and try to figure out how she wants things done, to stay out of trouble. It's about a week from St. Louis to Kansas City, so I figure I can last that long. That's before the engine boiler blows and scalds one of the black men near to death and lays us up at a place called Boonville for three days, fixing it. That puts the captain in a bad mood, and it don't do nothing for Mrs. Boykin's disposition, neither.

"Don't be thinking you're on vacation, sister," she tells me. "We still got a crew to feed, moving or not."

"Yes'm."

"You come on here with your fine clothes, lookin' like you ain't done a lick of work in your life. Well, you might look fancy now, but someday you'll look like this." She holds out her chapped, wrinkled hands, her knuckles standing out like dresser knobs.

"Yes'm. Looks like you've worked real hard." I try to get by her to reach the sack of potatoes in the back corner of the galley, but she swats at me with her hand as I pass.

"Don't you sass me, you gutter snipe."

I turn and look her in the eye. "Ma'am, I don't want no trouble,but I wasn't sassing you, and you got no call to hit me and call me gutter snipe."

"I'll decide what I've a call to do. I run this galley my way. Captain thinks he's doing me a favor, taking you on, but you're more bother'n you're worth."

"If you'd tell me just what it is you want done, I'd do it. I ain't no mind reader."

She lashes out with the back of her hand and catches me right in the mouth. The wires are still there on my teeth. I don't know how to get them off. So my mouth starts into bleeding right away.

Right then the captain walks by the galley door.

"Cap'n!" she yells. "This here little bitch was sassing me, so I learned her a lesson."

The captain takes one look at my bleeding mouth and nods. "Right enough, Mrs. Boykin. She's your charge." He goes on down the promenade.

I turn back toward the sack of potatoes, meaning to start peeling, but Mrs. Boykin steps in front of me. "See? Now I guess you know better'n to sass me!"

"I wasn't sassing you. I just said you had no call to hit me, and you still don't."

Her hand slaps me hard across the face, and this time the blood flies. I been smacked around before, but not like this. This woman seems to take joy in hurting me, so I stand to.

"Don't hit me again, Mrs. Boykin."

"Why you little trollop. I'll see you off this boat in a minute."

Boonville, Missouri looks like a no-account town, but I can't stay on board of this boat and put up with no more of this woman. I push past her, and she grabs my hair. I turn and jab her in the gut with my fist. It winds her, and she pulls back, gasping for breath. I take advantage of the chance and lay into her good, pouring out all my anger and frustration through my fists. All the ruckus brings the captain and crew running.

"All right, young lady. I took you on as a favor, and this is how you repay my kindness. Off with you! Told you I'd put you off if you didn't measure up."

I pull away from Mrs. Boykin and head for my bunk. I drag my bag out from under and go untie Soot from the rail. I step down the gangplank into Boonville without a single idea where to go or what to do. It's a cold, rainy April, and I don't have food or shelter for Soot and me. He licks my hand and whines, like to ask "What's next, Nell?"

All of a sudden being out on my own don't feel so good. I miss that big, warm, comfortable house in St. Louis. I miss Jeremy. Maybe they're right about me. Maybe this is just a dumb idea of a dumb girl. I run my tongue around the wires, tasting blood. I wish I was anyplace but here.

Chapter 19

In the twilight, Soot and I wander down the street that goes along the river in Boonville, Missouri. The water is high and brown, and the rain don't know when to quit. The whole world smells like sodden earth. I think of Granny's little cottage back in Ohio and long for someplace warm and dry. Soot walks along beside me, head down, bedraggled. The town don't last long, and I'm past the edge before I know it. Off to the right I see a old log barn, and I make for it. No house around, no tracks. At least maybe it'll be dry.

I find a pile of old, musty-smelling hay in one corner where there's still a roof, and I make a little nest for Soot and me. My mouth hurts and I'm hungry. Been living the good life so long I forgot about making sure to always have some provisions. Soot's wet and stinky, but I don't care. He's all I got, and we snuggle down in the hay and go to sleep.

Morning dawns cold—but dry and sunny. That lifts my spirits. I go outside and look around for a house, but there ain't nothing but open fields and the town a ways back. I don't want to have nothing to do with that steamboat, so I'm relieved to see it chugging slow upriver as I make my way back to the town. It's a river town, so they's always a steamboat or two in port, and I think to try to hire on another one. I'm standing on the wharf sizing them up when I hear someone call my name.

"Nell! Nell! Over here!"

There on the deck of an upriver steamer docked to take on wood is Andrew Morgan.

"Andrew! What are you doing here?"

"Looking for you! Dr. Beckwith sent me to find you and bring you back."

I look around for a quick escape, but he's already taking the gangplank in about two strides, and Soot has seen him and is pulling on the rope in joyful recognition.

"Andrew, I can't go back. Please don't tell them you found me."

He takes one look at my swollen face and tells me to open up. I do, like he's the boss and it's my job to obey. I feel real dumb, standing there on the wharf letting him look in my mouth like he's buying a horse.

"What happened? Who did this to you? If you think I'm going to let you get away, with things like this and worse happening to you, you can guess again."

"I'm okay. It was just this nasty woman on the boat. She's gone now."

He looks at me from under a shock of unruly brown hair. "Nell. Now, listen. You can't just walk out on Dr. Beckwith after all he's done. You need more work, and he's the only one who can take the wires off your teeth."

"You could, if you wanted to."

"Well, I *don't* want to. Besides, Dr. Beckwith would never forgive me if I found you and let you go again."

My stomach lets out a powerful growl. "You got any money? Me and Soot ain't had nothing to eat since yesterday noon."

"Yes. There must be a boarding house around here." He leads the way up a street away from the river and, sure enough, there's a house with a sign up: "Room and Board." Andrew steps up on the porch and holds the door open for me. It's still breakfast time, so the landlady just tells us to sit.

The table is long, and there's some empty spaces where others have already eat and gone to work. There's oatmeal and biscuits and coffee and bacon. The smells mix all together and make my eyes water. You can have a egg if you pay a extra penny. Andrew gives three extra pennies and gets two eggs and extra bacon. You can have as many biscuits as you want. I eat as much as I can hold, and then put away some biscuits in my pocket for Soot. We don't talk much while we eat, but I know Andrew will take up his cause as soon as we're done.

I try to head him off before he gets started. "I can't go back with you, you know. I'm out to find my mother, and I won't quit till I do. So you can just go back and tell Dr. Beckwith I'm beholden to him, but I can't quit now. I've come too far."

Andrew fixes a steely gaze on me. Gray eyes look like that. Like the steel of a railroad track. "I hope I don't have to force you, Nell," he says quietly.

"If you force me, I'll just run off again."

He sighs a deep sigh and reaches into his inside coat pocket. "I guess then I'll have to give *this* to you." It's a letter, addressed to me at Dr. Beckwith's. From Jeremy.

Dear Nell,

I am sorry I've been so elusive in the past months. I don't have a passable excuse, at least not in your eyes. I made some money gambling with Ethan Banks, but one night, just before Christmas, the people we were playing with accused us of cheating. There was a ruckus, and we both got arrested. I've been in the St. Louis jail since Christmas Day. I get out next Tuesday, and I expect you will be wanting to move on up the Missouri about then. I'm still up for the trek to Deadwood if you are. Please look for me around the wharf near your doctor's house. I'll be there.

Your Friend and Traveling Companion,
Jeremy Chatterfield, Esq.

I'm so excited to hear from Jeremy, I ain't even too mad that he was dumb enough to get himself put in jail for cheating at cards. I look at Andrew and see he's guessed what the letter's about.

"All right. I'll come back with you, but I'm not staying. As soon as I find Jeremy, we're gone again. I'm sorry, but that's the way it is."

Andrew looks kind of put down, but he nods and reaches into his coat pocket for another letter. This one's from Dr. Beckwith. He already knows what it says: how Dr. Beckwith respects my need to find my mother, in spite of he thinks it's folly, and wishes me well.

That I'm always welcome to come back there anytime I feel like it, and that they love me. There's a five-dollar bill tucked in between the sheets of paper. Andrew calls it mad money. Says it's to help me get back to St. Louis if things don't work out with Jeremy and me.

"You and the folks back there don't have much reason to like Jeremy, especially after he's been throwed in jail, but I know him. He ain't a bad sort—just don't have good sense when it comes to taking up with strange people. I think he's a little weak in the head sometimes."

Andrew looks away when I talk about Jeremy. He don't seem to like hearing about him at all. I guess the Gilpins and Dr. Beckwith have turned his head.

He stands up and pushes in his chair. "I'll settle up with the landlady. Meet you on the porch."

I go outside and feed Soot his breakfast biscuits. He's so grateful he wags his tail and licks my hand. When Andrew comes, I've tucked both letters in my bundle and wait to see what he plans to do. He ain't slow about telling me.

"There's a train for St. Louis at ten o'clock. Let's go buy our tickets."

Well, what do you know? Me. Nell Cannary. Riding on the cars just like real folks. I can't get over it. They let Soot on the train, and he lies down at my feet like he's done this a hundred times before.

After we're under way, Andrew turns to me. "I can take those wires off your teeth now, if you want."

He produces a tiny pair of pliers, familiar to me as instruments of torture. But he uses them to twist the wires off and drops them into his pocket handkerchief. Then he reaches into his pocket and produces two more whalebone disks, carved and shaped to fit me.

"Your mouth will heal pretty quick if you stay out of fights."

"I'll try."

Then Andrew does something real odd. He takes a mirror out of his vest pocket and hands it to me. At first I think I must have a smudge on my nose, but then it dawns on me he wants me to see how I look without the wires on my teeth. So I do. It's only a little mirror, and I have to move it around to get the view of my whole face, but

I'm different. I'm still Nell, but I'm different. I smile into the mirror and take note of my straight, even teeth. No need to pull my lip down anymore. It's a miracle.

Andrew is watching me, quiet like. "You have no idea of the change he's wrought."

"I know. It shames me to walk away after all he's done, but I sure hope to be back there someday to thank him proper."

I guess I act a little giddy after that, because Andrew seems even more serious than usual. He don't take no joy in my delight. He just sits there staring out the window studying the countryside as the train clickety clacks its way back to St. Louis. At the depot, he gives me a questioning glance.

"Coming back to say hello?" he asks.

I shake my head. "It'll just be harder to leave again if I do. Anyway, this here's Tuesday, ain't it?"

He nods.

"Give them my love and my thanks. Tell them I'll be back," I say.

"I'll walk you to the wharf. I want to make sure he's there."

We come around a corner and there he is, Jeremy, standing on the wharf beside a stack of crates. All around him folks are busy loading freight onto the boats. I want to run to him, but I don't, because of Andrew. We walk up to Jeremy slow and dignified, like I'm not jumping out of my skin with delight.

Jeremy sees us coming, but he don't make no move. He just watches me and Andrew like he's not sure what to expect. Then I remember that day in the tearoom. He probably thinks Andrew's my beau.

"Hello, Jeremy."

He nods. "Nell. I guess you got my letter."

"Yes. You remember Andrew Morgan."

He nods again, standing back like he ain't sure whether to stay or go. He looks awful. He's lost weight and his clothes are dirty and torn. His shoes are about wore out, and he needs a shave. "Looks like jail don't agree with you," I tell him.

"You looking to go upriver still?" he asks.

"You still hanging around with that Ethan Banks?"

He looks around, real uncomfortable-like. "No. He's still in jail. He got a heavier sentence than I did."

"You don't say," I counter. "Wonder how that happened."

"He got two years for assault. He beat up a man pretty badly. My crime was just cheating at cards."

I stand there looking at him for a long time. He looks thin and tired. Threadbare. I guess the association with Ethan Banks was costly. It's an awkward moment, standing on the wharf. Jeremy still don't seem to know what to make of me and Andrew.

Andrew comes to his rescue. He nods and bows slightly, backing away as he watches me turn to Jeremy. Those steely gray eyes never leave my face until he's backed into a piling and turned to catch his balance.

"Don't forget what I told you to tell the folks. I'll be back. I promise," I call after him.

We watch Andrew make his way up the street toward the now familiar white house on the corner. I feel a tug at my heart, but I know I have to go. I turn to Jeremy.

"You're a sight for sore eyes. I was going, anyway, but it sure helps to have someone to travel with."

He smiles that beautiful smile, and my heart flutters at the sight of it. I wonder how I look to him. He don't say nothing, so I can't tell. He steers me up the gangplank of a steamer headed upriver. "I took the liberty of signing on as a deck hand. We might have to pay your passage as far as Kansas City. I don't know."

The boat is old and about wore out. The steamboat business is sinking fast with the railroads hauling most of the freight and about all of the passengers, but some folks just can't get it in their heads that the world is changing, so they stick to steam boating long after it stops making sense.

We go up to the captain, a young-looking man, kind of handsome in a rough sort of way.

"Captain Marsh, this is my sister I told you about. She's a good worker. I wonder if there's any need for kitchen help."

I don't like the way the captain looks at me. Like he's thinking dirty thoughts. I want to pull Jeremy aside and wait for another boat, but the captain speaks up real nice. "Sure, son. Your sister's welcome to work her way along, too."

He don't say nothing about what kind of work, and I feel real uncomfortable about that. I don't want no more face slappers.

"Stevens! Show these two where to stow their goods." He turns away, and we're led down the promenade by a smallish man wearing a sweater and a seaman's cap to a tiny bunkroom with four beds built into the walls on either side of the door.

Stevens gives me the eye as he points out a top bunk to Jeremy. Reminds me of the tormenters. I look to Jeremy, but he's already been called out by the captain to heave to.

"You come with me," Stevens directs.

I follow him to an inside passage. He opens a door to a room no bigger than a privy and smiles a ugly smile at me. "This here will be *yer* quarters."

There's a tiny bunk and a wooden chair. No window. A kerosene lamp hung on the bare, rough wood wall. It smells dirty, like they stored wood in it or something.

"What about my work? Who do I work for?"

That ugly smile again. Crooked, yellow teeth. "You work fer me, honey babe. You work fer me."

"Doing what?" I don't know whether I'm more scared or mad, which. I move to get past him out into the passage, but he blocks the door.

"Doing anything I tell you, that's what."

Turns out this boat still carries a few passengers, and Stevens is in charge of them. "Steward" is what he calls himself, and his duties—or mine, as it turns out—is to clean the cabins, make the beds, carry their meals to them, and wash their clothes if they ask you to, which one old lady does—every day, and empty their slops into the river. Stevens is good for telling me what to do and watching me do it. I don't much care for the watching part, but it appears watching is what he does best.

I don't see much of Jeremy, except at table. Then he sits with the crew and we're both busy eating, so we don't have time to talk much. He looks skinny and wore out. Hard work don't seem to agree with him. One evening, after supper, we stand at the rail and talk for a few minutes.

I look out over the black water swirling along beside the boat. "Best thing to say for this here boat is it keeps going."

Jeremy snorts at that. "Barely. I think everything that can break has either broken or is getting ready to. I've been so busy fixing, I haven't had time to do anything else but sleep."

I see Stevens hanging around the promenade, watching us. "That one makes my skin crawl," I tell Jeremy.

"Yeah, I know. Well, it's only a few more days to Kansas City. Then this boat will pass into history."

"I hope I never see *that* one again."

Then from the shadows—"Girl! You need to make your evening rounds. Get to it!"

I move away from Jeremy and go forward to turn down the beds and light the lamps. Every time I look up, Stevens is standing in the doorway, watching me. I try to ignore him, but it ain't easy. I got this cold feeling in my gut, like the way I felt around Valoreous Cates. Wish Jeremy's bunk was closer to mine.

Chapter 20

I get done with my rounds quick and head for my bunk. It's extra dark, and I whistle for Soot as I make my way along the promenade. He's free to roam the boat as long as he don't bother no one. He comes up and licks my hand in greeting. I keep him in my bunk with me at night. I hate being scared, but just knowing Stevens is on board gives me reason. Kind of like the tormenters all over again.

When I get there the door to my bunk is open a crack, and I search my memory for whether I closed it or not. Soot don't seem bothered by it, so I go inside and Soot flops down in the corner, like usual. I undress and hang my clothes from a wooden peg on the wall across from the bunk. I can lie in bed and almost reach the other wall. What with the chair and Soot, the cabin is about full up.

I lie real still, listening to Soot snore. Except for that and the rumbling of the engines, all is quiet. I'm starting to drift off when a scratching on my door sends me bolt upright. I think it might be Jeremy, so I get up, but Soot's low growl, gives me to know it ain't Jeremy. I stop and listen. The scratching comes again, and this time Soot barks, low in his throat, kind of quiet. Then there's a knock.

"Who's there?" I ask. No answer.

I reach for Soot, but he ain't got no rope or collar, so he's hard to hang onto. He into barking real loud. Comes another knock. This one louder. I want to light the lamp, but it's too dark to find a match.

"Who is it?" My voice quavers. I hate that.

"Me. Stevens. Open up."

"What d'you want?"

"Open the damn door! Now!" He talks real tough, but low, so nobody hears him over Soot's barking and the rumbling engines.

I'm afraid to open the door and afraid not to. My hands are shaking and cold as ice, and I look around for something to use as a weapon. The room is bare, and so dark I can't find my own face, let alone a weapon.

"What do you want with me?" I ask, struggling to control my shaking voice.

Suddenly he rams his shoulder into the door, and it breaks open like there ain't no latch. He lunges at me, smelling like a brewery. Grabs my arm and twists it behind my back. I guess I scream. I'm so scared I take leave of my senses. Everything goes black for a second.

"Come on, girl. You know you want it," he growls, leaning me against the wall and trying to kiss me. His breath is so rank it almost makes we want to spew. I jerk away and grab for the bedstead. Soot tears into him, growling and snarling, and sinks his teeth into Stevens' leg. We put up a terrible noise—enough to wake the dead, and I hope that includes Jeremy.

It does. Jeremy and the captain and the rest of the crew and even some of the passengers. The captain tears in and pins Stevens to the wall outside my bunk, and I pull myself free. I see Jeremy over the captain's shoulder and run to him. He pulls me close and holds my head while I tremble, stroking my hair and whispering soothing words.

"It's all right, Nell. I'm here now. Don't worry. I won't let him hurt you again."

"Thank God for Soot." I'm still shaking, but I'm powerful conscious of Jeremy's words and his caress.

The captain hauls Stevens off to another part of the boat and the rest slowly return to their bunks. Jeremy comes back with me and sits down on the chair. We leave the door open and talk for a while.

"What'd I do, Jeremy? How's come he picked on me?"

"No telling. You're the only young female on the boat for one thing. And you're not unattractive, for another."

I ponder that for a while. Nobody's never told me I was anything but ugly. Dr. Beckwith seems to have wrought a miracle. Still, I ain't comfortable with it. So used to being ugly I can't really believe otherwise.

Jeremy rises and reaches for my hand. "You all right now?" he asks.

"Guess I will be," I tell him, and he goes off to his bunk and leaves me to ponder the meaning of "not unattractive."

Morning ain't no relief from my fears, for as soon as I go in to breakfast I see Stevens sitting there with the rest of the crew, like he's respectable or something. I thought the captain would lock him up or put him off, but no. Here he is, big as life and twice as mean, laughing and talking like a innocent man. I see Jeremy sitting at the crew's table, but he keeps his head down, don't bother with me.

I slide into my place and have my face in my oatmeal when the captain stops at my table and says loud enough for everybody to hear, "You want to keep to yourself and not be flauntin' your female charms around and tempting my crew. You hear that? Stevens told me how you been acting."

I sit staring into my oatmeal, my face burning. How far is it to Kansas City? I keep my eyes down as the crew files out, but I can't resist a glance at Jeremy. He passes by me, head down, but lets his hand touch my shoulder. I look up and see his face all red and puffy, his two eyes blacked.

Through the whole morning I go about my work quick as I can and avoid Stevens at every turn. At lunch I keep to myself, and Jeremy don't show up while I'm there. Stevens does. He sits down the bench on the other side of the table, leering at me, laughing too loud and clapping the other crew members on the back like they was his best mates. The boat steams slow up the Big Muddy, like it's almost standing still. I swear I seen that same tree a hour ago. I don't get a chance to talk to Jeremy, but I can guess what happened to him. I tie a rope around Soot's neck and keep him by me.

In the afternoon, Stevens and I cross paths a couple of times, and I see him eyeing Soot like he'd like to throw him overboard.

"You best keep that dog in tow. I get a chance at him, and he's a drowned dog," he warns.

"You better keep your distance from me," I tell him. "I'm pretty mean when I'm riled."

He leers at me and grins. "I'll just bet on that." He smiles that yellow-toothed smile. "Maybe I'll just find that out for myself."

I shiver like somebody just stepped on my grave. I ain't never had the creeps like he gives me, not even from the tormenters or Valoreous Cates or Ethan Banks. None of them. I ask one of the lady passengers how much longer till Kansas City.

"Tomorrow, dear. We should arrive about noon."

One more night. I wait until after the crew has had their supper before I go in and sit down at the table alone. I don't know where Jeremy is. My guess is he's trying as hard as I am to avoid Stevens. I don't hardly have no appetite. All I want is to get off this boat as fast as ever I can. I grab up Soot's rope as I leave the galley and go right to my bunk. Soot don't growl or nothing when we get there, so I guess there ain't nobody inside. I'm wrong. I get in and close the door, and before I can light the lamp, I hear Jeremy's voice.

"Nell, it's me. I'm hiding under the bunk. I'm going to stay here all night in case Stevens takes a notion to come back."

I get down on my knees and peer under. It's so dark, I can't hardly see him.

"How'd you get in here?"

"He broke the latch last night. All the more reason why I thought I should stop over."

"What'd he do to you?" I ask.

"Beat me senseless. That's all."

"Why didn't nobody try to stop him?"

"They're all afraid of him, I guess."

"Think he'll come looking for more trouble tonight?"

"I'll be surprised if he doesn't, but I'm ready for him." He shoves a couple of stout barrel staves out from under the bunk. "Between the two of us, we can take care of him."

I feel a deep sense of relief. "Thanks, Jeremy."

I undress in the dark, not talking for fear someone will hear us. Soot worries around in a circle a bunch of times, then lies down with a flump. I feel almost safe with him and Jeremy to protect me. I lie down on the bunk and drift off to sleep.

The knock comes hours later. It ain't even a knock, really. Just a bump against the door. Soot into barking, real loud, and I reach down for my barrel stave. When I touch it, I feel Jeremy's hand around my wrist. I get up and move toward the door. It's quiet out there for a long time, but Soot knows something's up. He don't leave off sniffing around the door. I figure Stevens'll have some way of dealing with him this time, so I'll have to move fast.

Waiting in the dark, I sense Jeremy skittering out from under the bunk. It's right crowded in here, with two of us, our barrel staves and Soot. The crash is sudden and loud. The door breaks apart, followed by a chair, followed by Stevens. He stumbles over the chair and straightens up in the doorway, so drunk he can hardly stand up. My barrel stave comes down on his head before he has a chance to take a step. He reaches for the broken chair, swearing real loud and snarling. Jeremy comes at him from the other side, and after another whack from his stave, Stevens' legs fold under him and he sinks to the floor.

Jeremy grabs my arm. "Come on, Nell. We might have killed him."

I grab my bundle and Soot's rope and we run to the rail. The river's dark and treacherous, but we ain't got no choice. We have to get off this boat. I tie my bundle to Soot's rope and jump over the side before I give myself a chance to think about it. The river is freezing cold, and the current is swift. I feel it dragging me downstream faster than I ever imagined. I see Jeremy jump and hope Soot follows, but by now I'm fighting to keep my head above water.

I ain't never learned to swim, but I ain't scared of water, neither. I struggle, weighted down by my clothes. Panic sets in and for a few seconds I give myself over to it. I go under once, feeling like I can't move anymore in the freezing water. Then something inside tells me to think. Let the water take me where it will. I give up all hope of ever seeing Jeremy or Soot again and go limp on my back.

Chapter 21

In a few minutes, I feel the swift current ease up and I turn over and look around. The sky's starting to get light, and I can just barely make out the dim outline of some kind of land, so I make for it for all I'm worth. My wet clothes drag me down, and it's all I can do to keep kicking, tangled up in my skirts like I am. The Big Muddy is a treacherous river, full of sand bars and changing currents, but this time it's on my side. My feet find a sand bar and I wade in to land, shivering and scared but alive. Glory, Hallelujah!

I can't tell if this is a island or real land. I just know it's the north side of the river. I stumble up the bank and huddle down beside a tree. The sun's coming up, but not soon enough for me. I think to freeze to death before it gets tolerable warm. As the light climbs, I make out a road not far away, but I stay put. The sun'll dry me out, and I'll feel warmer huddled up here until it gets up high. I hunker down, shivering so bad my teeth rattle, but at least I'm alive. I calculate it must be getting on to about seven o'clock when I hear a wagon rumbling down the road. I get myself up and stumble over to hail it. The driver is a colored man, and he has a boy with him—about ten years old.

"Where you come from, ma'am? Land 'o Goshen. You cold." He reaches down to give me a hand up, and I take a place in the wagon box among bags of seeds.

"I fell off a river boat. I ain't got nothing but the clothes on my back." I tell them.

"I Zachariah, and this my boy, Luke. We going to plant corn today. Ain't going far, but you can ride if you like. Luke, give her some 'a that there cornbread."

The boy reaches into a cloth sack and brings out a sizable chunk of cornbread, which he hands me with a solemn look. Luke's just a slip of a boy, coffee colored, big eyed, and already serious about the world.

"My name's Nell. I'm on my way to South Dakota to find my mother, Calamity Jane," I tell them as I gnaw on the lump of nourishment.

"Calamity Jane your mother? Well, I declare. We's got us a famous person riding with us, Luke. I heerd of Calamity Jane once or twice. You?" I like Zachariah right off. His voice is deep and soothing, like you don't have to be afraid with him around.

Luke nods a solemn nod and turns back to looking at the road. I'm shivering mightily, but there's nothing to cover up with. I sit with my knees drawn up, hugging them, cold and forlorn, like I ain't got no future. Suddenly Zachariah pulls back on the reins, and his mule comes to a stop.

"What you make of that, Luke?" He points to the left, near the river, where a dog struggles and whines, tangled up in the underbrush. Soot!

"That's my dog! Soot! Oh, thank you, sir, for finding him!" I jump out of the wagon and run to Soot's side. His rope and my bundle are wrapped around a bush and a log, but he's right glad to see me. I untie the rope, and he into jumping for joy. Zachariah and Luke get a good laugh out of his capers, and I do my best to assure him that I'm as happy as he is. My bundle, soaked and muddy, is still securely tied to the other end of the rope. Lucky me.

"How your dog fall off the boat same time as you?" Zachariah asks when I've pulled Soot up into the back of the wagon with me.

"I guess he jumped when he saw me fall."

"Tie that bundle to him and jump, huh?"

I look at him under lowered brows, not sure what to say. Luke saves me the trouble of making up another lie. "Sure, Papa. She prob'ly tie that bundle to the dog and then to a post to keep him from falling off the boat, but he pull free when he see her fall in. Dogs is like that."

"Yeah. That's just what happened," I say. I pull Soot to me and snuggle up to him. We're both wet, but snuggling warms us some.

The wagon lurches as we start off again, but it ain't long before we get to a tiny town, not more than a handful of houses. Zachariah pulls up the mule in front of a white clapboard house and goes inside.

"That Mr. Wallace house. We share croppers. He own the land, tell my papa what to plant and where." Luke is warming up to me, feeling free to talk.

"What's the name of this place?"

"This here Missouri City." He says it like it's an important place or something.

"City? It don't look like no city." Hardly looks like a town, or even a village. "That's a fanciful name."

"Mr. Wallace a fanciful man. That prob'ly why he live here. Want to be big."

I heard about people like that before. Not much account anywhere but at home. Like to think they're big, but put them up against real big, and they wilt. We wait around for about a quarter hour. "How far's Kansas City?" I ask Luke.

"'Bout fifteen mile. Give or take. What you wanta go there for?"

"I'm just following the river. Trying to work my way on the boats, but that ain't been going so good. I got no money, so that's about the only way I can go."

Luke nods his solemn nod, like a old man, wise beyond his years. "That a good dog. You might could sell him for a little in Kansas City."

"No. Soot's my best friend," I say, with a sad thought for Jeremy. Ain't much hope of ever seeing *him* again.

Zachariah comes out of the house, walking bent over, and stops to talk things over with his mule. I guess he's promising a comfortable stall and a measure of corn in return for the day's work. Then he pulls himself up into the wagon and we go lumbering off down the road.

He turns to talk to me. "We only go another half mile, then we turn off to the fields. Sorry, miss."

"It's okay. You found my dog. That's the best part. And thanks for the ride."

"You is surely welcome. I hopes you find your ma, and hopes she's good and kind as you picture her to be."

They let me off by a dirt track that leads to their field. I stand aside, holding Soot's rope and my wet bundle, and wave as they head for their labors. The dew is about dried off the grass, and the sun is starting to feel warm on my back. I set off down the dusty road that I expect will lead me in time to Kansas City. Here I am again without no plan.

Around noon I stop in a little riverbank grove and untie my bundle, which smells mightily like the river. I got two more dresses, some under things, a shawl and another pair of shoes. It's all wet and muddy, but my main thing is that gold piece Granny gave me. I find it tied up in a handkerchief in the pocket of my yellow gingham dress, same with my locket, right where I put it. The five dollars from Dr. Beckwith is in the toe of one shoe, and the letter from Jeremy is tied up with my under things. Soggy, but still readable. I spread the dresses and stuff out to dry. The dress I have on is about dry already, except for the seams. I try to comb out my hair, but it's matted pretty bad. I work at it for about a hour before it's untangled. Soot sleeps nearby. I sure am grateful to have him back. Seems like if we have to, we can go it alone.

"Mighty pretty hair."

I jump at the sound. "Huh?"

"I said mighty pretty hair. Seen you combing it. Pretty color. Almost red, but not quite so noisy. Quieter than red."

The speaker is a real tall feller, and I wonder why Soot never barked at him. I look over, and there he is, snoozing like he ain't the world's greatest watch dog.

"Thank you for the compliment," I say, watching the guy careful to decide if he's up to no good or not.

He's kind of funny looking—his clothes, I mean. Pants the color of mustard with red and black running through—plaid I guess. His shoes are real big, and the same mustard color. I ain't never seen mustard color shoes before. He's wearing a yaller shirt and a big bright red bow tie, and his hair is as red as fire, and standing straight up.

"You from a circus?" I ask, more to explain his outfit than to be nosy.

He grins and nods. "How'd you know?" he asks.

"Your clothes."

"Oh. I wear them every day, so I forget they're odd to some."

"Where's your circus?"

He shrugs over his shoulder. "Camped in the woods over there. Everybody's napping. I like to get out and walk when I can."

He seems like a nice sort, so I explain about falling off the boat and drying my clothes.

"Must be the day for it."

"Day for what?"

"Falling off boats. We picked up a feller this morning who said he fell off a boat, too."

Jeremy!

I'm up and running toward the circus camp without even getting the feller's name. As I approach the circle of wagons, I'm amazed at the beautiful colors and fancy designs on them. There's three, painted up like St. Louis ladies of the evening, only respectable, all red, green, and gold. The camp is quiet, and I don't yell for fear of poking a beehive, so I go around looking for Jeremy. There's two wagons that are cages. In one is a big brown bear sound asleep. In the other, a big yellow strip-ed cat, pacing. I ain't never seen the like of that before. Don't even know what to call it. I round one of those cage wagons and come up on a huge, gray beast with a tail on each end— one big and the other little. Then as I stand there, the big tail grabs up a bunch of hay and shoves it into its mouth. I guess that's the front end.

I'm about to drop my teeth when I hear Jeremy's voice. "Nell!"

There he sits, on a log, with his legs stretched out in front of him, looking like the biggest toad in the puddle. I half expect him to let out a croak, he's that comfortable. There's a couple of women sitting on another log, hanging on every word that comes out of his mouth, and one or two boys on the edge of the group, like they'd rather hang around Jeremy than work.

"Jeremy! I thought you was dead!"

"Not at all, my dear. Come meet my new friends." That's it with Jeremy. One minute he never saw you before in his life, and the next minute you're best friends. I don't know how he does it.

He stands and sweeps his arm around the group. "Meet Stella, the trapeze artist, Jezebel, the tattooed lady, and Esmerelda, the mistress of the Arabian horse. These young men are Jiggs and Tex. They're roustabouts. Folks, this is my sister, Nell. We both fell off the same boat last night."

They all smile and greet me like a long lost friend. I can see how Jeremy would thrive on all that attention. I guess they don't care to question how my brother Jeremy got his face all smashed up, or why he talks real fancy, and I talk like a ignernt Pennsylvania girl, or how we both come to fall off of the same boat on the same night. Fine with me. I take a seat on the log near Jeremy just as the tall young man comes up, with Soot trailing after.

"I didn't get your name," he says to me, sitting down on the log.

Soot sniffs up Jeremy real good to see where he's been and who he's been with, tail wagging so hard his whole rear end swings.

"I'm Nell. Sorry to run off like that. I was in a spin over Jeremy."

"Yes, I figured." He sits down beside me and offers his hand. "I'm Regis Pennypacker."

"Hello. What's your job with the circus?"

"Thin man. They put me up beside Annabel Lee—she's the fat lady."

He is outrageous skinny, I'll say that. More'n six feet tall and must weigh less than a hundred weight. His wrists are about as skinny as mine, and every bone he's got shows through his skin. He's got a Adam's apple that looks like he swallowed a peach pit, and his shock of red hair stands straight up and makes him look like a big, long-burning match.

Jeremy ain't been here more'n three hours, and he's already everybody's pet, talking to the whole crew like they knowed each other for years and he's the circus expert. Even the owner seems taken with him. They sit in his tent most of the afternoon, talking about how Jeremy can fit in with the troupe.

I go back and pick my dry clothes off the bushes and tie them up again. Soot seems to like the circus people, but he ain't at all sure about that big cat. I get the feeling Soot'd make a tasty morsel for lunch, so I keep a good eye on his comings and goings. The elephant fascinates him. He don't know which end to bark at, and the trainer tells me to keep him away so he don't upset Dora. That sounds like a funny name for a elephant, but the trainer says almost all circus elephants are named Jumbo, so Dora is special.

I bide my time waiting to get alone with Jeremy. The chance don't come until after supper, when the troupe is bedding down. They're bound for Kansas City tomorrow, with a show tomorrow night, so everyone wants to get to bed early.

They put me in a tent with Jezebel and Esmerelda, and I watch Jezebel touch up her henna tattoos, which are all flowery and full of curlicues, and all over her. She tells me they last a few weeks, and she can redo them between towns. Her real name's Catherine Borden and she was raised on a farm in Wisconsin, near a town called Baraboo. Says it's a real circus town, and she grew up planning to run off and join a circus since she was six. I ask her if Baraboo is anywhere near a place called Bear Valley, but she don't know of it.

It's after dark when Jeremy finally comes around. He stands in front of our tent and calls my name. I go out to meet him, and we walk around the camp in the dark, talking.

"Did you get hurt when we jumped?" I ask.

"No. I was pulled under for a second, but I'm a strong swimmer. You?"

I tell him about my morning, then ask my question. "You're not thinking of traveling with this circus, are you?"

"Why not? They need a barker and a sleight of hand man, and I can do both. They're going all the way to Omaha, so we might as well sign on. We'll make some money and have our stomachs fed."

"What about me? What can I do? They won't want me just hanging around."

"I already talked to the owner, Mr. Jordan. He says they'll find something for you to do. Maybe help Huddles."

"Huddles? Who's that?"

"I don't know, but I guess he's got an important job. Jordan says he needs as much help as he can get."

"I hope it don't have nothing to do with that there strip-ed cat. It scares me, and Soot don't have no time for it neither."

Jeremy flashes his handsome smile. "No, Nell. I don't think they'll put you to taming the tiger just yet."

I sit and pout a bit. I ain't so excited about traveling with the circus as Jeremy is. "Seems like this'll be a mighty slow way to get to Omaha, wherever that is, stopping in every other town for a show or two."

"It'll do until something better comes along. I don't care much for river boats anymore."

"Me, neither."

We sit on the same log I found him on this afternoon. The camp is quiet. The night is starry, and I feel good to be alive, considering where I was when I woke up this morning. Suddenly a loud female shriek rips the air.

"HUDDLES! I told you I hate soup! Get me something decent to eat and be quick about it."

Chapter 22

The screaming is followed by the clunk of a pan against a rock and more screaming.

"Can't you get anything right? I swear, I've told you a thousand times, you stupid man, I hate soup. I need something more substantial for my bedtime snack."

Then there comes some quiet mumbling and a man steps out of one of the wagons down the line and picks up the pan. He wanders off in the direction of the cook wagon and comes back a few minutes later with another pan, this one wrapped in a towel, steaming hot.

I turn to Jeremy. "Is that Huddles?"

"Yes, I think so."

"I'm gonna work for him?"

Jeremy raises an eyebrow and gives me a scowl. "It's not a marriage, Nell. Omaha can't be more than two weeks travel from here, shows and all."

I'm used to Jeremy being off in his judgment some, but this here is more than some. Here we are almost into May, and he wants to travel at a snail's pace with this silly circus, when we could get to South Dakota in the time he's thinking to get to Omaha.

"Then you'll be wanting to stay for one more town or one more show. I know you, Jeremy Chatterfield. You turn me by inches."

Just then, here comes this Huddles man, carrying a bucket of slops with both hands, trying not to spill it before he gets to the riverbank. The smell gets into my nostrils, makes my eyes water. I look over at Jeremy, but he makes like he don't smell nothing.

Huddles dumps the pot and rinses it in the river. He turns and walks toward us with little steps, like he's afraid he's gonna fall, then stops to pass the time of evening. The bucket don't stink no more, but I don't want to look at it neither.

"You must be my new assistant," he says, kindly. Everything about him seems timid. He ain't very big, and he's kind of pale, and he don't look you in the eye when he talks to you. "I'm glad to have you. Lord knows, I need help."

"Yes, sir. I guess I am. I don't know how much help I'll be—not knowing what your needs are. And we won't be staying beyond Omaha." I say it firm, with an eye to Jeremy.

"That's all right," Mr. Huddles replies. "I'm grateful for any relief." He picks up his bucket and makes his way off into the night.

The next morning I get answers about Mr. Huddles. He wanders into the cook tent, looks around like he don't know nobody, and sits down by me, looking weak and worn out. I guess a night's sleep didn't help.

"Morning, Mr. Huddles," I say between spoonfuls of oatmeal sweetened with honey. "How are you today?" I learned the ways of polite conversation in St. Louis.

He smiles a feeble smile and nods. "Right enough, I expect. Fair to middling, anyway." He takes a bite of applesauce and turns his head, but not his body, toward me. "You ready for your training?"

"Training? Yes, sir. I reckon I am. Hope so, anyway."

He rises, picks up a tray with a cloth over it and leads the way out of the cook tent down the line of wagons all the way to the far end. There, pulled a little aside from the others sits a wagon with red, blue and yellow wheels, painted up real fancy, and canvas sides that look like they roll up and down. The canvas sides are covered with pictures and writing about "Beautiful Annabel Lee—the Fat Lady." They show this big lady maybe five feet tall and six feet wide, sitting on a velvet couch with a box of bonbons on a table beside her. She looks real comfortable on that there velvet couch, and smiling, but the noise coming out of that wagon would scare a badger.

"Huddles, you lout! Get in here! How long do I have to wait for my breakfast?"

With a look of apology, Huddles scrambles up the three narrow wooden steps into the wagon with the tray. I stay outside, looking at the canvas pictures and wondering if I'll have to get yelled at like Huddles.

It turns out, yes. My duties are to do anything Miss Annabel Lee tells me to, and to do it faster than fast and perfect the first time, 'cause I'm lucky to be in her presence for free.

The first time I step inside the wagon, she takes one look at me and yells. "Come here, girl. Hand me that brush. My hair needs brushing." She takes up the brush and starts in, but I can tell she ain't got much gumption about her. She lies back in what looks like a swoon and lets the brush fall. Then she opens one eye and looks at me. "Pick that up," she commands.

I pick it up and try to help her to her feet, but she yanks her hand away. "Get away from me, you simple soul! Lord above, what do I have to do to get good help?"

I go outside and Mr. Huddles shows me the way of things, taking care of Miss Annabel.

"My wife sits or lies down all the time. She can't get up, and she can't walk."

"How's she get in and out of the wagon?"

"She doesn't. The wagon was built when she wasn't so heavy and could still get around," he says with a sigh. "The wagon is our apartment. The sides roll up so the paying customers can see her."

He walks around to the back end of the wagon and opens it up. He shows me how to set and remove the slop jar which sets under a hole in her couch.

"You can get in from here and give her a bath or change her dress, or attend to her needs, but she never gets out."

"Never?"

He shakes his head sadly. "No. Not anymore. She stays there all the time. Moving her would take two or three men and some kind of cart."

"All day, every day?"

He nods, and I shake my head. Who'd believe that if you told them? Too fat to move. I declare.

"Huddles!" Her loud voice pierces the air. "Get in here right now, and bring that silly girl with you. It's time for my bath."

Miss Annabel Lee fancies herself a star and demands everybody treat her like one. She eats all the time, and it takes a great deal of time and attention to keep her clean and happy. Poor Mr. Huddles sweats and worries his way through every day, trying desperately to satisfy her every whim. Reminds me of a dog chasing its tail. Pretty soon I'm wondering how long I can put up with her meanness, but I resolve to try to at least get to Omaha.

In Kansas City, Miss Annabel calls me in and hands me a piece of silk cloth. I ain't never touched anything so fine before.

"Take this to Mrs. Anderson on Plum Street. Tell her I need something just like it made into a kimono that opens down the back. Huddles! Give the girl my measurements."

I get the measurements, which is ample, and head out. When I get to her shop on Plum Street, Mrs. Anderson ain't overly glad to see me. See she's worked for Miss Annabel Lee before, and her memories ain't pleasant.

"I'm not sure I can get enough of this silk to make anything for her," she sighs. "And get ready to run back and forth a thousand times trying to please her. She's never satisfied."

After about a week of wrangling with Mrs. Anderson, the new kimono is ready. Miss Annabel sweats a lot, and I'm always sifting talcum powder into her creases. It helps the cloth slide better. I help her into the kimono for the show, but not without a serious struggle, pushing her rolls of fat this way and that and adjusting it to make her comfortable while she wiggles and squeals that I'm pinching her. See, there ain't no back in the kimono. It just slips over the front of her. Makes it easier to get in and out of. All her dresses is like that.

Here's the way the routine works. Mr. Huddles gets her breakfast every morning. My first job, after she eats, is to give her a bath, so I heat water as soon as I'm done eating. Not too hot and not too cold, or I get yelled at. Then we open the back of the wagon. Mr. Huddles has rigged a curtain to hang out over so I can get in there and wash her down. While I'm washing her, she eats bonbons. I like it best when she's eating, because then she's not yelling at me to do this, do that, don't do this, don't do that. I get a lot of sympathetic looks from the other circus people. None of them will go near her.

Jeremy is curious about Miss Annabel, and he stops by almost every afternoon during her "rest time" to see me and get the latest report on her antics.

"What do you do all day, Nell? I never see you out and about," he asks me as we sit on a log under an oak tree.

"After her bath, I powder her down and help her into her dress and her little red slippers, which she'll never wear out,'cause she can't even walk. Then I open the curtain so the people can file past the front of the wagon and gawk at her."

"That doesn't sound so bad."

I glare at him. "I'd just like to see *you* give her a bath. Just once. Then you'd decide if it was so bad or not."

He grins and jukes like he's afraid I'll hit him.

"She sits on a velvet bench all day, eating and smiling and nodding to the people like as if she was nice or something. People pay good money for the treat and make lots of comments, which Miss Annabel makes like she can't hear because of the window, and that's a good thing."

Jeremy listens to my rant with half a smile. He still thinks it's funny, but I don't. And neither does Mr. Huddles, even if he don't say nothing. *Nobody* could put up with her meanness for long.

"Her side show is open even when there's no circus performance, so she makes a lot of money for Mr. Jordan," Jeremy tells me, like I care about how much money she makes. "So what's the rest of your day like?"

"I draw the curtains for lunch and a nap, and then the show starts all over again at two o'clock and goes until four thirty. Then I give her a rubdown with oil and sift more talcum powder on her, help her out of her dress and into her night robe, which is also real silk."

Jeremy chuckles over the image of me oiling Miss Annabel. I shoot him another glare, but then Mr. Huddles shows up carrying a tray covered with a napkin.

"Her tea," he explains with a slight bow to Jeremy.

We're sitting near the edge of the camp. All around there's a lot of stuff going on. Mr. Zanzir, the animal trainer, is working with that there big brown bear. I look around for Soot and make sure he's tied up when that one is out. It looks all nice and cuddly, like it wouldn't hurt a fly, but Soot ain't buying that. He into barking every time he sees that bear, and I don't even want to know what he thinks of that there strip-ed cat.

Regis Pennypacker wanders by and stops to visit with me and Jeremy. He's Miss Annabel's opposite in every way. When her wagon is open, he stands by her window and welcomes the paying customers. He smiles and talks to folks, tells them about Miss Annabel. By himself, he ain't much of a attraction, but up against Miss Annabel, he brings a balance. He's so nice and real, you can't help wondering what kind of person the two of them would make, put together. Kind Regis in his long skinny stove pipe pants and his red hair, and nasty old Annabel in her yards and yards of fine silk cloth.

Jeremy moves over on the log so Regis can set down. "What's she do for the rest of the day, then? Nothing?"

Regis rolls his eyes. "She rests until dinnertime. After dinner, if there's an evening show, she'll let her wagon be opened up for one hour, no more, before the show, but she prefers not to work evenings, and Mr. Jordan doesn't push it, except in the big towns."

He sits quiet for a while, his chin on his hand, which is on his elbow, which is on his knee. He's so skinny and sharp-cornered, he looks like a rail fence with a punkin on top.

"You know," he says, real thoughtful-like, "I don't know how that man keeps going."

"What man?" Jeremy asks, like we ain't just been talking about Miss Annabel and Mr. Huddles.

"Huddles."

"Oh. Yes. Well, I guess the pay is good." Jeremy again, always thinking about money.

He's thriving in the circus. Every evening on the midway, I hear him talking up the charms of Jezebel or Esmerelda or any of them. Sometimes he sets up his little, wooden table outside Miss Annabel's wagon. He moves around peas and walnuts like lightning, all the time keeping up a steady stream of talk, talk, talk. The people—Jeremy calls them "Rubes"—line up and pay to try to guess where the pea ends up. Then one day, nice as you please Miss Annabel sends Mr.

Huddles to shoo Jeremy off. She likes her quiet, and she likes being the only attraction at that end of the midway.

We make our slow way upriver—past St. Joseph, Nebraska City, Plattsmouth—all the way to Omaha. It takes the better part of a month, and I'm about to tear my hair out over Jeremy. He's having so much fun, I begin to wonder if I'll ever see South Dakota. In Omaha, we play three days, two shows a day, and I am about wore out with Annabel Lee. I find out the next big town, Sioux City, is about a hundred miles. I ain't sure how I'm going to get there, but I know it ain't going to be in the company of Miss Annabel. I don't know about Jeremy.

The last night in Omaha, we're camped along the river, and everybody seems in a party mood because they've worked hard for about a month straight, so they get a big fire going and everybody comes out and they sing songs and pass a bottle around and talk and holler until real late. Mr. Huddles comes out twice to ask everybody to be quiet because Miss Annabel can't sleep with all the noise, even though her wagon is about as far from the party as it can get.

"Come on, Huddles," one of the roustabouts shouts. "Come have a drink. You work too hard."

Mr. Huddles waves a weak hand and turns back to the wagon, but about a half hour later, he returns to the party.

"She's asleep now. You can holler all you want. She sleeps like the dead."

By this time, most of the company is pretty drunk, but me. I don't hold with letting go of my senses, so I just watch and talk to whoever ain't too drunk. Soot stays real close by me, and I like that, 'cause of that there big cat and the bear. Mr. Huddles sits down on my log and takes a drink out of a bottle offered by one of the roustabouts.

"She used to be so pretty," he tells me. "Pretty and nice. I thought we'd have a good life together."

I nod. "Guess you got more than you bargained for."

"Yes." He takes another drink.

"You need help, Mr. Huddles. Someone to do the heavy work. You must have some money put by. Why don't you buy a little house someplace warm and settle down?"

He shakes his head with more vigor than I thought he could muster. "I couldn't stand it. She'd drive me wild. At least, here I get some relief, some change of scenery. Some kindred company. The woman is a scourge."

It sounds strange to hear poor, dear Mr. Huddles give voice to such mean feelings. He goes about his days so meek and mild, you forget he has any feelings at all.

We set for a while, and then Soot and I get up to go find Jeremy. Mr. Huddles stays put, half a bottle of good Nebraska whiskey in the crook of his arm. Jeremy's in the cook tent with a bunch of the circus people he's challenged to a game of cards. I worry about him and cards, so I keep pretty good track of his comings and goings. They're gathered around one of the tables, drinking, cussing, yelling and laughing. I step in and Jeremy looks up.

"Hello, sister. How's your evening going?"

"Fine. You tell Mr. Jordan this is our last night?"

He looks a little uncomfortable. "Not yet. I thought I'd tell him in the morning when I pull my pay."

"Uh huh. Jeremy, you got no intention of leaving this circus, do you?"

"Now, Nell. Of course I do. I only signed on to Omaha. You know that."

"I know that and a lot of other things. I'm going to bed. And I'm moving on tomorrow. You can go or stay. I'm tired of arguing with you."

I turn on my heel and walk out. It's a nice summer night. The frogs are singing in the moonlight which comes and goes as the clouds pass over. I go to the tent I share with Jezebel and Esmerelda, but nobody's there. Still partying I guess. I think to tie up Soot and go by Miss Annabel's and check on her before I go to sleep.

When I get there, I hear quiet voices inside the wagon, so I hesitate. It's Mr. Huddles talking to Annabel. She must've woken up. She's grouching about something, and he's talking real soothing to her.

"All right, dear. Yes, yes. I'll take care of it. You're right to be angry with me. I never seem to get things right. I'll try to do better."

"And you've been drinking. You come in here smelling to high heaven. How many times have I told you, you can't drink? You useless fool! Hand me that box over there."

"Yes, dear. I know. You're right. I shouldn't drink." His voice sounds choked, like he's crying. I stand in the quiet night, wondering if I should just go on back to my tent. What a sad man. Then I hear a rustling sound, like somebody's struggling to get free of something. Like a tussle. The wagon rocks a bit, creaking. It lasts for maybe a minute. Then the night is silent again; even the frogs have stopped their croaking. It's a creepy silence, too silent for me.

I stand there for a long time, but there's no more sound. Then the door creaks open and Mr. Huddles lets himself down the three steps to the ground, all quiet, like a ghost. He walks with his head down, stumbling along, still a little drunk. He's crying. He almost bumps into me before he sees me.

"I'm sorry. I shouldn't drink, you know. It makes me angry when she says I'm useless. I shouldn't drink."

"What do you mean, Mr. Huddles? What happened?"

He tilts his head back toward the wagon, sitting in the silent darkness. "I'll have to go tell Mr. Jordan. I've killed the goose."

Chapter 23

I go back to the tent, but I can't sleep. I lie there staring at the canvas the rest of the night, afraid if I close my eyes I'll see Mr. Huddles, with a pillow in his hands, hovering over Miss Annabel Lee. Not that I blame him. She sure was mean. But I'm powerful upset by it, and when morning comes, I round up Jeremy first thing.

"We gotta get out of here right quick," I tell him.

He's on his way to breakfast, not all the way awake yet, so when I tell him about Mr. Huddles, he shakes it off like he thinks I dreamed it or something and heads off for the cook tent. When we get there Mr. Jordan has called a meeting of the whole company. He looks mighty serious, and I know why.

"We're packing up and moving on right away. Eat and pack. Fast."

A murmur ripples through the troupe. "What's he so in a hurry about? We thought to have a day off today." But they do his bidding, and before we're packed up and heading off, the rumors start to fly.

"Somebody beat up a townie last night and the cops are out after us."

"Mr. Jordan ain't paid his accounts in Omaha, and his creditors are coming to collect."

"The county animal inspectors are coming to take the tiger away."

There ain't no activity around Miss Annabel Lee's wagon. Mr. Huddles hitches it up just like normal and we get on the road. I wonder how long it takes a dead body to start to stink. We roll out by ten o'clock, me and Jeremy riding on top of the hay wagon they use to haul feed for the animals. The rest of the troupe are scattered among the other fancy painted wagons. Everybody has a serious look about them, but they ain't got no notion of why. I'm glad Jeremy has sense enough not to talk about what I told him. I want to part company right away, but he says they're headed north, so why not go with them a ways?

We ain't gone ten miles when Mr. Jordan gives the order to turn off and head west. After jolting and creaking about a mile off the main road, he stops and calls another meeting.

"We've had a tragedy among us," he says. "Our dear Miss Annabel Lee died during the night. Rather than deal with the authorities, which would hold us back considerable, I chose to move out this far and bury her here. Men, pick a place and set to work."

Digging a grave for a four-hundred-pound woman ain't no easy task. I ain't never seen such a big hole, which it takes four men the better part of the morning and some of the afternoon to dig. Mr. Huddles sits on the wagon seat, watching, tears streaming down his face. I think he must have one gallwalloper of a headache. The rest are real nice to him. I guess they think Miss Annabel Lee died of heart failure or apoplexy or something. I don't feel hateful toward him, just struck dumb by the way things happen. I keep my peace.

The roustabouts have a hard time getting her out of the wagon. They have to take some of the boards off the back to get at her. Then they hook one end of a chain around her and the other end to Dora, the elephant, to pull her out of there. The smell is pretty awful by then, and I'll never forget the picture of Miss Annabel being dragged to her grave. Folks are gagging over the smell, and some are crying, but others just want to get the job done and get out of there. Soot puts up a howl, like he's lost his last friend.

Once the body is under ground, a huge mound, they say some prayers and sing a hymn about gathering at the river. The smell is dying down by then, so people stand around a while and talk about her like she wasn't the meanest person they ever met up with. Then Mr. Huddles goes into the wagon, and after he comes out a few minutes later with a trunk and a carpet bag, they set it on fire. We don't stick around long to watch it burn.

Mr. Huddles climbs up in the lead wagon beside Mr. Jordan and we head back for the main road. We move along right smart, trying to put some miles between us and the burnt out wagon. Before long it's getting dark, and we move off the road again and set up camp in a woodlot near a nice farm. The folks are real excited to have us there, and they sell us food they've put up and hay for the animals. The kids play with Soot when they ain't standing around the cages gawking at the tiger and the bear. We go right on about our business as if this was just another day at the circus.

I grab Jeremy as he's walking by on his way to see Mr. Jordan. "Get our money, and let's get away as soon as the sun's up."

He gives me one of those, "Oh, Nell" looks, rolls his eyes and nods. "Okay. Okay. We're gone, but I don't see why we can't stay with them. They're headed north, and we're headed north, so what's the difference?"

I put my nose right up to his and say, "Jeremy, if you can't see no difference, your head's thicker'n I thought. This here travel is *slow*. Too slow. It's almost June. I gotta get to Deadwood, find my ma, and decide what to do next."

I can tell Jeremy's tired of hearing about Deadwood and Calamity Jane. He's right. There ain't nothing in it for him but maybe a little adventure. Good thing he's always up for a little adventure. Thing he ain't up for is discomfort.

"Come on. The sooner we get to Sioux City, the sooner you can find a bed to sleep in," I tell him.

"Ahhh," he says, rubbing his hands together. "That would be fine."

He goes into Mr. Jordan's tent. Ten minutes later he comes out with some folding money in his hand. He stuffs his into his pocket and hands me mine. "We could take a train to Sioux City, you know."

"I know, but I want to save my money. When this is over, if I have to, I'll take the train all the way back to St. Louis."

"You planning to settle down back there? With that Andrew fellow?"

"I've thought on it some. Al and Mrs. Al want me to. I don't know about Andrew." I watch for a reaction. I want him to say, "Oh, Nell, don't go back there. Let's get married and settle down near your mother in Deadwood." He don't.

"Thought I'd go on out west after Deadwood," he says. "I hear San Francisco's a great place. I'd like to see it, and be able to say I've crossed this whole country."

"You ever think on going back to England?"

He shakes his head. "No. I've been there. Next, I want to see Australia."

"Australia? Where's Australia? I swear, Jeremy, you make up places just to aggravate me."

"I didn't make it up. It's way across the Pacific. Settled by English convicts. A very interesting place."

"Humph. Can't be more interesting than here. Bet they ain't got no woman the likes of Calamity Jane."

Jeremy hefts his pack up on his shoulder and smiles. "No. I guess not," he says, and we head on up the road with Soot trailing after us.

We ain't two miles along when the circus wagons lumber up behind. Jeremy's of a mind to hop on the last one and ride for a while, but I give him the evil eye, and he thinks better of it. Following the procession is Regis Pennypacker all bones and angles on a little burro so small his feet would drag if he didn't have rope stirrups to hold them up. He gives us a sad wave as they disappear around a bend.

We trudge along in silence most of the afternoon. Jeremy ain't in a very good humor, and I just want to keep walking. I ain't sure walking to Sioux City is such a good idea anymore, and I can tell Jeremy don't think so. Way off in the distance down the road ahead of us, we see a black thing walking, and we into speculating about what it is.

"Looks to me like a black bear," Jeremy allows.

"Prob'ly Valoreous Cates, back to being a preacher man in a black cape," I say.

Jeremy chuckles at that. When we get close enough, I catch my breath. Who'd think to run into a nun out here in the wilds of Nebraska?

Nuns still give me the heebies, so I'm for passing her right on by. She's walking at a pretty good pace, kind of like a goose, bobbing along, leading with her head. She turns to greet us and I see she ain't no pullet. Her hair is tucked away, but her wrinkly face gives up her age.

"Hello, fellow travelers!" She seems right glad to have company. "Are you bound for Sioux City, too?"

"Yes'm. And beyond."

"How far beyond?"

"Clear to Deadwood in Dakota."

"Ohhh, Deadwood. I loved it there."

I look real hard at her. "You *been* there?" I ask.

"Oh, yes, dear. I did the Lord's work there for years. Sister Mary Agnes, Dominican Order." She don't slow her pace none, and she fingers a rosary as she walks. You can see her lips moving when she ain't engaged in conversation, and if you want to talk, you better keep up the pace.

Jeremy walks along behind us, real quiet. It's turned warm for May, and Jeremy don't take to carrying a pack. He's got my stuff and his own in a canvas haversack like the soldiers carried in the war. I don't know where he got it, and I don't ask. I'm just glad he's willing to carry the stuff. Not thrilled, but willing.

I ain't never seen a nun out on her own before. Mostly, if they go out at all, they go out in pairs. So I question her. "If you don't mind my asking, what's a lady of God doing out here in the wilderness all alone?"

She turns her long goose neck and looks at me. "The Lord's work, dear. We Dominicans go about the world and preach the gospel. I've worked with the Indians and the miners and the buffalo hunters most of my life. They're good people. Just need a little prodding now and then."

"You actually lived in Deadwood?"

She purses her lips. "Oh, my yes. Went there in '76 when it was naught but a muddy mining camp and stayed until '81 or '82. I don't rightly remember. They got statehood in '89, but some time before that the Lord called me to Omaha for a spell. Now I'm off to Sioux City to work with the Indians again."

We walk along in silence for a while, but I can't help myself, I have to ask. "You ever met Calamity Jane?"

"Oh, my dear, yes. Jane was quite well known in Deadwood while I was there. Notorious, I'd say."

"She's my ma," I tell her.

She stops and turns to me, peering into my face. "Your mother? Really?"

I shake my head up and down, looking her right in the eye. "She had to let me go when I was a baby 'cause Deadwood weren't no place to raise a child." I watch her real careful to see how she's taking this.

"She was right about that," the nun says. "I heard tell of something between Jane and Wild Bill Hickok, but I just thought it was one of Jane's stories. She's prone to making things up, you know."

"I've heard that, but I don't mind if she does. I know she's my ma."

The old nun steps to the side of the road and sets down on a big rock. She takes off her shoe, dumps out a stone and sets there rubbing her foot.

"Did she send for you?" she asks.

"No. She don't know I'm comin'. I aim to surprise her."

Jeremy lets down his pack, and we all share a drink from the nun's big canteen. "You each need to get you one of these in Sioux City," she tells us. "It gets mighty dry out there in the Badlands."

She opens her bag and takes out a slab of cheese and some bread, cuts off chunks and hands them to me and Jeremy and Soot before she serves herself.

"I'll tell you this about your mother—she's a good woman, never mind what anybody says. A woman of compassion. When the smallpox came through in '76, she nursed a passel of men through it in a little cabin out from town. Everyone else was afraid to go near them, but Jane. She has her faults aplenty, but nobody can take *that* away from her. She's a good woman."

I shiver with pride and glance at Jeremy. He smiles, like he's knowed all the time my mother's a kind, caring soul.

"So where do you think Jane is now, ma'am?" Jeremy's all interested.

"Don't know. I been gone from Deadwood for years, but I heard she was off to Denver or Arizona—someplace—to get married a while back. Fellow named Burke, if I recall."

I'm put off by the thought that Jane might not even be in Deadwood no more, but I ain't got no choice but to start looking for her there. "I sure hope I get to find her, or at least somebody that knows her real good. Knows about me. See, I been looking a long time."

She peers at me from under unruly gray eyebrows. "Well, if I was looking for Calamity Jane, I guess Deadwood's as good a place as any to start. Now, let's get back on the road. I want to make it to Blair before dark."

She pulls herself up from her rock and tucks the rest of her bread and cheese into a cloth bag. "If I was going to Deadwood and never been there before, I'd get me a guide. That country out there can be treacherous."

We fall into step beside her. She sets a fast pace, and out of the corner of my eye, I see Jeremy's worked up a sweat. He ain't saying much. Prob'ly too thirsty to talk. Off in the distance, the river stretches along between two green banks, broad and wide, like a brown satin ribbon shining in the sun. I like rivers. So does Soot. He's happy as long as he can smell one.

Blair, Nebraska, is a dusty little town set back a mile or so from the river. There's one hotel, but Sister Mary Agnes passes on it and goes knocking on doors until she finds herself a Catholic house—or a charitable Protestant one.

"Well, here's your chance to sleep in a real bed, Jeremy."

He lets down his pack and grins at me. "Not only a bed, but a bath, too, I'm guessing."

He goes into the hotel, which ain't much, and gets us two rooms. There's a tub in a room downstairs behind the kitchen, but that's extra. They have to pump water, heat it up and carry it for you. There's even a place to tie Soot out back, and a butcher shop down the alley where Jeremy finds some bones in a barrel. I rest and look to my bundle while Jeremy enjoys his bath and Soot enjoys his bone. I get the tub after Jeremy, and my toes are tingling just thinking about it. Our clothes could use a wash, so I go downstairs and ask the hotel keeper's wife if I can buy some soap.

It's late afternoon, and I figure to wash our clothes and hang them up to dry overnight. The lady shows me to some wooden washtubs on a bench out back, and gives me a washboard. I go upstairs and gather up my clothes. Jeremy's door ain't locked, so I go in and get his clothes, too. I reach down into the haversack to get his socks, and I feel something hard down in the corner. I pick it out—it's a little, black, carved wooden case. I know it ain't no business of mine, but I can tell it's a tintype or something. I try to keep from it, but next thing I know it's open, and I'm looking at a picture of a right pretty young woman. Stylish. Fancy. Not some country bumpkin like me.

I sit down on his bed and study it for a long time. Jeremy ain't never said nothing about no woman—sister, aunt, mother nor sweetheart. That last one sticks in my craw. Sweetheart.

Chapter 24

That night I toss and turn on that cotton-tufted mattress until the dawn finally appears. I'm vexed with myself. What did I think, anyway? That Jeremy didn't have no life before him and me met up? That all his adventures didn't take him where he'd meet women? What if the jail story was just made up? What if he was with somebody else the whole time? What if she died, tragically, of typhoid fever or diphtheria? Worse, what if there was someone back in St. Louis or Cincinnati—or even England, waiting for him?

I go down to breakfast in a foul humor. Jeremy don't come down right away, and then I remember our clothes hanging out back and rush to take them down. I carry them upstairs and knock on Jeremy's door. He's still in bed when I go in.

"Here's your clean clothes," I tell him.

He stretches, lying on his back with his arms behind his head. "Thanks, Nell. Just put them over the chair."

I do it and bite my tongue to keep from wading into him over the picture. I drop my clothes off in my room and head back down for breakfast, feeling spiteful and guilty at the same time. Jeremy comes down about fifteen minutes later all clean and shaved, looking almost respectable—and beautiful in a way no man has a right to be.

"I really must get some new clothes in Sioux City. These are threadbare at best," he says, sliding onto a bench beside me. Always thinking about how he looks. That's Jeremy. The landlady brings us breakfast, and he dives in like it's been a week since he ate.

I'm quiet through the meal, but Jeremy, being Jeremy, don't notice. I swear I'd have to hit him between the eyes with a plank for him to notice anything about me. The landlady is taken with his looks, and commences to sweet talk him, right while I'm still there. If my back wasn't up already!

I excuse myself from the "Hon and Dearie" talk, and go up to the room to get my stuff. While I'm up there, I sneak another peek at the picture. She's just as beautiful today as she was last night. I snap it shut and shove it back into the haversack. When I get back downstairs, Jeremy and the land lady are sharing a cup of coffee like they been friends forever.

"Jeremy!" I say it so loud, he jumps and I even scare myself. The landlady looks at me kind of sour and gets up to clean the table. "Are we going or not?" I ask that more quiet.

"Sure. Just getting my stuff."

I wait on the porch, Soot lying at my feet, and watch the dusty street until Jeremy reappears with his haversack. I see Sister Mary Agnes come walking down the middle of the street, Mother Goose on a mission. She spies us on the hotel porch and stops.

"Good! I haven't missed you. I was thinking about Calamity Jane last night and thought of something else to tell you. There was a story that she saved a stagecoach that was being robbed and brought it safe to Deadwood. Jumped on and drove it when the driver was killed. Don't know where I heard it, or if there's an ounce of truth to it, but if it's true, that's a woman with some gumption."

I grin with delight at every morsel about my mother. For a minute or two, I even forget about that there picture in Jeremy's haversack. "Thanks, ma'am," I tell her. "It sure is good to talk to someone who actually knew my mother once."

"Yes. Well, everything you'll hear about her won't be good, but I think it's best to repeat the good when you can. I can't say I approved of her going around in men's clothes. A woman is a woman. Man's helpmeet. God's own creation. A body shouldn't dispute that." She turns her long neck to look about her. The street is near about empty, so she don't mind standing there in the middle chewing the fat.

"I'm off for Sioux City. You walking my way?"

Jeremy speaks right up. "No, thank you, ma'am. I'm not walking to Sioux City. There's a coach. I'm for riding."

I turn and look at him like he must be daft or something, but the look in his eyes tells me arguing would be a waste of time. "Okay. I guess we can afford it."

Sister Mary Agnes gives us a nod and takes up her trek again. The bottom of her habit is already dusty. She don't seem to mind the walking. Her lips take up the rosary as she steps off toward the north.

Jeremy hefts his haversack up on his shoulder. Seeing that sack—knowing what's in it—sets me off again, and I bound off the porch two steps at a time and strut off up the street ahead of him.

We turn at the next corner and head for the Wells Fargo office. Jeremy takes my money and his to buy the tickets. It costs each of us five dollars for the fare to Sioux City. That's all I earned in almost a month with the circus. I fear it might be a while before I can earn that much again, but Jeremy don't give it a thought. The coach don't leave until 11 o'clock, so we sit down on a bench outside the freight office to wait.

"Jeremy?"

"Yes, Nell."

"You don't never talk much about yourself. Where you come from. Your family and all."

"There's little of interest to tell. I was born in Bury St. Edmunds, the youngest of three sons. My mother died when I was seven. My father remarried when I was nine, and I hated my stepmother, so I looked for every possible way to get off on my own. Left home at thirteen. Came across when I was seventeen. Spent some time in New York, then Philadelphia—then on across Pennsylvania to Johnstown, where I met you." He rattles it off real fast, like he's making a speech and can't wait to get done.

"You ain't got no girl relatives?" My mind's on the picture.

"No. Both of my brothers are married, but I've never even met their wives."

"You got a lot of schooling?"

"The average amount for an English lad. Through grammar school. But my travels have given me great opportunities to broaden my view of the world. Travel's an education in itself."

"What about your pa? What'd he do?"

"He was a vicar. Still is, I suppose. I wouldn't know if he were alive or dead by now." Something in his tone tells me he don't care to know, neither.

174

"What's a vicar?"

"A minister of the Church of England."

"Oh. You don't seem real fond of him."

Jeremy looks uncomfortable—like he don't like where this talk is leading. "He was—is—a harsh man. I didn't care much for him." He turns away like that's the end of the talk.

"What about your brothers?" I know I'm pressing a little close, but curiosity makes me push the limits.

He hesitates, then answers. "One's like him. A vicar. The older one—Richard. The other, Benjamin, is a schoolmaster. He's more like me." He rises and steps down off the porch. "I need to stretch my legs before the long ride," he tells me, and walks down the dusty street. "Think I'll search out a public house."

I sit there on the porch of the Wells Fargo office with our stuff, puzzling over Jeremy. He ain't much of a one for drinking spirits— especially before noon. Guess my nosiness got under his skin. I sigh.

When he's out of sight, I take advantage of the chance to look at that there tintype one more time. I open the haversack and reach all the way to the bottom, feeling around for the little wooden case. I take it out and study it in the light of day. She's pretty, all right, and fashionable—at least to me she is, but then I don't know much about fashion. Just the kind of fancy girl I'd expect Jeremy to like. Not plain and common like me. I study it for a long time, but there ain't no words on it nowhere. I can't tell if it's old or new or if the girl is English or American. When I see Jeremy coming back up the street, I stow the picture away again and sit prim to welcome him back.

He ain't surly now, but there's no talk in him. We sit on the Wells Fargo porch until the stage rumbles up the street making a dust cloud behind it.

The stage ride to Sioux City jolts us almost senseless. Even Soot, riding up in front with the driver, seems annoyed by the rough ride. He bounds down, wagging his tail and looks at me at every stop, like to say, "Are we there yet?" It takes us a full ten hours, and we don't get in until nine o'clock at night. It's dusty and hot for late May, and I wonder what makes Jeremy think it's worth all that money to get our brains jarred out of our heads, but I don't ask. I just know this is the last coach ride I'll afford until I get to Deadwood.

Sioux City's a busy town. Kind of smelly, too. Lots of stockyards and meat packing. And railroads. It ain't glamorous, like St. Louis, so I don't worry so much about Jeremy getting into trouble over some money-making scheme. They's Indians aplenty around, and a few soldiers. The Indians remind me of Addie. I ain't thought about her in a while. I wonder how she is and if her baby came all right.

We sleep the first night in a camp at the edge of town. It's peopled by drifters and lost souls, but we ain't got no money—leastways, I don't—none that I want to spend, anyway, and Jeremy appears to be holding onto his. He looks around at the various folks squatting along the riverbank and makes a face.

"I don't mind telling you I'm not comfortable in this company."

"It ain't a marriage. Just a night." I root around in my bundle for something to cover up with. Wish I'd saved the whores' petticoats. I lie down on the ground and flump the bundle under my head for a pillow. Jeremy stays standing up.

"You want to go spending your money on hotels and hot meals, go ahead but it's a long way to Deadwood, so we might as well get used to camping out."

"Deadwood? Did someone say Deadwood?" A voice out of the darkness.

"I did," I answer.

"You bound fer Deadwood?" The voice is attached to the most grizzled, hairy, dusty creature anyone ever conjured up.

"Maybe. Maybe not." Jeremy steps up to head off this stranger before he gets too familiar.

"Cause if'n yore goin' to Deadwood, I'm yore man. I know more'n anybody 'bout the Badlands. You want a guide? You got him. The best there is. Obadiah Watkins, at yer service." He thrusts a blackened hand toward Jeremy.

Jeremy takes a step back. "We ah—weren't expecting to need a guide. Thought we'd follow the river to Yankton and maybe on up to the White," he stammers.

I'm more than amazed at Jeremy's grasp of geography. Where's he find out all this stuff?

The man laughs a loud, kind of crazy sounding laugh. It's a making-fun-of-you-city-folk kind of laugh. Not mean exactly, but more mean than nice.

"Well, you're welcome to try it on your own, but I wouldn't advise it. Easy to get lost. You get lost in the Badlands, you could stay lost for a century or two."

"Yes, well, we'll think about it and let you know tomorrow if we need your services." This is the closest to haughty that I've ever seen Jeremy act.

Obadiah Watkins grins a gap-toothed grin, barely visible in the firelight. "You think on it. I got a job of work to do in town, but I'll be here in the evening."

Jeremy lays down his haversack beside me on the riverbank and lays himself down with his head on it for a pillow. It occurs to me we have to fit ourselves out for the trip. Canteens, like the nun said, and provisions. Maybe even a map, if there's one to be had. I go to sleep pretty quick with my arm around Soot. Good old Soot. He's a lot easier to deal with than Jeremy.

The camp wakens early in the morning. I guess there's some that has work to go to, and others that want to move on. Somebody makes some coffee, and I smell bacon. I roll over and see a woman holding some over the fire on a stick, letting it drip on a piece of bread. It smells delicious. I roll back to see if Jeremy's awake. He ain't there. Probably got up early to tend to his private needs.

Soot is dying over the smell of that bacon, and I get up and go over to the woman and ask if I can buy some of her bacon bread.

"Sure, sweetie. No need to pay, though. We help each other around here. What one has, we all have. Git your own stick, though."

She's kind of skinny and none too clean, but there's kindness in her brown eyes, and I reach out with gratitude for a piece of bread and look around for a stick. When the bread's heavy with bacon grease I sit down on my bundle and share it with Soot. He licks his chops like it's the best meal he's ever had. I'm wondering where Jeremy is, but in a few minutes I see him coming down the path from the town with a loaf of fresh bread under one arm and a bag of coffee beans under the other. I tell him about the woman's kindness, and he cuts the loaf in half and gives it to her. Then she gives us each a cup of hot coffee, and Jeremy gives her a handful of beans.

"Where you folks bound for?" she asks, shading her eyes against the rising sun.

"Deadwood," I tell her.

"Deadwood? Why'd you wanta go there?"

"To find my mother. She's Calamity Jane."

"Calamity Jane's your mother? My land. I didn't know she had a child. Don't tell Obadiah that or he'll start in telling Calamity Jane stories and buffalo hunting stories and mountain man stories till the prairie dries up."

"Obadiah Watkins? The man who offered to be our guide?"

"The very one. Crazy old coot, but he knows the Badlands better'n anybody."

"How do you know him?"

"We was companions once. But he'd get to drinkin' and get nasty, so I keep shut of him now, most of the time. We kind of travel together at a distance if you get my meaning."

"Where is he now?"

"Gone into town for a job of work. Them stockyards needs workers ever' day. Keeps a man in liquor."

When Jeremy and I finish eating we gather up our stuff and wander on into town. Jeremy ain't got no intention of spending another night in that camp, but I'm set on fitting us out with provisions for the trip, so if that uses up all our money, so be it.

"How much money you got?" I ask. Seems to me he's usually right casual about his money. Comes too easy.

"Some," he answers, looking away.

"I got five dollars Dr. Beckwith gave me." I don't tell him about my double eagle. Not that I think he'd steal it or nothing. Just, it seems special—between me and Granny—and I've sort of made up my mind not to ever spend it.

"I've got forty-five dollars, give or take."

"Forty-five dollars! Jeremy! Where'd you get that much money?"

"My pay from the circus, and the rest I won at cards from the roustabouts."

He reaches into his pocket and brings out a handful of paper money. I forage in my bundle for my greenback and hand it to him.

"How much you think it'll cost to get us outfitted to go on?"

"I don't know. Let's find a general store and see what we need."

We ain't in that store more'n twenty minutes and we come out near busted. We got us two canteens, two bedrolls, a canvas shelter, beans, more coffee, flour, corn meal, salt, meat, a little bit of sugar and some baking soda. The store keeper says it should last us about a month, and we figure we've got about five hundred miles to go. Jeremy figures. I ain't got no sense of the lay of the land. All I know is Deadwood is somewhere far to the west and a little north.

Turns out it's a right heavy load, and it taxes both of us to get it back to the camp along the river against Jeremy's intentions. We divide it up even so he don't have all the carrying. I'm for starting out right away, but Jeremy allows he'd like to talk more to Obadiah Watkins, so we set ourselves down by the fire and wait for him to come back from his work.

The woman who travels with him—her name is Sally—comes over and sits, talking to us while we wait.

"Obadiah knows the country, sure enough. He can guide you better'n anybody."

Jeremy sets out his case. "We're temporarily short of funds, you see. We can't afford his services, but we thought we could exchange some provisions for a little information."

"Right enough," she replies and turns to see Obadiah come stumbling into camp. "Oh, dear. He's been at the bottle already."

Obadiah Watkins is one of them puzzlements you meet once in a while. He can't stay away from the drink, but he's a wise man, full of knowledge, even when he's drunk. Trouble is, he's something of a mean drunk, and the truth is not in him. To say he's given to overstating things would be understating Obadiah.

He wanders in all rheumy-eyed, a bottle hung from his belt. It's about three fourths gone, and Obadiah don't look like he's been sharing. Sally takes one look at him and starts into picking up her stuff in preparation for leaving.

"When he sobers up, tell him I'm for Vermillion. He knows where to look for me there." She stows her stuff in an old, beat up carpet bag, pours the rest of her coffee on the ground, and stuffs the blackened pot into the bag. She makes her solitary way out of camp in the late afternoon, her moccasined feet making gentle tracks in the dust.

Jeremy looks at me, then at the old buffalo hunter struggling to keep his balance against a spinning world. He raises an eyebrow in question. I look around and shrug. What choice do we have? I unpack the canvas shelter and start to make camp.

Chapter 25

Even when he's drunk, Obadiah Watkins knows the lay of the land. Him and Jeremy got their heads together till dark, drawing maps in the dust with a stick. I take it all in, knowing how Jeremy can forget what he come for easy as that, 'specially if he sees a chance to get his hands on some money. Not that he's likely to come across any in the Badlands, but I need to know everything he knows. This part of the trip seems off-putting, given that we're about to leave civilization behind and test our mettle good. I worry about how Jeremy'll do. He tends to like his comforts, and according to Obadiah, comforts is going to be sparse on this journey.

The two of them talk way into the night, even though Obadiah ain't one bit more sober when he goes to sleep than he was coming in. At least he don't show no nastiness, and I feel sorry for Sally, off by herself someplace along the river. I ain't had a lot to do with drinkers, and I count myself lucky. I got my own concerns, lying there in the canvas shelter while Jeremy and Obadiah lay out their plans. I know I got us into this, and from what I hear, the Badlands are just that. My mind is shadowed by doubts about why I'm even doing this, and taking Jeremy and others along to boot. This Calamity Jane thing could be what they all say it is, the yearning of a poor, motherless child. I don't want to believe that, but the prospect of crossing those Badlands gives me pause—scares the dickens out of me.

By morning, Obadiah's dried out some, but the smell of him would make a skunk cringe. He's slept on the ground and wakes up creaky. Can barely get around for a hour or so. Then he finally notices Sally's gone.

"Goldern that woman! Always ready to absquatulate when you need her. Who's gonna make my coffee? Who's gonna make the biscuits? I'm hungry!"

"You can join our fire, Obadiah," Jeremy assures him. "We're pulling out as soon as we finish eating, but you're welcome to anything we've got."

Obadiah settles himself on a log by the fire and commences to drink hot coffee out of a tin cup. Burns my mouth and hands to watch him. He pours down near about half the pot before he turns his rheumy eyes on me. "That Sally say where she was goin'?"

"Vermillion. Said you'd know where to find her."

"Best I clean myself up a bit first."

I ain't about to argue with that. He disappears among the bushes along the riverbank amid splashing and thrashing, with an occasional glimpse of bleached white skin. When he reappears, he's wearing the same buckskin pants and cloth shirt, but they've been scrubbed clean in the river. He asks Jeremy for the loan of some shaving gear and sets about shaving his face without a looking glass. I could offer to help, but I don't. I think he should have to reap his own harvest. When he's done shaving, he asks for a comb, which Jeremy also provides. I see him wince just a tiny bit at handing over his ivory comb to that mat of wool. It takes some time, but Obadiah turns out looking almost fit for human company, hair pulled back and tied with a string, face shaved clean.

"Well? We ready?" he asks.

Jeremy nods, and we load up our belongings and head up river. Sioux City should be a short walk through, but Obadiah allows he's in need of a dram shop, and Jeremy seems bent on agreeing with everything Obadiah says and does. They stop for a drink, which seems to set Obadiah to rights, and we proceed through town. We ain't a mile beyond when Obadiah hollers up, real loud: "There she is! The cussed strumpet. Leave a man in his time of need, will you?"

I look where he's looking and see Sally sitting under a tree with a basket in her lap and her carpetbag by her side. She stands, hands on hips, to return the tirade. "You randy old scalawag! Don't you talk to me like you was my master. You leave off the drinking and I'll stick around. You make your choice."

I chuckle that Sally's sassy enough to match him. I catch Jeremy's eye, and we grin over their strut and display—like a couple of prairie chickens in mating season.

Without making any bargains about guiding or even traveling together, the four of us head on upriver to Vermillion. Crossing into South Dakota's a real milestone for me. Makes me feel close to my ma. Vermillion ain't just another river town either. They got a college there. It's a little smaller and a little quieter than other river towns. Kind of genteel. We set up camp along the river south of town and plan to see if there's any boats for Yankton in the morning. After supper, Jeremy and Obadiah elect to go into town looking for fun.

I grab Jeremy's arm and give him the evil eye. "Don't you go getting into trouble, Jeremy. And keep Obadiah away from the spirits, you hear me?"

He gives me one of his cure-all grins and follows Obadiah up the track to town. Me and Sally sit by the fire and talk.

"Where you come from, anyway?" she asks.

I tell her about my travels from Pennsylvania all the way to here. "I been off on my own now for about a year. Done all right for myself, too. Bet the nuns'd be surprised I didn't get myself killed or worse. Heck, I doubt they'd even recognize me."

Sally nods. "Been on *my* own since I were thirteen. Now I reckon I must be about twenty-eight. Been with Obadiah three—four years now. He's not the worst of them, I can tell you. Some of these old buffalo hunters ain't got the least idea of how to get on with a woman." She pokes at the fire with a stick, rearranges the rocks and sets the coffee pot to boil.

"Where do you live come winter?" I ask.

"Hole up wherever we can find shelter. Sometimes it's an old soddy somebody left. Sometimes it's with the Injuns. Summers we just roam."

"You like that life? I mean, don't you ever wish you could settle down and have a house and raise a family?"

She looks off at the river, kind of sad-like. "I try not to want what I can't have. Don't do no good. Just makes you unhappy. Like you and that there Jeremy. I can tell you want that with him. Settin' yourself up for heartbreak. He ain't the settling down kind."

"What you mean, settin' myself up for heartbreak?"

"Just what I said, honey. You got stars in your eyes you can't hide. But I'm just sayin' he's got a whole 'nother look on life, and it don't include no woman."

I'm taken aback by her honesty—not at all happy to know what she thinks, but struck by how she can know stuff about folks they don't know themselves—or can't admit, leastwise. I sit quiet, thinking on what she said. Ain't no sense to argue with her. She thinks what she thinks.

After a while, I bring myself to take up the conversation again. "What about you and Obadiah? He sure ain't the settling down kind. You gonna foller after him till you're both old?"

"Doubt either of us'll live that long. This here ain't your civilized east. This here is a hard land. I reckon I'll foller after him till he kills himself or kills me, one."

Sally looks a lot older than twenty-eight, but twenty-eight seems pretty old to me. It's easy to see she's had a hard life. Her face shows it. But there's something else there, too. Not book knowledge, like Dr. Beckwith, but a purchase on life like nobody I've knowed before. She looks it right in the face and calls it what it is: uncertain. I trust her judgment, even if I don't like it. Don't want it to be true.

Around midnight we're awakened by loud singing, and along come Jeremy and Obadiah shouting to the treetops about "Old Dan Tucker." I don't have enough trouble keeping Jeremy on the straight and narrow, he has to take up with a drinking man. I'm all set to give him a piece of my mind when he flops down beside me, laughing out loud, and pulls a wad of paper money out of his pocket.

"Oh, Nell, you should have been there. It was so easy—taking money from those college boys. I swear they never played poker before in their lives, and every one of them was afraid his friends would find him out for a rube." He's clearly delighted with himself, and Obadiah sits in admiration of every word he says.

"Shore were fun to fleece them there college boys. Think they're so smart, but get 'em drunk and they ain't no different from the rest of us, only more so."

I wonder if we're safe here tonight or if the college boys'll get the constable out after us. But it appears they're too drunk to notice they been fools, or maybe too embarrassed to admit it, because we get up and get on our way upriver early and nobody says nothing to us. We elect to walk instead of taking a boat. Guess Jeremy and Obadiah want some maneuvering room in case the college boys come after them. Yankton is a good day and a half upriver, and the walk is hard on Jeremy and Obadiah, but I figure it serves them right. The wages of sin, so to speak.

Along the way, Jeremy starts in to counting his money, and he's right pleased with the amount. Talks all the way to Yankton about how he's gonna get a bath and buy some new shoes—boots, he says— and some clothes fit for the Badlands. I let on like I don't hear him. I swear a fool and his money are lucky to get together in the first place.

We get to Yankton around noon the next day and make our camp along the river and, of course, it don't take Jeremy and Obadiah more than five minutes to come up with a reason to go into town. I take the afternoon to wash clothes and spread them out to dry. Sally wears a buckskin dress and moccasins like a Indian. Braids her hair, too. She don't never look as dirty and scraggly as Obadiah.

"I wish I had a sun bonnet," I tell her as we lounge along the riverbank trying to catch a fish for supper.

"Well, go in town and get one," she replies.

"I ain't got no money," I say, mindful that I'm lying.

"Yankton ain't that big a town. Go find Jeremy and ask him to get you a sun bonnet. You pull your own weight. It's the least he can do for you."

I think on it for a while and allow as how she's right. "Come on, Sally. Maybe Obadiah'll buy you something, too."

We ain't a mile up the road when we run into the two of them riding in a rickety two-wheeled cart pulled by mule. It ain't the finest beast I ever seen, but it's a lot better'n I ever expected Jeremy to own.

"Where'd you get this?" I ask as they pull up beside us.

"Bought it from a settler who's keen to go back east. Says he got the mule from the army. Willing to sell for next to nothing," Jeremy says, puffed up like a rooster. He's wearing new buckskins and new boots, and he's got a red kerchief tied around his neck. That's Jeremy. Can't let himself pass unnoticed. Obadiah's decked out, too, in new boots and a new shirt. His hair is braided and he smells better than I ever thought he could.

"We was looking for you to see if we could get us each a sun bonnet," I tell Jeremy.

"Sure." He reaches in his pocket and comes out with a greenback dollar. Get yourself a nice one. You'll need it later on."

Obadiah matches Jeremy's gift, and Sally and I step off up the road to town feeling rich. As we pass by the cart, I notice a keg stowed in the back. I don't have to ask what's in it.

That night, we sit around the fire and make our plans for the next part of our journey—up the Big Muddy to the White River that flows into it around five days from Yankton. Obadiah keeps himself well oiled with drinks from the keg. It appears he ain't able to get on very far without it. The weather's getting pretty hot, and we think to travel early, rest for a few hours in the afternoon, and then push on until about dark. We'll follow the river, for water and fish. There's an abundance of prairie grass for the mule, so it's cheap to keep. Soot'll eat fish if he has to, but I try to pick the bones out for him. Obadiah knows the lay of the land, and we follow his advice. Drunk or sober, he knows more than we do, so we set out for the White on more or less of a track along the river.

Traveling by mule cart ain't very fast, but it sure beats walking. We don't have much stuff, so it don't tax the beast to haul two of us at a time, slow or not. In the first couple of days out of Yankton we pass a little town or two, but then I'm struck by the emptiness of the land. There ain't nothing but prairie grass and the river. Hardly no trees except right by the river, and then not many, mostly cottonwoods. My eyes would welcome a mountain or two.

Obadiah goes into a daily tirade about how the buffalo are all gone. "Used to hunt 'em, and them herds stretched out as far as the eye could see. First come the railroad, then come all those city folk, shooting them from trains. Railroads encouraged them—didn't like it if a stubborn buffalo took up on the tracks and slowed down their train. On the other hand, they was scared to death of a stampede." He gets all irate—his face red and his eyes real little, like he's squinting in a dust storm. "Damn 'em. Kilt off the buffalo sure as Ned. Bastards." It strikes me he contributed his fair share to their demise, but I figure arguing with a drunk makes about as much sense as arguing with a pig, so I keep my peace.

One afternoon after we've started up the White River, which is a great ways smaller than the Big Muddy, not near as deep or wide, we take our rest in the shade of the cart while the mule wades up to his belly in the sea of prairie grass. At first the river bank is gentle enough, but after some distance the river has cut itself a deep channel out of the prairie and we travel way high above, looking down into a crevice that looks like somebody come along dragging a great big hoe behind. Still it's water and a trail to follow, but the water ain't very plentiful and likely to get scarcer as the summer progresses. Late one afternoon, we stop to set up camp on the edge of the scar where there's a rough path leading down to the water. Sally has the cooking well in hand and Jeremy and Obadiah are playing a dice game in the fine sand. Soot has found his way down the bank, gone wading and got himself good and soaked, and lays down beside me to share his wet dog smell. I'm setting on a piece of old buffalo robe of Obadiah's, which don't smell much better than Soot, when I notice something is bothering the mule. He into braying and stepping about kind of frantic, head up, nostrils flared, pulling on the rope tied to his stake. Then Soot takes it up—barking and whining and nudging his nose under my arm. I sit up and look around, but far as I can tell there ain't nothing out there but the endless grass. Then I see it. The smoke. Far off to the west and coming toward us. "Fire!"

Obadiah jumps up when I cry out and starts in to making preparations. He grabs onto the mule's halter and hitches it up in the midst of loud and stubborn protests. Jeremy, Sally and I load up our stuff in the cart. We look for a way down to the river that's wide enough for the cart and not too abrupt, but we have to go on almost a mile toward the fire before we find a grade we can navigate. Obadiah coaxes the mule down to the river bed amid loud protestations and severe resistance. I lead Soot down and tie him up to a tree by the river to keep him from running off. Then Obadiah drives the mule and cart right into the water, which at this place ain't more'n a couple feet deep.

The mule is terrified, and Jeremy and Obadiah tie ropes around tree trunks on opposite banks to keep him from tearing off. We wait for the fire, above us now, sweeping across the prairie, and hope it will keep to the flat land and not swoop down the river channel. Obadiah sets me and Sally to work dousing the cart with water. We watch as some of the tall cottonwoods upstream burst and crackle into flame. Soot stands in the water, bedraggled, pulling on his rope and looking at me like he never imagined I could do him so mean.

Obadiah turns to Sally and me. "Here," he says. "Tie these over your noses." He hands us each a wet cloth and we do as we're told. The fire is closer now and roaring so loud we can't hear each other. I feel the heat when it's still a ways off, and see the flames leap up ten or twelve feet above the lip of the canyon. Higher than you'd dream with only tall grass to feed off of. Me and Sally look like bandits with rags tied on our faces, but we keep wetting them to keep off the heat and smoke.

The roar is deafening as the fire draws nigh. We can't even hear the mule braying or the dog barking. All we can do is stand in the river and watch them writhe and pull on the ropes that bind them. The smoke is thick and black and it rolls down into the river bottom, choking us and burning our eyes. Then the fire is upon us, and there's naught to do but duck under the water, hold our breath, and hope it jumps the gully without killing us. It would be a shame to get this far only to die in a prairie fire, and my mother never to know that I was coming. Makes me sad to think of it.

I hold my breath and squint my eyes shut, holding tight to one of the cart wheels to keep myself from running off in a panic. My lungs feel like to burst, and when I know I can't stand it no longer, I open my eyes, take a breath, and look for a place to run. The fire all around above us keeps licking at the cottonwoods, but there's only smoke in the riverbed. The mule is kicking and jerking against the ropes. I can't even see Jeremy, so I close my eyes again, grit my teeth and hold onto the cart wheel, sure I'm going to die.

Then, just that quick, it's over. The fire has passed, blown on its way by a powerful wind. The grass is blackened and pockets of smoke rise out of the hot spots on the prairie above us. We untie the mule and Soot and pull the cart up onto a high spot on the river bank, where we camp for the night, grateful to be alive. I lie awake a long time, the smell of burnt grass singeing my nostrils. I roll my bedroll closer to Jeremy, who's sleeping like the innocent, and reach out to touch him. My hand finds his, and I hold onto him for a long moment, glad we're both still alive. Good old Soot crawls over and snuggles up to my back. Now I can sleep.

The next morning we're up and out early, dragging ourselves up out of the river channel when off in the distance we see some people coming toward us.

"Injuns," according to Obadiah. "Prob'ly rode out the fire in the river just like us."

I look at Sally. "Should we be scared?"

She shakes her head. "No. They're probably just hungry. Or want to trade. Not much going on with them since Wounded Knee."

"Wounded Knee? What's that?"

"You ain't heerd of Wounded Knee? A massacree. Just after Christmas. Out at Pine Ridge. Knocked the fight out of the Sioux."

A bolt of lightning strikes my heart. "Pine Ridge? Ain't that where the Lakota Sioux are from?"

"I guess so. I don't know that much about the Sioux. Lakota, Dakota, Oglala, Blackfoot. A Injun's a Injun far as I'm concerned."

Addie. Addie going to Pine Ridge to have her baby. Addie and Robert, hell bent to get there to help her people. I turn to Jeremy, but he don't know Addie. No sense to bother him about her. I gaze out over the blackened prairie with fear in my heart.

Chapter 26

Obadiah waits until the Indians get close and then he walks right up to them and starts in to talking like they're old friends.

"Does he know them or something?" I ask Sally.

"No. Like as not, they ain't never met, but Obadiah knows how to talk to 'em. He'da made a good agent. Never woulda had to fight 'em, if it was up to him."

The Indians are a sad and pathetic troupe. They have one horse, bone weary and old as Methusala, dragging a thing made out of two long poles tied together with rawhide, and piled up with whatever poor belongings they have. They look like they've been dragged behind that thing themselves. An old man, two women and two little ones. I'd warrant they hadn't eaten in days. They stop near us and the man talks to Obadiah for a bit.

"They're bound for Lower Brule," he tells us. "They's a reservation there. They need some food. Ain't et in three days. Hope to find their men at Lower Brule"

I stand back, watching and remembering Addie needing so bad to help her people. I wonder how she is and if she might be somewhere out there, like them, hungry—or worse.

We dole out some flour, corn meal, salt and coffee. One of the women gives me a beaded belt she's made herself, to pay for the food. I tuck it in my pack with my other clothes.

"Obadiah. Try to find out if they know anything about Addie, my friend from St. Louis. She was going to Pine Ridge last fall with her husband. Addie was going to have a baby. Ask them did they know her?"

Obadiah turns and speaks with the old man.

"He says most everyone died at Wounded Knee. If she was there, there ain't much hope for her. A few escaped, but the winter might of took care of them."

I send up a silent prayer for my friend, my sister, Addie.

There ain't much to talk about, and after a little while the Indians take up their burdens again and head north. We keep on for the west, following the river but keeping to the flat land above. The travel ain't too hard—just jolting over the blackened prairie, and after a few boring days, we keep on west following the White. We go a good ways before we come into the Badlands, 'cause Obadiah tells us he knows the best way through 'em, and he takes us skirting the southern edge to where he says they're narrowest. Says we could go around them, but since we're with him, it won't be necessary. The Badlands are nothing but cliffs and peaks and gullies and something Obadiah calls buttes -- steep, rugged, flat-topped mountains that jut up off the prairie floor one by one. Beautiful to look at, but treacherous to travel through. There ain't no track or nothing to go by but the sun, and it's mighty strong. There's rocks and gullies and washes everywhere you turn, all pink and white and gray. We're slowed to only a few miles a day, and I'm ready to bust with fearful uneasiness, always looking for a way around or through, even though I know we're in good hands with Obadiah.

Obadiah's a decent sort, in spite of his drinking. He's smart, that's for sure. Knows all about a lot of things. I feel pretty sure of us with him along teaching Jeremy what he needs to know. Long as we keep him away from the keg, he's fine, but even when he's drunk he seems to have control of his senses. But he does get mean. Says a lot of things he wouldn't never say sober. 'Specially to Sally.

One night we're camped along a dry wash, and Obadiah's treating himself to some whiskey. He's been fairly reasonable in his consumption up 'til now. I keep a wary eye on him. The evening is quiet, but the sky to the west looks pretty dark. Once in a while a flash lights up the sky. Obadiah studies it and shakes his head. "Storm comin'," he says. The air cools down considerable, and we sit on a flat ledge above a wash, enjoying the breeze, but Obadiah's restless. He keeps getting up and staring to the west, pacing around the edge of the camp, like there's something out there he don't like.

He don't say much more, but he's watchful. A while back he turned us into a path that looks to go through a narrow canyon, but I ain't sure. I don't want to question Obadiah's judgment, but I don't like the look of this canyon. It could lead right on through, or it could just lead to nowhere.

The sky gets dark pretty sudden, and big purple clouds blow up out of the west. Obadiah, he into pacing. "Gonna be a gully washer," he says, and starts searching out a good place to ride it out. There ain't none. We need a flat place on higher ground, but flat places is hard to come by, 'specially on higher ground.

The mule is skittish as the evening wears on—braying and testing the rope that holds him to a scraggly tree. Obadiah goes over and talks real quiet to him, and he settles down for a bit, but soon as Obadiah walks away he into braying and jerking on that rope again. The lightning and thunder crack and roll to beat all. When it starts to rain, they's big drops, like to wash your face with one. I turn mine up to it and wash the dust off, absolute joyful to be cool and wet and even something like clean.

Obadiah's still in a caution. He don't stop pacing and talking to the mule. All of a sudden, the storm blows wide open, raining and pouring down like a dam opened up. Reminds me of the flood back in Johnstown, and I get pretty nervous watching these little narrow side canyons fill up with rushing, grayish water. Obadiah yells to make for higher ground. We can't hear him over the thunder and the downpour, but we get the message by his gesticulations and gather up our bundles, tie Soot up with a rope, and scramble up the rough rock sides against a million gushing streams. Our shoes suck in the slop, and we can hardly manage to climb faster than the swirling, muddy water.

Obadiah goes to hitch up the cart, maybe back us out of this canyon we're in, but the mule into braying and kicking every time Obadiah gets close enough to touch him. We can't hear it, but we can tell Obadiah is talking to him again, soothing like. The mule ain't cooperative, but against all my expectations, he gets the job done.

By then it's too rough to get the cart out anyway, so Obadiah tries to turn the mule and head for higher ground on the other side of the canyon, but no. That mule ain't going to do nothing but stand there and let it rain on him. Jeremy lets himself down from our ledge and makes his way, head down, to where Obadiah is struggling with that mule. He don't know nothing about horses or mules, so I'm scared for him. I try to call him back, but the thunder forces the words back down my throat.

The rain washes all manner of sludge down the sides of the buttes so that the mule stands up to its belly in deep, swirling, gushing water. What with the thunder and lightning, the frantic animal rears and bucks every time Obadiah goes to touch it. Jeremy tries to hold its head while Obadiah moves to unhitch it so it can be free of the cart, which by now is floating behind it. They can barely hold on while the animal kicks and bucks at whatever's in reach. Jeremy loses his grip, falls backward into the rushing water and struggles to get hold of one of the cart wheels to pull himself back up against the current. Then that mule lands a kick on Obadiah's chest, sends him flying, and he lands with a thump on a rocky point on the opposite side of the wash from us. The lightning flashes show Obadiah's face wearing a look of surprise. The rain beats down harder than ever, but he don't move.

Jeremy struggles to get by the mule and cart to help Obadiah, but he can't breach the torrent that separates them. He turns and claws his way back up the rough rock, but just as he seems to be getting a solid hold, a huge gushing torrent pours down over the rock and washes his feet out from under him. I yell out his name, but he just goes slipping and sliding down the gully, helpless to stop himself. Now I'm scared. Obadiah still ain't moving, and I can't even see Jeremy. Sally is screaming and gesturing toward Obadiah, but I can't hear a word of it. The rain is beating on us now so hard we can barely see Obadiah where he lays.

I inch my way down toward what now looks like a river gushing from one rock to another, not sure how to try to help. Obadiah is on the other side, so there's no hope of reaching him. I look around for Jeremy and see him clinging to a rock about fifty feet downstream from where I saw him last. His face is all white, his eyes bugged out. I can't even find a tree limb to try to reach him and if I get into the water, it'll drag me away, sure as Ned.

I look across at Obadiah again, but he just lays there still in the rain while the mule kicks and kicks until it's free of the cart. The thunder's so loud you can't even hear the racket of the cart breaking up. Once the mule's free, it runs off down the canyon where we came from to God knows where. The cart, mostly pieces now, floats along in the torrent and lodges against a rock where the canyon curves. I see Jeremy trying to reach it for something to hold onto. Sally sits with her knees drawn up in the pouring rain, lit up by the lightning, watching Obadiah's still form, waiting for the storm to end.

Next thing I see, Jeremy's lost his hold and is being carried downstream again. I watch, helpless, as he gets bounced back and forth in the current and up against the far bank. Suddenly, he's in a calm spot, and he drags himself up out of the water and sits up against a rock to catch his breath. I can only get a clear look at either of them when the lightning flashes, but before long I see Jeremy trying to creep back up over the rocks toward Obadiah. There ain't nothing to hold onto as he goes. My stomach rears up sick watching him inch his way to where Obadiah lies still. There's a gully washing down between them, and when he gets to the edge of it he stands up as if he's going to jump. I let out a scream, but Jeremy can't hear me. He rears back and jumps across the raging water, barely makes it to the other side. I can see he's hurt by the way he spares his left leg, trying scramble up the rock to where Obadiah lays. The water's still rising, and I'm scared it'll wash both of them away. Jeremy reaches Obadiah, touches him and tries to rouse him, but nothing doing. Then he looks across at me, as hopeless as I've ever seen a man look. Obadiah's dead.

Sally knows it, and she into wailing, rocking and keening. Jeremy climbs up to a higher flat place above Obadiah's lifeless body. I can't hardly see him over there, and I fight waves of panic that he'll get washed away. We sit there, drenched and bedraggled in the pouring rain, staring across a raging chasm. The water in the ravine rises steadily, and the rain pours down like to drown everything on God's earth. I ain't scared for myself. I just want Jeremy back on my side of that torrent. After a while sitting there with the dead man, Jeremy puts his head down on his folded arms. It looks to me like he's crying.

When morning finally dawns under sunny skies, Obadiah's body is gone, washed away with the storm. Sally cries out that we have to find him and give him a decent burial, but Jeremy is still on the other side, and we have to get him back with us or cross over ourselves before we can do anything else. The water falls a lot slower than it rose, and we have to wait for a long time before it's safe to even try to cross. Jeremy waits for us over there, and I can tell he's hurting. Once Sally and I cross over, I grab onto him and hold tight. His ankle is swollen, probably broken, and there ain't even scrub wood to make him a crutch. We can't waste no time now. We've got to get out of these here Badlands while we still have what little provisions we hauled up the rocks with us. No mule. No cart. No Obadiah. He don't say so, but I get the feeling Jeremy is on the edge of giving up, and Sally ain't no better. Guess that leaves me.

We have to go tramp a long way over tough ground to get back to the trail we was following yesterday, and we ain't even sure it's the same one, washed out as it is. Jeremy stumbles along, leaning on me, limping and wincing in pain. As soon as I find a stick of wood, I wrap a piece of my petticoat around the top of it for a crutch.

Soot walks along, head down, like he can't believe how bad his life is turning out, and Sally is beyond comfort—glassy eyed and numb. I feel so hopeless without no guide or nobody to tell us if we're even lost or not. Jeremy don't say much, but I can tell he's scared, too. I stick close to him and Soot sticks close to me, while Sally hangs back, alone with her grief.

We don't see no one the whole day. That ain't rare. We ain't seen hardly a soul since we turned west along the White. We don't know if we're in Indian territory or what, so we just keep on going west. The walking is hard at best. Most of the time it's nigh impossible. We stumble and slip and end up with skinned knees and turned ankles, but late in the afternoon we come to a shallow river and a more flat prairie that looks to go on forever, so I think we're out of the Badlands. Jeremy's ankle is all swole up to twice its size, so I elect to set down under a scraggly tree to rest against the heat and let Jeremy prop up his leg.

Without Obadiah, I'm real afraid we could be going the wrong way and wandering around in circles even, but I figure whatever happens is up to me. All I know is to head west, keep the sun behind me in the morning and ahead of me in the evening, and hope it gets us to civilization. I'm real scared for Jeremy. Sally ain't no help at all, and our provisions are meager. My judgment is I ain't got no choice but to keep going, but I'm feeling guilty about bringing all of us into this fix. If it weren't for my stubborn hard-headedness, we'd all be safe and Obadiah wouldn't be dead.

Chapter 27

I know we ain't going to get out of here with Jeremy in the shape
he's in, so I elect to leave him and Sally on this river bank with a
few trees for shade and try to find help. I'm hoping this here river will
take us to Rapid City, the last place Obadiah talked about. Jeremy
says he remembers it should be northwest of here. I'm not sure how
to calculate northwest, but Jeremy helps me figure it. I hope if I
follow this river, I'll find someone to help us. I take Soot and strike
out pretty much on my own along the river, but it ain't long till I come
on a crick flowing in from what I calculate to be the northwest, so I
elect to follow it. Looks to me like the river is headed just plain north,
and I'm out of food, so I just keep walking and try to keep my belly
full by drinking water. This here is big woods—pine trees as tall as
you can think. Lots of rocks bigger than a house, and rough walking
along this here crick. It's getting dark when I come to a rugged old
cabin that I'm not sure if there's anybody living there or not so I go
up and knock on the door. The trees towering over make you think
it's getting dark before it really is.

A man opens the door, a hairy, tough, rugged looking feller with
real deep-set eyes and a frowny face. Scares me just to look at him,
but I'm that desperate.

"Howdy," I say, forcing a smile. "My name's Nell and my friends
are hurt, lost and outa food out there." I motion over my shoulder.

The man reaches behind the door and brings out a gun. I get a
cold feeling in my stomach, but when he steps out the door, I see
there's a woman behind him. She's lean and rangy looking, but one
look at her face tells me there's kindness there.

The man stops in the door yard, looks all around like he wants to
make sure I'm alone and turns to me. "How far?'

"I ain't sure, but I think I been walking a day and a half.
Followed this here crick, up from a river on back."

He nods and turns to the woman. "Give her some grub—and the dog, too. I'll make up a pack. You mights well come along."

The woman smiles and invites me in. The inside of the cabin is cozy—hung with a lot of animal skins, but some nice woven blankets and things, mostly traded from the Indians, I guess.

"I'm Melissa Reed. Folks call me Liss. Tom's my husband. You?"

"Nell. My name's Nell. Cannary, I guess." I feel embarrassed to call myself Cannary out here in the west where somebody might have knowed my folks. Might question my claim. Might not believe me.

Liss Reed don't bat a eye. She just turns to a pot over the fire and dishes me out some stew. I'm so hungry I don't even bother for a spoon. I drink the stew right out of the bowl until I get to the vegetables. Then she hands me a spoon and I get right into it.

She sits down at a table, motions me to sit, and watches me eat. "You sure are hungry, girl. What's your story?"

I tell her as much as I can about our travails since we left the Big Muddy. I'm so worried about Jeremy I jumble up my words, but she gets the gist of it. She's real pretty—nice, gray eyes and blondish hair. Talks like she's from the east, so I ask her.

"Where you from?"

"Boston. We've been out here for some time, though. Tom's a trapper, hunter, miner, mountain man, scout, whatever makes him happy and free. I just come along to keep him from killing himself."

Tom comes in the door, still carrying his gun, with a pair of leather saddle bags over his arm. "Tom never goes anyplace without his gun," Liss tells me. "Don't pay him any mind."

He hands the saddle bags to Melissa and starts gathering up bullets and stuff for his gun. "You think you can guide us back to your friends?"

I nod. "Just follow the crick down to the river. That's where I left them."

"Liss, get them some potatoes and a chunk of that bacon out of the shed. I'll fill the canteens."

"Can I do something?" I ask.

"Roll up all the buffalo robes you see. We'll need them for sleeping."

I roll up five buffalo robes and tie them with rawhide strings Liss gives me, while Tom gets the rest of his pack together. Then he goes back outside, still toting his gun, as Liss comes in with a gunny sack full of food. Tom loads two of the rolled up buffalo robes on the mule, balanced on either side. Then he gives one to me, one to Liss, and takes one himself. They got leather straps on them so you can slip your arms through and carry them on your back. In about a half hour, we've loaded a mule with provisions and set out in the gathering darkness. I wonder why we don't just wait until morning, but this Tom seems to know what he's about, so I don't question. We make about five miles downstream before Tom holds up and makes camp. It's a moonlight night, so we can still see to walk, but not that well. I'm right glad to stop before I step in a hole and break a leg.

We each roll up in a buffalo robe to go to sleep. I like a buffalo robe. It's soft and warm, and these have kind of a nice smell. Too bad you have to kill a buffalo to get one, but I don't have much time to mull that over, 'cause I'm asleep in less than a minute.

The sun ain't even up when Tom nudges me with the toe of his boot. "Up with you, girl. We got no time to lose."

I'm up and got my robe rolled up before he can give me a second nudge. Liss hands me two cold biscuits and a piece of beef jerky and we're off down the crick.

Around mid-morning we come to the river Tom calls the Cheyenne. "This is it. This is where I started to follow the crick. They should be downstream not very far."

We turn south, a straggling company of mule, man, woman, girl and dog. Soot's feeling better having his belly full, so he lopes along, tail wagging, behind me. We pass some landmarks I remember, but the whole trip seems much shorter going than coming, and it isn't long after noon that we see them, propped against a tree, one of my old dresses spread over the branches for shade.

"Jeremy!" I run to him and hug him on my knees. He don't hug me back. He's too weak. His face is pale and his eyes look dim, like he can't seem to make me out. He raises a hand in greeting, but that's about all he can do. Sally sits beside him with a glassy-eyed stare. Tom and Liss are quick to minister to them, getting them to drink water and eat a bite or two. Jeremy's ankle is swollen black and blue and green and yellow. I wonder if he'll ever regain the use of it. But Liss goes to the saddle bag and brings out some kind of salve, smears it around his foot and leg, and rips up my old dress to make a bandage. Next, they hoist Jeremy up on the mule's back, but he can barely sit up, so they take turns walking beside him to keep him from falling.

Sally perks up pretty quick with the water and food, so she can walk alone, but not too fast. She still don't want nothing to do with me. Guess she blames me for Obadiah. She might be right.

We trek back to the crick before we make a camp. Tom and Liss seem to know the territory pretty good, and they can make a camp quick as that, but Tom is watchful and never without his gun. I ain't sure just what it is he's so watchful about—could be lots of things—Indians, animals, outlaws. This is the west, so it could be almost anything. Liss feeds us good and then turns to Jeremy. "You got a bad break there, boy," she tells him. "I'm not much for setting bones, but if that heals the way it is, you'll be a cripple."

If Jeremy had any color in his face, it drains at that. He winces. "How far to a real doctor?" he asks.

"'Bout a day to our cabin and another two or three to Rapid." Tom replies. "But we can't go to Rapid with you. You're on your own to get there from our place."

That ain't what Jeremy wanted to hear, but the prospect of being a cripple sounds worse. "You know what to do?" His voice is weak with fear and pain. My heart is breaking for him. All my fault.

Tom nods. "Done it before. It won't be fun, but it's pretty much your only choice."

Liss goes to the saddle bags and brings out a bottle of whiskey. "Here. You'll need this."

Jeremy takes the bottle and pulls out the cork. He raises it to his lips, his eyes finding mine above the bottle. He flashes the cure-all grin, weak, but determined, and takes a deep swig. After about twenty minutes of nips at the bottle, he's out of his senses, and Tom moves in, gives Jeremy a stick to hold between his teeth. He unwraps the cloth from around Jeremy's ankle, takes a good hold of his foot and yanks down with all his might. A scream rends the woods, a bone cracks, the mule skitters, Soot lets out a howl. I cringe at the edge of the firelight. Jeremy's fainted.

While he's out, Liss binds his ankle as tight as she can around two curved sticks to keep it from moving. She covers him up with a blanket and puts a sack of cornmeal under his head. Then we all lie down, wrap ourselves in our buffalo robes, and go to sleep. Sally takes her robe a ways away and lies down by herself.

The next morning, we break camp early and set off along the crick for Tom and Liss's cabin. Jeremy is on the mule again and Sally is still hanging back, but we make our way along in pretty good time. When the shadows lengthen we come into the clearing, glad for the comfort of a roof over our heads. But Jeremy is feverish, and Liss goes into her herb cupboard to make him some tea. I'm feeling so low down over Jeremy, I sneak out after dark and sleep in the stable, where they won't hear me praying to God to save him.

We spend the next three days at their cabin while Jeremy fights his fever, shivering, flailing, and calling out in delirium. Now here we are so near to Deadwood, and I can't even think about my mother. All I can think about is Jeremy and what I've put him through. When the fever finally breaks, I feel like turning back, but I can't get a purchase on back where. Liss tells me Jeremy needs a long time to mend, and suggests maybe I should go on to Deadwood by myself.

"I ain't even sure why I'd be going," I confess. "It don't seem so important to me now."

Liss smiles at that. She and Tom have been real polite about my Calamity Jane story, but I can tell they think it's stuff and nonsense. Tom even allows he knew Jane once a long time ago in a army camp. Says he's not sure I'd want to be her daughter if I knew all about her. A few months ago, that'd have got my back up, but now. ..

I linger in the woods with them for another day, watching Jeremy close, and decide I might as well go on and face whatever it is I have to face. Sally is itching to get to Rapid, where she says she's got friends. She's beyond herself in grief, so I gather up my stuff and some provisions Liss gives me, whistle to Soot, and set out with her. She still ain't talking any more than necessary, but I don't care. I've got my own thoughts to contend with. We follow the crick for a couple of days, all the way to a dirt track that a sign says leads to Rapid—it'll be a welcome sight for footsore travelers. My shoes is wore out, Sally is all the way barefoot, and Soot is about lame, but at least we find people. This ain't like no eastern city, for sure. Mining town. Not very old. Still a long way to go to live up to its name. But a welcome sight for all that.

We barely stumble into town, lost in our minds and weary in our souls. Sally's set on finding her friends, who knew Obadiah, too, so we part company at the edge of town. She ain't even got the gumption to thank me or wish me well. I hug her and tell her I hope she'll feel better soon, but it's like hugging a sack of dirty clothes. Empty.

This town is full of growing pains. Some houses, some tents, a school of sorts, a couple churches, and a passel of saloons. The hotels are more brothel than berth, so I head around the corner off the main street and find a boarding house that ain't fancy but looks clean. I arrange for a room and a bath with money Jeremy gave me.

I'm so weary and sad. I think I got the blues from Sally. Funny, the closer I get to Deadwood, the wormier I feel inside. Like how it is before Christmas. You think on it and think on it, but then when it comes, it don't never measure up to your hopes. That's how I feel about Jane. Scared of what I'll find when I do get there.

I go to my room and unwind my bundle. Everything's still there, but dirty and mildewed from being wet so often. The locket and my double eagle are snug in the toe of my only other pair of shoes. I get them out and look at them for a spell. The only ties I got to anything. The dime novel is in there, too, damp and moldy but still readable— what started me on this quest. I take it out and start reading for about the fiftieth time, but now it seems made up. Kind of silly, like it was wrote for little kids or something. Jane's exploits don't fascinate me like they used to. I put it away, gather up my clothes, and go to wash them in a tub I saw outside the back door. I take off everything but my shift. Don't care who sees me now.

I go down the back stairs and ask the landlady for the loan of her washtub and some soap. These old rags of mine could use a good long soak. I'll be surprised if the washboard don't make shreds of them.

There I am, out in back of the boarding house, scrubbing away, when here comes a young boy about twelve years old wandering by. He stops and watches me for a minute, then sets down on the porch bench to whittle a stick. He don't say nothing, and I just keep scrubbing the clothes.

"You work here now?" he asks after a few minutes.

"No. I'm just passing through. On my way to Deadwood."

"Deadwood?" He gets real excited. "Take me with you? I got a aunt in Deadwood, and I hate this here town. My pa's always losing at cards, and then he beats me 'cause he's mad about it. .. and I'm handy."

"I can't take you away from your pa. But I reckon you *could* run away yourself if you was of a mind to. Couldn't stop you from that."

"Well, if I was to go the same direction as you only just a few steps back, that wouldn't be like you was taking me, would it?"

I stop my scrubbing and look at this boy. He's right handsome for a frontier kid. Brown hair, kind of unruly. A few freckles, and a longish head. When he grins, his brown eyes have a knowing look about them. I detect some mischief there, too, and I like him right off.

"I ain't sayin' you can come with me or not. That's up to you. I'm leaving tomorrow morning, early, but I ain't stayin' there. Just goin' to meet my ma and then I'm back off down the crick I come up on."

"Why? Got somebody waiting for you?" He gives me a knowing grin.

"You might say."

"Why ain't he with you now?"

"Cause he's sick and hurt and can't travel." I'm getting a little irritated with all these questions. "You're a right nosy sort."

"You married to him?"

"No. He's just a friend."

"You been traveling together, I guess you're more than friends by now."

"That ain't none of your concern," I tell him in clipped words. "Come if you want to, or stay. No difference to me."

"Okay. Sorry. Didn't mean to get your back up."

"My back ain't up. You're a little bit cheeky. What's your name, anyway?"

"Harry. What're you gonna do in Deadwood? Your ma live there or what?"

"Maybe you've heard of her. Calamity Jane."

He slaps this thigh and almost doubles over in a fit of laughter. "Heard of her! Everybody in Deadwood knows about Jane! She was the drinkingest woman God ever made!"

"Was? What do you mean was? Did she stop?"

He's still laughing so much his face is red. "Calamity Jane's your ma! Now that's a good one. Who'd ever bed that one, *I'd* like to know!"

By now I feel a urge to slap this little urchin silly, but I step back to the washtub to wring out my clothes. He sets down on the bench and commences to whittle, but every now and then a titter escapes him, and it gets my ire up again.

"She ain't there, you know." He says it like he knows what he's talking about.

"Well, maybe she is and maybe she ain't, but I guess somebody there'll know where to find her. I come this far, so another league or so won't kill me." I haul my wet clothes over to a clothesline strung between the house and a little stable out back. The boy follows me, still whittling on his stick.

"I guess Sister Jennie would know."

"Sister Jennie? Who's she? A nun?"

He haw-haws at that. "Hardly. She's a madam. Friend of my aunt's."

"What's a madam?"

He into laughing again. "Gawd! You don't know nothing, do you? A madam runs a whore house. Jennie has the oldest house in Deadwood. She's retired now, but she still keeps track of her girls. Knows everybody."

I give this Harry-boy a study. "If I let you travel to Deadwood with me, will you take me to meet this Jennie lady?"

"Sure. I just want to get shut of my old man."

Then from around the side of the house comes a mean-looking, rag-tag man about thirty-five, unshaven, and wearing what was once nice clothes, but that's beyond memory.

"There you are, you little bastard! Come here! I been looking all over for you, you good-for-nothing."

He lunges for Harry and barks his shin on my wash tub. He grabs the boy by the shoulder and smacks him across the ear with his open hand. Harry's grin is gone. He looks up at the man, terror in his eyes.

"Pa! Don't hit me, Pa! I ain't done nothing." He struggles to free himself, but the man holds him in an iron grip. "Honest, Pa. I'll be good!"

"You bet you will, you little cur!" His hand lashes out again, catching Harry full in the face. "I told you to stay by the saloon. You know how I hate having to go look for you." He shoves the boy so hard he falls backward into the dirt, blood streaming from his nose.

I step up. "Hey, mister. You got no call to be beating on that boy."

"He's my son. I'll beat him if it suits me."

Harry picks himself up and backs away, wiping his face on his shirt sleeve, and I step up in the man's face. "He ain't done nothing. Leave him be."

The man reaches for the boy again, grabs him by the arm and starts to drag him away. Then he stops jerking on the boy's arm and looks at me kind of dumbfounded. "Who you?" he asks. "Who you to be telling me what I can and can't do? I'll beat him to a pulp if I want."

I step up real close and raise my right foot high and stomp it down on top of his arch like to break it. He yelps in pain and grabs his foot, jumping up and down on the other one. Harry's free, and he takes off running like the wolves was chasing him.

"There," I tell the man. "Serves you right. If you want to beat up on somebody, at least pick somebody who can give you a even fight."

He rears back as if to hit me, but I stand my ground. "Maybe you should think better of it," I tell him and turn on my heel and go into the boarding house. I find young Harry hiding under the steps, so I take him by the arm and drag him up to my room.

"Go see if you can wrangle us up a ride to Deadwood. If you can't, we'll walk. It ain't that far."

"Yes, ma'am." With that he's gone down the steps two at a time. He's back in about fifteen minutes.

"There's a freight wagon leaving at seven in the morning for Deadwood. The driver says he'll take us for nothing long as we sit on the freight

"Right enough. See you in the morning."

Sleep ain't in my fortunes that night. Soot comes up and licks my face, like he can't figure what I'm about, so I pull him close and hug his neck. Come all this way, and now I don't know what to think or what to do. I lie there wondering how it'll be, meeting my Ma, or leastways someone that knows her. Deep down I know I ain't got much to claim her with. If it ain't right, this feeling in my gut, I'll be left without a purpose or a prayer. Soot lies down with a flump on the floor and I turn over on my back and stare at the ceiling for long hours 'til dawn.

In the morning, I bundle up my clothes and look around for young Harry. He don't show, and I wonder if his old man beat him up too bad last night. I'm worried, but when he still ain't showed by seven o'clock, I go find the freight wagon and me and Soot climb up. We head out of town toward the northwest and, just as we pass the last building in Rapid City, a boy comes out of the shadows and hops up on the back of the wagon, big as life. Harry! I sure hope your pa ain't up yet.

Chapter 28

I think that there ride on that there freight wagon is the longest ride I ever had in my life. I feel all giddy inside. Like I can't wait to get there, and like I hope some earthquake comes along to keep me from it. Harry keeps up a constant chatter about this and that, that if I had a flour sack, I'd stuff it in his mouth. He's not a bad kid, but sometimes a body needs quiet to think on things.

I'm thinking, all right. What if she looks at me and laughs? What if she says I ain't hers? What if she says I am? They say she drinks some. What if she's drunk and don't even remember me? What if she says she wishes I'd stayed in Johnstown and she don't want nothing to do with me? What if she ain't even there? In Deadwood, I mean. According to Harry, that's likely. I stare at the track behind and try to keep my feelings from running away with me.

Deadwood ain't much of a town, for sure. Mostly wood and throwed up at angles above the gulch, houses perched on hillsides, sticking out every which way, like crows on a branch. Kind of flimsy and temporary, to my mind. Only two streets, mostly, and even though there's some nice new brick buildings downtown, there's still a lot to remind you of a mining camp. But they got a railroad—two of them, in fact—and even electric lights. It's clear they're striving to be like a big city, 'cept they've still got a ways to go. We get there in mid-afternoon, and Harry takes off running as soon as the wagon stops.

"Harry!" I yell. "Here. Take Soot with you. Bring him back tomorrow." I point to a hotel with a upstairs porch that looks over the main street.

I get down and stretch my legs, go up the front steps of the hotel, and get a room. They's a real bathroom down the hall from my room, with a porcelain tub and a water closet. I ain't never seen the like of that, not even in St. Louis. In my room I open my bundle and shake out my last dress. My second pair of shoes are beyond repair, and I'd like to get new ones to meet my mother in, but since I ain't sure where this is going to take me, I elect to hold onto my money. I take a real long bath and put on my cleanest dress before I go downstairs for supper. I feel real grown up, like a lady of the world, staying all by myself in a hotel and eating in a dining room.

As soon as the sun goes down, things start to liven up in Deadwood. There's piano music coming from more than one saloon, and folks, men mostly, wander around the street yelling at each other and clapping each other on the back. It ain't even Saturday, and they're rowdy as young bulls already. I'm thinking the best place to watch the show is from that upstairs porch, so I git on up there and pull a straight-back chair out of my room to sit on. It's like watching one of them plays that used to come to Johnstown. All kinds of characters, each louder and fuller of brag than the rest. The stores is all open and people are coming and going like it was the middle of the day. I guess miners have to do their business in the evening cause they're working all day.

I go back in the room and decide to wait until morning to go looking for this Jennie lady, but it's hard to stay here in this room waiting. I think about Jeremy. Wish he were here. Wonder how he's getting on. Suddenly I find myself crying. Over what? I don't know. This feels for all the world like the end of something, but I can't say what. A dream, maybe. More than one dream, maybe. A knock on the door interrupts my tears. I wipe my eyes and open it to Harry with a envelope in his hand.

"It's from Jennie, the madam I told you about. I think it's a in-vite. I told you I could make a connection for you."

"Thank you, Harry."

He looks around the room and then notices my tear-streaked face. "Guess I come at a bad time, huh?"

"It's all right, Harry. I was just thinking about my. .. uh, friend. Did your aunt greet you? Is Soot all right?"

"Yes'm. He's fine. My aunt loves dogs, so there ain't no trouble there." He gives me a polite bow and turns toward the door. "My aunt's got supper on."

When he's gone I sit down on the bed, trying to get my thoughts sorted out. I wish I could go for a walk, but this ain't the kind of town a lady goes for a walk in alone after dark. A lady. Me. Some stretch.

I light the lamp and open the envelope Harry brought. It's a invite to come visit tomorrow at two o'clock. My hands are shaking, holding the card in the lamplight. I feel so alone and far from home— now where's that, pray tell? Not the convent in Johnstown, for sure. Not in some tent meeting with the likes of Valoreous Cates, and not in some flea-bitten circus. I'm pretty sure Deadwood ain't going to be home, neither. Nor Granny's cottage in Ohio, or Dr. Beckwith's house in St. Louis. Just wish I had *somebody*. That brings Jeremy back to mind, but it ain't really a comfort. Just a uncertainty, like always.

I've known for a while now that the chances of finding my mother are slim and getting slimmer. Funny. I never *really* thought I'd find her, but it kept me going all the same. Now here I am on the doorstep, and I feel the hope springing up again. Maybe this Miss Jennie will know something—will even welcome me as Jane's long lost baby girl. No matter what anybody says, I ain't ready to let go of that yet.

I step out on the upstairs porch and study the street below. It's a dirt street with wooden sidewalks under the store roofs. It's getting dark, and the moon is rising over Mount Moriah. Harry pointed that out to me on the way into town. Said Wild Bill Hickok, a Wild West gun slinger, was buried there. Supposed to be a friend of Calamity Jane. I get out the locket with the picture and the lock of hair in it, and hold it real tight, like holding it will make it what I want it to be.

Somewhere down the street there's more laughter and piano tinkling. The air smells like dry summer. I watch a Wells Fargo stage come around the corner and stop in front of the office. Four people get out, two men and two women. They look wore out from traveling, and they get their trunks handed down and head straight for the hotel I'm watching from. Below me a man crosses the street, head down, holding a baby. Strange for a man to be all alone holding a baby, especially in Deadwood. I cough and the man looks up—and I gasp in recognition.

"Robert! Robert Quinn! It's me, Nell! Where's Addie?"

I turn and run through the room, out the door and down the stairs. Robert is standing in the public room of the hotel when I get there, holding the baby, wrapped in a dirty blanket. He looks even more gaunt and wild eyed than I remember. His clothes are all dirty and tattered, and he ain't seen a razor in many a day.

"Where's Addie?" I repeat, looking around behind him.

"Gone."

"Gone? Gone where?"

"Dead. Gone with God." His voice breaks with the words.

The baby peers out from the bundle of soiled blankets, and it don't take me long to figure out it needs some attention. I reach for the child. "When? How?"

"Just after Christmas. Wounded Knee. The damn soldiers."

"Oh, Robert, no!" A picture of Addie runs through my mind. Beautiful, pregnant Addie, in love with Robert and her people. "When was the baby born?"

"Just a few weeks before. Addie had her with her. Her and her mother. I was gone off trying to round up some strays and bring them back to the reservation for the winter." His eyes are bitter, and I understand why. I heard about Wounded Knee.

"I didn't get back until two days later, and I found Addie thrown up on a pile of frozen corpses. My beautiful angel, Addie, frozen stiff, staring at nothing. A poor old Sioux woman had the baby. Picked her up from under her mother's dead body."

"Her? She's a little girl?" I'm flooded with emotion—something I can't name—for a poor motherless little girl child.

The baby smiles at me and reaches a little brown hand out of the blankets.

Robert nods. "Her name's Nell."

"Nell! After me?"

He nods again.

"How kind of Addie."

He stands there silent, brooding, full of grief, fingering the rough blanket that holds his child. His eyes have a haunted, far away look. He ain't the same Robert who come looking for Addie last summer. I can't name it, but it ain't just grief. It's giving up. It's a "just let me die, too" kind of look.

After a while he speaks, his voice so full of emotion he chokes on the words. "So beautiful and so good. I should have left her in St. Louis. If I'd done that, she'd still be with us." He raises a hand to his forehead. "Why? Why did they have to be so brutal? Women and old men. Babies. Why?" His shoulders shake with grief.

I ain't one for hanging on to what might have been, and I don't want to go down there in that grief hole with him. Right now I can see this baby needs a mama. "What're you going to do, Robert? With the baby, I mean?"

He shakes his head. "I don't know. I can barely keep myself together, let alone take care of her. I had an Indian woman for a while, but she walked out of the lodge one morning and never came back. Probably died of the cold."

"What are you doing to keep yourself?" My mind always turns to practical matters when people get helpless.

"Trapping. Hunting. I thought to go back south and try to gather up supplies for the Indians. There's more sympathy for them since Wounded Knee."

I want to tell him, "Don't count on it, Robert. Most folks away from here ain't even heard of Wounded Knee, or if they have, they think it's heroic what the soldiers done." but I don't say nothing. I sit down in a chair there in the main downstairs room of the hotel and reach for the baby. Robert hands her to me and sits down in a bent hickory rocker across.

"Hello, Nell," I say to her. She lights up, her dark eyes dancing, and struggles to get free of the dirty blanket. She's a mighty pretty baby—looks for all the world like her mama, and less like a Indian than you'd think. But then she's only a quarter Indian, so I guess she's more white than anything. Irish white, too. Robert's Irish, and so was Addie's pa.

I snuggle my nose in her neck, and she lets out a giggle. My heart is gone the moment I touch her.

Robert watches us nuzzle and coo, no reaction from him. He's so distraught he can't even take any joy in his child. Then he asks,

"Nell, I hate to ask, but—Addie would have wanted this. Could you take her? And raise her, I mean? I don't know what to do with her. The Indians are too poor to take her in, and most white women don't want to be bothered."

Another poor, unwanted baby girl. I wonder how many of them there are—how many throughout history. My heart aches for her. I rearrange the rough bundle, blanket torn and smelling like pee, clothes even worse. Men are such bumblers. Robert sits watching me, waiting for an answer to his plea.

"Yes, Robert. I will raise my sister's child. You wait here while I get some things for her."

I hand the baby back, rush upstairs and rummage through my bundle looking for my double eagle. I grab it and run back down. Robert is sitting in the rocking chair with Little Nell, while she plays contentedly, chewing on a wooden darning bulb.

"I'll be right back," I shout as I head out the door, hoping it ain't too late to get to the mercantile.

I run down the street looking on both sides for a store. There's one. I run up on the wooden sidewalk and dash in, breathless. "Where's the baby stuff?" I ask.

The store man jerks his head to the rear, and I go back and pick out blankets, nightgowns, undershirts and a whole bundle of diapers.

"You don't need those," says a voice over my shoulder. It's the store man, followed me back. "Most folks just use old rags."

"Not for this baby," I say. "You got any bottles for milk?"

"Bottles?" The man looks confused. "Most women. .."

"I ain't most women," I tell him. "So where's the nursing bottles?"

Never mind. Maybe Robert has something for that. "You got any cornstarch? Or scented talcum powder? How about a length of muslin for a towel?"

I gather my purchases and hand him the double eagle. I can see Granny smiling at me all the way from Ohio. Good way to spend your double eagle, huh, Granny? I wait for my change and am out the store and up the street before the store man barely finishes wrapping my goods.

Robert is still sitting there in that chair, but Baby Nell is sleeping on his chest. He looks wore out and sad. I doubt giving her up is really what he wants, it's just that he's too wrought up to know what he wants, let alone what's best for her. I make a silent vow that he'll never be sorry for giving her to me. I reach over and pick her up off his chest and shoulder my other bundle. Without another word I climb the stairs to my room.

Robert stands and watches me. His face and his posture tell it all. He raises a hand as though to wave good-bye and brings it down to wipe his eye. He stands there, prayerful, for a minute while I watch him from the balustrade. Then he moves away into the dark streets of Deadwood.

Upstairs, I lay the baby down on the bed and commence to unwrap her. She awakens and stretches, her little brown feet drawn up against her wrinkled under things. I carry her down to the kitchen and ask for some warm water and a basin to bathe her in. The cook is a fat, black woman, who smiles knowingly and fills a basin with warm water and even carries it upstairs for me. I follow with the baby.

She ain't a fat baby, but she's mighty cheerful, even with her nap interrupted. I bathe her and wash her hair. She's got a powerful lot of it—black, thick, and standing straight up. Someday it'll shine like black gold—like her mama's. I powder her and dress her in her new clothes, and she gurgles and talks to me like she's knowed me all her life. I can see Addie in her bright little eyes, and I hug her to me and sing to her.

"Baby, I make you this promise. I will tell you all about your mama, so when you grow up, you'll feel like you knowed her."

She takes a little milk from a spoon I got from the kitchen and curls up against me like she's sleepy. I take a drawer out of the dresser and lay her down in it on a pillow. She turns on her side, puts her thumb in her mouth and drifts off to sleep. I sit watching her for a long time, holding my breath so she keeps on breathing. Joy creeps over me, filling me with its promise. I ain't alone no more.

Chapter 29

Little Nell sleeps through the night, and in the morning I take her downstairs to the hotel man and ask him if he's married. He nods. "Is your wife here?"

Another nod.

"You got any kids?"

This time he laughs. "Kids? Hell, yes. We got a passel of 'em. Whatcha need?"

"Some lessons."

"Emma!" he roars. "Em! Come on in here. Somebody to see ya."

A short, sturdy woman pushes a curtain aside and enters behind the desk. "Mornin'," she tells me.

I'm quick about explaining my situation, and she's more than kind to help me. She gives me some oatmeal to start with, already cooked for her own brood. "Sweeten it up with a bit of honey, and she'll take it right down. I think I got a nursing bottle around here someplace from my last one."

When Baby Nell and I return to the hotel room, her with a full tummy and me with the satisfaction of knowing more than I knowed when I woke up, Harry is there, sitting on the chair by the window, looking at me with a questioning frown. "Where'd you get that?" he asks.

"It's Addie's baby, my half Indian friend from St Louis. She died at Wounded Knee. Her husband, Robert, gave the baby to me. Said Addie would have wanted it."

Harry screws up his face in a scowl. Injun baby? What you want with a Injun baby?"

"Her mother was my friend. She needs a mother now, and I'm it," I tell him. "Besides, what's wrong with a Injun baby?"

"Grow up to be a Injun, that's what."

"Where do you get ideas like that? People are people. A baby's a baby, and this one needs me."

"Okay. Okay. I'm just letting you know how folks'll be. Not everyone likes Injuns."

I want to smack him right there, but I guess he's just spouting what he's seen and heard.

"I might need you to watch her while I go see that Jennie woman this afternoon."

He makes a pitiful face. "Better not. I wouldn't know which end to tend to if she cried. Take her with you. Jennie won't mind. All women love babies." That's a man for you. Useless as pocket lint.

My visit with Jennie has faded in the face of my new responsibilities. I root around in my bundle for the locket and get myself and Baby Nell ready early. Harry has let himself out, so I start out down the street looking for him 'cause I ain't got no notion of where this Jennie's house is. Harry ain't nowhere around, so I stop by a milliner's shop to get a sunbonnet for Little Nell and ask.

"Jennie?" the lady simpers. "Oh, yes. Jennie. Well, I wouldn't know, but I've heard her house is just around the corner on Gold Street." She gives me my change and eyes me like she thinks I'm a new girl looking for work.

I carry Little Nell around the corner to a house that sits up kind of high with a big, wide front porch and fancy, fringed window shades pulled down against the light. I go up and knock at the door. A young girl answers—right about my age. I tell her my name and that I'm here to talk to Miss Jennie. She takes me into a real fancy parlor with big furniture and tables covered with fringy cloths and lots of pictures hanging out from wires hooked to a wooden rim around near the ceiling, and all kinds of vases and figurines and flowers setting everywhere. It's about the fanciest room I've ever been in. Even richer than Dr. Beckwith's house. Everything's velvet and lace and doilies. I wait, balancing Little Nell on my lap. She grabs the fringe on the table cloth and yanks it to her mouth. I have my hands full tussling to get it away from her.

It's about fifteen minutes before Miss Jennie comes in. She smiles and comes right up and shakes my hand and talks real nice to Little Nell. She's all dressed up in a dark red gown, with her hair piled up high, and she's got rings on most of her fingers, and ear rings and necklaces and bracelets to throw away.

She turns to me. "Now, what was it you wanted to see me about, dear?"

"It was about. .." Here I am a couple thousand miles into my trek, and I'm tongue-tied. "My ma." I say. "I think Calamity Jane might be her—er—my ma that is. You know her?"

"Indeed I do. Come. Let's move into my office and have some tea and biscuits while we talk."

Her office is as plain as the rest of the house is fancy. All business here. A desk with lots of compartments, each neatly labeled. A waste basket, two chairs, an oil lamp. No clutter. She offers me the straight upright chair and takes the big, old, tilting, oak armchair on wheels for herself. She picks up a talking piece and says, "Alice, please bring in some tea and biscuits for my guest and me."

Then she leans back in her chair and looks me over real good. "What makes you think Jane is your mother?"

I tell her about being left at the convent and not having any roof in my mouth and running away and the dime novels—all of it. "Most folks think I'm crazy to think it, but I'm *sure* she's my ma. Got to be. Ain't no two ways about it." My old zest is re-awakened.

I dig down into Baby Nell's bundle and take out the locket. "Here. This here was pinned to my blanket when I was left at the convent. I figure that's my pa. You recognize him?"

I sit breathless while she studies the locket picture. Her brow wrinkles, and she turns it this way and that to get the best light. "Can't say as I do. But then I didn't know every man Jane knew, so. .."

"Do you think she'll be glad to see me?"

Alice brings in the tea, and Miss Jennie pours. She's still pretty, even though there's lines in her face. You can tell she was once a beauty.

"I think Jane would be delighted to know she has a daughter, especially one as bright and self reliant as you. But Jane's not here now. She's been gone for a long time—a dozen years or more. Last I heard she was moving around the railroad towns in Montana. Jane don't stay put long." She hands the locket back to me.

"Well, could you get word to her that I'm here looking for her?"

She leans toward me and takes Little Nell from my lap. She cuddles the baby, smiles at her, and tickles her under her chin. Baby Nell gurgles back, just like they're having a real conversation. Miss Jennie hugs her and spreads out her blanket on the floor. Then she lays her down, gives her a little wooden dog to play with, and comes back and sits down right close to me. She leans in and takes my hand in hers.

"Nell. Is that what you said your name was? Nell?"

"Yes'm."

"Jane and I were friends years ago, but I've never known anything about her having a daughter. Not a real one anyway."

"What do you mean?"

"Well, Jane makes things up. Lots of things. Ever since they started writing about her in the dime novels. Some of her stories have a tiny bit of truth to them, but most are just things she'd *like* to be true. So she's claimed to have a child more than once."

"That's it! That's what I heard, too. And I'm just about the right age. See? Don't that man in the locket look just like someone you knew back a long time ago?"

She casts her eyes down and shakes her head, ever so slightly. "I knew Jane pretty well in those days, and, unless she kept you under the bed day and night and had the cat take care of you when she went on a week-long bender, I never saw any evidence of your existence."

I feel the bottom slip out of my hopes. Just like that, everything I hoped and planned dwindles away. Now I feel empty and alone. Nothing to hang my hopes on. Regret over putting Jeremy through all this. I want to cry, but I can't let this Jennie woman see that. I get down on the floor beside the baby and make like I'm tending to her. Then I wipe my eyes where Jennie can't see. "But, couldn't you just ask her? Couldn't I just meet her?" My voice quavers. Gives me away.

Miss Jennie is real kind. She reaches over and pats me on the shoulder. "No, dear. She'd claim you. She'd parade you all over with a sign on your back: Calamity Jane's Daughter. She'd make up outlandish tales about you and her snagging outlaws. And she'd break your heart—and you hers."

She picks up a long, gold taper, holds it over a lamp, and lights a slim cigar. She blows smoke up into the room, and her bracelets jingle when she sucks it in. "Jane's a good person, a fine human being. You could be proud to call her your mother on her good days. But she's a drunk and a liar, and she'll grab onto anyone who tickles her fancy and make them her own. Trouble is, people get tired of old drunks. Man or woman. And the drink is more important than anyone or anything else, so the glitter always wears off." She lets out a long stream of smoke. "I'd advise you to go back to wherever you came from and forget about Jane. Even if she was your mother, you'd be better off not knowing, and so would she."

I sit there bewildered, foolish, disappointed. "I guess I knew it wasn't true, but it kept me going, made me think I was somebody." I struggle with the words. It hurts to admit I've been a fool.

Miss Jennie holds my hand and smiles at me. "Looks to me like you have a greater purpose now," she says, looking down at Baby Nell.

"Oh, she ain't mine. I mean, she is, but her ma's dead. Wounded Knee. Her pa gave her over to me. I'm gonna be her ma."

"Gave her to you, just like that?"

"Me and her ma was friends back in St. Louis. Her ma was Lakota Sioux, but her pappy's white."

"So, now what? Will you settle here?

"No, ma'am. I got friends back in St. Louis. They knew her mama, too. We'll be welcome with them."

She hands me a hanky. I wipe away the last of my tears. Talking about Baby Nell pushes the hurt down.

"You got the money to get back to St. Louis?"

"Not anymore. I bought stuff for the baby." I look down at Nell, drifted off to sleep in a patch of sunshine on the office floor.

Jennie opens a desk drawer and takes out a deep blue velvet reticule. She reaches in and takes out not one, but two double eagles and hands them to me. "Think of this as a gift from your mother," she tells me. "She'd want you to have it. Now get on back to St Louis and never look back. You have a good life ahead of you. I know this."

She rises with a smile and I know the meeting is over.

"Um, could I stay here until she wakes up?" I ask, looking at the sleeping baby.

"Of course." She opens a door and disappears into the rest of the house. I sit there on the straight chair, fingering the two double eagles, thinking on the way things are. I know what to do now. It's plain as the nose on my face, as Sister Mary Patrick would say. Only one more task before me.

Chapter 30

Back at the hotel, Harry's taking a nap in a chair in the lobby while he waits for me. He sits up and grins when I give his shoulder a shake.

"Well?"

"Well, I guess she ain't my ma." I say it quietly, evenly. "Jennie don't think so, anyway, and she'd know."

He studies my face for a sign of sadness or self-pity, but I left that at Jennie's. He stands up and stretches. "So, what now?"

"Guess I'll head back down to Rapid and on down the crick to find my friend Jeremy again. You stayin' here?"

He screws up his face in a boyish sneer. "My aunt don't want me around. She's afraid my pa'll come looking for me and beat us both up. Don't 'spose I could come with you, do you?"

I smile. "Wouldn't mind if you did. You could use some grooming, and I could use some help with a dog and a baby."

Harry's face lights up. "It's a deal, then." He offers his hand for a shake.

"Might as well gather up our stuff, buy some food and get going." It's mid-afternoon, and if we're lucky we can bum a ride on another freight wagon bound for Rapid. Harry takes the lead on that. With Soot on a rope, he steps right up to the driver and says, "Give a kid a ride, sir? Help you unload in Rapid."

The teamster gives him a nod and Harry motions to me to climb on.

"Hey, wait a minute. I just meant you, not the whole damn family!"

"It's okay, mister. They won't be no trouble." And he and Soot bound up in the driver's seat, just like they belong there. That easy, we leave Deadwood behind us. Deadwood and half of my dreams. The other half is waiting in a cabin by a crick below Rapid.

Getting back to Jeremy is my only goal left, and I wish I could move that old freight wagon faster. It bumps along a rugged track, pulled by a team of eight oxen. Ain't nothing fast about it, but we do get to Rapid before dark. Harry stays to help the freighter unload, as promised, and I look around for a camp site. I find one along the river and wait for him. He'll know where to look. Jeremy'll wonder what possessed me to take charge of a twelve-year-old boy, but I know what it's like to be alone and unwanted, so I'm an easy touch. Besides, he's a good hand to help, and he's company.

Harry's a bright boy and kind of funny. I get a kick out of him making his way by wheeling and dealing. I think he'll be all right wherever he ends up. If Jeremy thinks I've gone daft by picking up with Harry, what'll he think when he sees this baby? He didn't know Addie, so there's no connection for him. I sit down by the river to think about what happens next. What I want to happen is for Jeremy to love me and want to marry me and think it's fine for us to have a ready-made family, but I know in my heart that ain't the way it's going to be. If Jeremy doesn't want to settle down with just me, he sure ain't gonna want a baby and a kid. It appears to me I've sealed my fate.

Getting back to Tom and Liss's place ain't easy, even with Harry's help. I get me one of them papoose things the Indians carry their babies in, but Little Nell wants no part of it. She hollers and screams and twists herself sideways every time I try to put her in it. Guess she ain't been used to that. I end up carrying her in a bundle slung over my shoulder, and, even though she ain't very big for seven months, she's a load to carry. Harry spells me every once in a while, but it ain't enough to soothe my aching back. We're two days trekking down from Rapid, but finally I see the rugged little cabin beside the crick and I make a whoop and run for it.

I been gone almost a week, and I expect to see Jeremy up and hobbling around, but I don't. I go up to the door and rap on it, but there's no answer. I go around and look in the side window, but it's too dark to tell if there's anybody there.

"Just walk in," counsels Harry. "They probably just went berry picking. They won't mind."

I follow his lead and we enter the cabin, letting our eyes get used to the dark. Then I make out Jeremy lying on the only bed in the place. "Jeremy! It's me, Nell. Jeremy! How are you?"

He barely moves, even though I'm almost yelling. "Jeremy!"

I can barely see him in the dim light of the cabin, but I'm scared already. He's skinny and gaunt looking, and so weak he can hardly say my name. "Nell."

I look around the cabin and don't see any signs of life. "Where's Tom and Liss?"

"Don't know. Gone. Three, four days ago." It takes all his energy to get it out.

"What? They just went off and left you? Why?"

Harry stands in the cabin doorway with Soot on a rope and Little Nell in his arms. He looks spent, so I move to take her and find some place safe to put her down.

"Soldiers," Jeremy whispers. "Soldiers came and took Tom. Said he was a deserter. Liss went mad and tried to shoot them, so they took her, too."

I'm going in three directions, getting Jeremy water, seeing to the baby, directing Harry to gather wood and bring in more water. The cabin is well stocked, so I manage to bake us some biscuits and fry up some bacon. By the time we're ready to eat, Little Nell has fallen asleep, giving me welcome relief to talk to Jeremy. It takes me about a half hour to give him the whole story of Harry, Little Nell, and my talk with Sister Jennie. He's still too weak to take it all in, and I elect to wait until morning to make it clear. I'm exhausted, and I fall into the bed beside Jeremy and sleep like the dead.

Morning brings sunshine and raises my spirits until I get a chance to take stock of Jeremy. He's a ghost. I get him up out of the bed and Harry helps me get him outside. He's nothing but a skeleton, can't even walk on his own. I set him down under a tree and go back in and open up the cabin as much as I can. I bring out all the buffalo robes and spread them in the sun. Then I gather up all the blankets and pillows off the bed and tell Harry to fill the big, oak wash tub. There's bugs and all kinds of vermin crawling on them. Jeremy has big welts on his back and legs from bug bites.

I build a fire in the middle of the yard and Harry helps me make a tripod out of oak saplings to hang the kettle from. I figure to scald the daylights out of those bugs. Once the water is hot, I load the blankets in and stir them with a long pole. I find some lye soap in the cabin and use it without sparing. I'm run almost ragged taking care of Jeremy and the baby, even with Harry's help. And behind all this activity is the deep fear that Jeremy's too far gone. That he won't get better. I put my head down and don't think about it. I can't. I've got to fix him.

I send Harry out with a gun to shoot some squirrel or rabbit. Anything to make a broth. He brings back one of each and I direct him to skin them and gut them and I put some water in the fireplace kettle to ready it for the squirrel today and the rabbit tomorrow. The root cellar yields some potatoes, two carrots and a head of cabbage. Their spring garden is just coming into itself, so there'll be vegetables to spare for a while.

Meantime, Jeremy just sits leaning back against the tree, barely moving, barely seeing what's going on. I think he must have picked up some disease worse than a broken ankle, but I ain't got an idea what it could be. I just wish Liss would show up. I know enough about how they treat deserters to know it will go hard with Tom, but I hope they let her go and she finds her way home.

For the next three days, we work to clean up the cabin, get rid of the bugs and find food. Harry steps up to the role of the hunter and fisherman, and I manage all right taking care of Jeremy and the baby. I tie a rope around her ankle and the other end to a tree near the door, so she can crawl in and out. She gets uncommon dirty, but at least I know where she is. Most of the time, Jeremy don't say a word. Just lies there watching me or the baby or both. He don't ask me any questions, and I ain't sure how much of what I've told him has sunk in. I just keep feeding him and letting him sleep and waiting.

A whole week is out when one morning I'm outside feeding Nell her breakfast and Jeremy appears in the doorway, hobbling on a crutch that Tom made for him. He still looks a fright—dirty, ragged and torn. I'm struck by the memory of the fine looking dandy he was, and by the knowledge that it was me got him into this state.

"Jeremy! Don't try to do too much now. Let me help you out into the yard."

He lifts his head in a weak nod and waits until I get there. He leans on my shoulder, and we cross the yard to a nice shady spot where there's some grass under the tree. He seems alert now, and my hopes rise with every breath he takes.

"Where's Tom?" he asks.

"The soldiers took him. Don't you remember? You told us that."

He nods vaguely. "Oh, yeah. I remember. Who's that?" He tilts his head in Harry's direction.

I tell him as much about Harry as I think he can take in. Then he sits quiet for a long time. I let him sit there while I tend to the baby, checking back every few minutes to be sure he's all right. He don't feel feverish no more. Just looks like the wrath of God.

Every day after that he eats more and seems to gain strength. We harvest the garden and wait for Liss to show up, but there's no hope in Tom's case. No wonder they liked living so far away from other people. Summer moves along, and I start to wonder how long it will be before Jeremy can travel. The swelling in his ankle has gone down, leaving a big bump on the outside that'll likely be there forever, but he can move it ever so little, and that makes me hope he'll be able to walk without a limp. Thank Tom for that.

I calculate it must be August before Jeremy can walk on his own, and then very careful. It's almost that long before his mind clears and he can make sense of what's happened. That's when he asks me about my ma.

"Well, you were right all along. She ain't my ma. Miss Jennie was right sure of that, and she ought to know."

He looks close at my face to see how I'm taking it, but all that has faded in the face of my new responsibilities. "I don't feel bad about it. I knew it was a dumb idea, but it kept you and me together for a long time."

He smiles. "And here we are, still."

"You up to a bath in the crick?" I ask, not wanting to pursue that subject just yet.

"Sure. I feel like I could shed this skin and grow a new one," he laughs.

I tell Harry to look after Little Nell and I gather some clean rags to use for towels. Then we grab hold of one another and stumble our way down to the crick. The water is cold as ice, turn you blue in a minute, but Jeremy don't seem to mind. He strips off his clothes without a blink at me, and I help him sit down on a rock with just his feet in while I undress, too. Then I step into the deeper water and ease myself down beside him, and he moves off his rock into my arms. He ain't very heavy, and the cold water seems to brighten him up. I wash him all over, and he takes a turn at me, but he's still too weak to do much of a job of it. It's enough to get my juices running, though, and I look up at him and smile.

"Want me to wash your hair?"

"Sure could use it," he answers. "And a shave after, if you please."

I'm downright joyful to be so close to him and have him getting better, so I take my time washing his hair. He lies back in my arms, his head against my breasts. I'm beyond joy.

"Let's get out and dry off." I feel like I'm above the edge of a cliff, ready to soar and ride the currents like an eagle, my heart alive with the joy of it.

When Jeremy stands, I look, expecting to see that he's interested in more, but no. He follows my gaze down his front, then looks back at me with a look of apology. "Sorry, Nell."

The truth slowly dawns on me. Jeremy ain't like other men. I always knew that—he's kinder and more genteel. But I get it now. How he's different, I mean. I heard about men like him—men who don't care much for girls. I don't get it, but there's a lot I don't get. I rise and grab a clean cloth for a towel and hand him one. We both feel better for the bath and we get out and spread our towels on the grass. We lie down, side by side, and Jeremy is the first to talk.

"I guess you know how it is now, huh, Nell?"

"Guess I do."

"I'm sorry. I know you wanted more from me, but I can't be what I'm not."

"You always been like this?" I ask.

"Yes. Always."

"That why you got beat up in Pittsburgh and put in jail in St Louis?"

He sighs. "Yes, Nell, that's why. Why I left home so early. Why I keep moving—avoid letting myself get entangled."

"Oh. Well, then, why did you stay with me?"

"Because in my own way, I love you."

That brings tears to my eyes. "I love you, too, Jeremy. Ever since I picked you off the river bank on the Conemaugh."

"I know." His voice is so gentle; it makes the tears flow free. "I knew then. I never wanted to hurt you. Never. You're the closest thing to a sister, mother, friend I've ever had. I stayed because I thought you needed protection while you ran all over creation looking for your mother."

I roll over on my stomach and look into his eyes. "You still love me after all this?"

"Yes, Nell, I do. I'd do it all again."

"Even the bad parts?"

"Even the bad parts."

"So where do we go from here?" I ask.

He sits up and pulls on his shirt over skinny ribs, bones sticking out everywhere. "I guess this is where we part. You've got your life." He nods in the direction of Harry and the baby. "And I've got my travels."

The words go through me like a knife. First one dream dies, then the other.

"Why? Where you going?"

"San Francisco. Then maybe Australia. It's a big world, and I want to see as much of it as I can. For someone like me, it's safer to keep moving than to stay in one place too long."

I get up off the towel and start getting dressed. "Now that I have a baby to care for, I can't go running off with you."

"I know, but you have a great life ahead of you. You've got a lot of people who love you back in St Louis. Everyone there will be happy to help raise Addie's baby, and who knows? Dr Beckwith might even turn Harry into a doctor."

"Yeah, but. .."

"And then there's Andrew, just waiting for you to come back so he can persuade you to marry him."

"How do you know that?"

His face breaks into one of those smiles that lights up the sky. "Anyone in his right mind could tell that just by the way he looked at you when I took you away in St Louis."

I lie back and mull that over for a while. I like Andrew. I really do. And here is Jeremy setting me free so I can learn to love again. We'll see. Maybe it will be Andrew. Maybe not. But it's not important for now. For now, I just want to spend every possible second with Jeremy until the inevitable parting of the ways.

Another two weeks goes by with no sign of Liss, and I worry for her but can't see a way to get in touch. Jeremy is mending nicely, and anxious to get moving. I know that means I'll have to move, too. So one evening we pack up our stuff, which ain't much anymore, and plan how we'll go to get to Rapid. I can get a train to St Louis from there, and Jeremy can go wherever it is he's drawn to. Denver, he says now. Then San Francisco. They got trains all over now. You can get just about any place on a train.

I leave a note for Liss in case she ever comes back, and we lock up the cabin and go. Rapid is two days walk, but we get there with little trouble, and Jeremy ain't long in finding him a bath and a shave. The next is a whole new suit of clothes, and before my eyes he's transformed into the handsome dandy I fell for back on the Conemaugh. My first, last and forever impression of Jeremy is, he's beautiful.

We spend one last night in a hotel, Harry and Soot in a downstairs room next to the kitchen and me, Jeremy and Little Nell upstairs. I'm glad for one last chance to pour my heart out to Jeremy.

"I been thinking on what you said that night at the cabin and about this here little one and I guess the best place for both of us is back in St. Louis. Al and Mrs. Al would make fine grandparents."

"And Andrew?"

I bite my lip and look into his eyes. "Maybe." I say. "Maybe."

He enfolds me in his arms, and I enjoy a moment I know won't come again.

"When will you go?" he asks, his voice rough.

"Tomorrow. Might as well get back and get the baby settled. She's been tossed around enough, and Harry needs a place he can call home. I bet Al and Mrs. Al would welcome a son, too. Anyway, how could I handle the baby and Soot without help?"

Jeremy grins and hugs me tight.

We spend our last night together as we have so many others. Snuggled up like spoons, Jeremy's face in my hair. I wake often to tears, but then I reach over the side of the bed and feel Little Nell's soft breathing on my hand, and my tears dry up.

The morning comes too soon, and Jeremy is up and about while I care for the baby. He leaves and comes back with the train schedule. The next train east leaves at ten o'clock. That's quick, but I call it a mercy. The longer I stay near him, the harder it will be to leave.

"You go buy the tickets," I tell him, and hand him the two double eagles.

"Where'd these come from?"

"Just say my mother gave them to me."

He grins.

"Better round up Harry, too. And Soot."

I take my time dressing little Nell and packing her things in her own little bundle. I keep talking to her to keep myself from thinking about what's coming. It ain't long before Jeremy's back with Harry and Soot. He hands me the train tickets—all the way to St. Louis—and the change from my double eagles.

"This feels like more change than I should get," I say, examining the handful of coins.

"Call it a gift from a friend," Jeremy says.

We troop out of the hotel and walk the block or so to the station, my heart pounding in my chest. I carry the baby, Harry handles Soot and Jeremy follows with our bundles. The train is setting there, puffing steam and smoke, and Jeremy helps us into the car and ties Soot at the back. Soot just lays down to sleep. He's been on a train before. This is old stuff for him. Harry's so excited he can hardly sit still. In fact, he can't. He's up and down, opening and closing the windows, testing the seats, checking how to pass from one car to the other. A man comes through with a basket of rolls and butter, and Harry, hungry all the time, asks me if he can have one.

My eyes are on Jeremy. He stands beside me, his hand on my shoulder. "This is a good thing you're doing, Nell. Life is going to be good for you."

My eyes fill up on me, try as I might not to let them. Jeremy leans down and whispers in my ear. "You are beautiful and you are loved. Don't ever forget that."

The conductor comes to the door. "All off but the paying passengers," he calls. The train starts chugging real loud, slow at first then faster, and Jeremy steps back, still holding my hand. His fingertips linger on mine until he has no choice but to jump off the moving train. Then he runs alongside for a piece, waving and smiling that smile. I watch him fade away through my tears.

By afternoon, Little Nell is napping and Harry has made friends with the conductor and is following him on his rounds. I sit and watch the world go by, remembering how hard it was to cross this country after we lost Obadiah. I feel peace come over me. I've learned a lot.

In all this quest to find my mother, I've found me a lot more—a granny, an uncle, a ma and pa, a sister, a daughter and two brothers—one older, one younger. Oh, yes. A brother. I will always love you, Jeremy. Always. For what you taught me and what we learned together about love.

What I learned about love is this: love is where you find it, and you need to grab on and hold on tight 'cause it may not be forever. And one other thing: it's better to *be* a mother than to *have* a mother. Least that's what *I* think.

***

The train puffs into the St. Louis station. Little Nell is restless. I don't blame her none. Trains is for grownups, for sure. But we made it. Much easier with Harry to help me. He leads Soot off the train, looking a little unsure of this big city. He gives me a hand down, and we stand on the platform while I search my purse for a coin to pay for a wagon to take us home. Then Soot into barking and wagging his tail, pulling on the rope. I look up and see them. Al and Mrs. Al, all decked out in their Sunday best, and Dr. Beckwith standing a little aside, beaming as much as they are. Behind them, holding a big bouquet of daisies, stands Andrew Morgan. How did they know? Who told them I was coming home? Then that beautiful smile flashes across my memory, and I know.

Afterword

1900

Bear Valley, Wisconsin

The post comes late this morning, almost eleven. There's a letter from Harry—all complaining about how hard he's studying to become a doctor, and what a hard taskmaster Dr. Beckwith is. I smile at the memory of my sore teeth. I know all about that. Dr. B. is thinking about retiring. Wants Andrew to come back to St. Louis to take over his practice. Not likely, since Andrew is the only doctor for half of Richland County—well, the only good one, at any rate.

The other mail is a package—small—like a letter, only sewn into a canvas envelope, the ends sealed with careful stitches, the flap glued tightly in place. There's a bulge in the middle, so it's more than a letter. Dull gray and worn, like it's been a long time coming. It's addressed to me—Mrs. Andrew Morgan -- Bear Valley, Wisconsin—in neat, careful script. There's no postmark, or if there was it's worn off. I hold it in my hands for a long time, study it, turn it over, run my fingers along the stitches. I knew who it's from. The hand is familiar. I've had many letters over the years, but this one is different. I know it's the last.

I'm in no hurry to open it. I sit on the porch in the late morning light with the packet in my lap. My children are playing down by the creek. As I listen I can hear their shouts, the calls of the crows, the soft rustle of the corn. They'll be coming up for lunch soon. I should open the letter, get it over with. Be done when they get here, but why not wait just a little longer? Wait until they've gone off on some new adventure and left me to my memories. I put the packet in my apron pocket and go into the kitchen to see about lunch.

My apron pocket sags, weighted down by the packet, and while I listen to the children's tales of catching turtles by reaching under the overhanging creek bank, my heart keeps going back to it. They eat ravenously, full of plans for the afternoon. A trip to China Walls. Not far. A favorite picnic and berry picking spot. Could they have a little snack to carry with them?

When I've sent them on their way, laughing and chattering, I feel a pang of guilt for not going with them. But this—this is urgent. It demands my attention. I wait until I can no longer hear their chatter, or tell it from the crows' cries. A soft, summer afternoon silence settles on the valley. Andrew is gone making house calls—won't be back until dusk. I climb the stairs to the widow's walk above the attic. I love to go up there and look out at the lovely Wisconsin countryside. I can still see the children off in the distance, the three of them, heads down, berry buckets swinging at their sides, bound for China Walls. I sit down in a wicker rocking chair I keep up there, the only furnishing except for a small table on which to place a cold iced tea. The packet feels heavy in my hands. I sit back and close my eyes, give myself over to the memories. I'm putting off the inevitable. I know in my heart it brings news I don't want to hear. I've brought a knife to slit it open—there'll be no breaking the seal. As I watch the children disappear among the trees along the creek, I sigh and pick the packet from my lap. The knife slides its way through the canvas, guided by my careful hand.

Inside is a black picture frame that opens like a little book. I've seen it before on the dusty plains of Nebraska. Jeremy's mother. The letter is neatly wrapped around the picture.

White Horse, Yukon Territory
November 1898

Dear Nell,

If you are reading this letter, you must know that I am no longer among the living. I've come to Alaska and the Yukon to find gold, but not in the usual way. You know me. I'll find a way to mine the miners. I've hauled my pack over the Chilcoot Pass and come down the other side, but I must admit it was exhausting. I'm not the man I once was, I'm afraid. I lie ill from pneumonia brought on by the cold and exertion. I've asked my friend Max Neuhauser from Cologne, no less, to post this for me.

I hope you and Andrew are living your dreams in Bear Valley, Wisconsin, and that you look forward to a long and happy life together. I hope above all that you are satisfied with who you are. I thank you for the greatest adventure of my life. I would gladly trade the Yukon River for the Ohio any day. I want you to know now and for all time that I love you. Have always loved you, and would have done anything—even take a ridiculous trek across America—for you.

Please take care of my mother's picture. I've no one else to give it to.

Thank you for loving me and for teaching me that your love knows no reason, no boundary, no end. Even in the face of the insurmountable, love persists. Stand tall and proud of who you are, for even if you never knew them, "your people" must have been fine folk. They made you.

With love and gratitude,
Jeremy Chatterfield, Esq.

I let the letter fall into my lap, and the tears flow. Oh, Jeremy, Jeremy. Impossible love of my life. I sit long on the wicker rocker, looking out over the cornfields and woodlots. This is a fine place to end up. With a fine man and three fine children. I would not have it any other way, and yet. ..

When I hear the children coming, I take the canvas packet downstairs to my bedroom and put it in a drawer. I check my face and hair in the mirror before I go down to meet them. Nellie comes first, trudging out of the tall corn stalks carrying a bucket heavy with raspberries. She's not quite ten, and her quarter Lakota Sioux blood dominates her appearance. Dark, round-faced and broad-featured, she reminds me more of Addie every day. The same sweet, quiet ways. A willingness to consider all possibilities. Accepting of others' shortcomings. Her brother Andrew follows with a walking stick and his pockets full of rocks he's picked up along the way, beads of sweat on his upper lip. Bright and serious, a little pattern seeker, he will study his way through life like his father. After a short interval the corn stalks part again, and the little one comes trundling across the lawn, a handful of drooping Black-Eyed Susans in his little boy grasp.

"Here, Mama. These are for you." I look down into his upturned face and smile my thanks. Blue eyes the color of a chambray shirt, sandy brown hair thick like a wheat field in summer. A smile that would charm the world with its beauty. I take the flowers and wrap him in a hug.

"Thank you, Jeremy," I whisper.

About the Author

Judith Redline Coopey was born in Altoona, Pennsylvania, and holds degrees from the Pennsylvania State University and Arizona State University.

A passion for history inherited from her father drives her writing. Her first book, *Redfield Farm* was the story of the Underground Railroad in Bedford County, Pennsylvania. The second, *Waterproof,* tells how the 1889 Johnstown Flood nearly destroyed a young woman's life.

Looking For Jane is a quest for love and family in the 1890s brought to life through the eyes of Nell, a young girl convinced that Calamity Jane is her mother.

As a teacher, writer and student of history, Ms Coopey finds her inspiration in the rich history of her native state and in stories of the lives of those who have gone before.

Preview of Redfield Farm

For Ann and Jesse Redfield, Quaker brother and sister, their hatred of slavery is as hard as Pennsylvania limestone. Ann's devotion to her older brother runs deep, so when he gets involved in the Underground Railroad, Ann asks no questions. She joins him in the struggle. Together they lie, sneak, masquerade and defy their way past would-be enforcers of the hated Fugitive Slave Law.

Their dedication to the cause leads to complicated relationships with their fellow Quakers, pro-slavery neighbors, and with the fugitives themselves. When Jesse returns from a run with a deadly fever, accompanied by a fugitive, Josiah, who is also sick and close to death, Ann nurses both back to health. But precious time is lost, and Josiah, too weak for travel, stays the winter at Redfield Farm. Ann becomes his teacher, friend and confidant. When disappointment shakes her to her roots, she turns to Josiah for comfort, and comfort leads to intimacy. The result, both poignant and inspiring, is life-long devotion to each other and to their cause.

Redfield Farm is a tale of compassion, dedication and love, steeped in the details of another time but resonant with implications for today's world.

The author brings a deep understanding of the details of the Underground Railroad, which lends authenticity and truth to this tale of a live well-lived and a love well-founded.

Preview of Waterproof

Fifty years after an earthen dam broke and sent a thirty-foot wall of raging destruction down on the city of Johnstown, Pennsylvania, Pamela McRae looks back on the tragedy with new perspective.

This fast-moving retrospective propels the reader forward much as did the flood itself.

When the Johnstown flood hit, it wiped out Pam's fondest hopes, taking her fiancé and her brother's lives and her mother's sanity, and within a year her father walked away, leaving his daughter—now the sole support of her mother—to cope with poverty and loneliness,.

The arrival of Katya, a poor Hungarian girl running away from an arranged marriage, finally gives Pam the chance she needs to get back into the world; Katya can care for her mother, and Pam can go to work for the *Johnstown Clarion* as a society reporter.

Then Davy Hughes, Pam's fiancé before the flood, reappears and, instead of being the answer to her prayers, further complicates her life. Someone is seeking revenge on the owners of the South Fork Fishing and Hunting Club, the millionaires who owned the failed dam. And Pam is afraid Davy has something to do with it.